Out of the Blue

Elise Noble

Published by Undercover Publishing Limited

Copyright © 2017 Elise Noble

v9

ISBN: 978-1-910954-38-6

Edited by Amanda Ann Larson

Cover art by Abigail Sins

www.undercover-publishing.com

www.elise-noble.com

To Uncle John, for making it this far through the series.

CHAPTER 1

THE HEAT OF the sun on my face woke me, and for a few seconds, I couldn't remember where I was. Certainly not at home because the converted attic I slept in didn't have any windows. I cracked open one heavy eyelid. An expanse of opulent plum carpet stretched out in front of me, all the way to a pair of glass doors, and silver railings around the balcony beyond glinted as the light caught them. The sun itself blazed high in a cloudless sky, a ball of fire that caused me to squint.

It all came back to me then. An airplane ride, Las Vegas, the sales jolly—sorry, symposium. My asshole of a fiancé. In daylight, the Strip didn't look quite so impressive. The hotel opposite was dusty rather than glitzy, the gaudy lights that lit it at night an illusion of glamour that didn't hold up under scrutiny.

This was my last day in the city, thank goodness. The three-day trip had been a chore rather than a pleasure. But at least the bed was comfortable. I cocooned myself under the quilt, hoping for another half hour of sleep on a mattress far more comfortable than my lumpy affair back home.

Getting up would mean a return to reality, or rather, to Norsville, Texas. The tiny town perched on the edge of the mainland just across from Galveston. In high school, the jocks had called it Snoresville and the geeks had called it Nowheresville. Two very different groups of people with one thing in common; they both left town the moment they could.

Some took jobs in Galveston or even Houston—anywhere with a bit of nightlife and neighbours who didn't get all up in your business. Others moved farther away to attend college, only returning for the holidays when family custom dictated that it was their duty to visit.

Not me. I stayed put. My life was going nowhere, or rather, staying there.

Because in a little under three weeks from now, I'd be marrying Wade Bruckman. Twenty days until my life got flushed well and truly down the toilet. Four hundred and eighty hours, 28,800 minutes, 1,728,000 seconds.

I'd hated Wade from the moment I met him, long before he blackmailed me into going through with this charade. The arrogant son of a bitch took after his father, who by some fluke of genetics had ended up owning half of Norsville and part of the neighbouring town too. Wade's grandparents had bought the land cheap decades ago, and now he used his birthright to make other people's lives a misery.

Including mine, although my stepdaddy helped him out there.

The thought of my upcoming nuptials made my stomach turn. I'd had a recurring nightmare for the past few weeks where I walked down the aisle and flipped my veil up, only to find Wade had turned into a grotesque monster with horns and a tail. Which wasn't too far from the truth, really. I screwed my eyes shut again, trying to block out the sun. Had I dreamed of the devil again last night? I couldn't remember.

An image flashed through my mind. Not Wade, but another man—muscular, toned, with blond hair instead of brown. Clearly I'd been reading too many of my sister's romance novels. I shook my head to erase the picture, and the faint throbbing in my temples signalled a killer headache just waiting to burst onto the scene. And that damn guy still lurked at the corner of my subconscious. I couldn't help licking my lips, but my mouth was drier than Death Valley itself, and the bottom half of my face felt like somebody had sandpapered it.

Water. I needed water. And Tylenol. I spied my purse on a chair in the corner of the room, an industrial-sized bottle of pills hidden safely within it. I'd been getting a lot of headaches recently—no prizes for guessing why.

A sigh escaped my lips at the thought of getting up, but it was no good. I needed to do it. I stretched my legs out under the quilt until my knees clicked, and then I did the same with my arms, reaching up until I hit the headboard behind me.

With the kinks worked out, I rolled over.

Or at least, I tried to.

A warm lump blocked my way, and I didn't know whether to hit it or run. What was it? Or rather, *who*?

Not Wade, that was for sure. I'd cited traditional values and refused to share a bed with him until our wedding day, even though that was only putting off the inevitable. He was safely ensconced in a deluxe suite on the twentieth floor while I was stuck in a "tier one" room on the eighth, which basically meant I got a bed and bathroom, albeit very nice ones.

Natural instinct took over and I screamed. Seconds later, a tousled head of blond hair popped out from under the quilt, a lazy smile quirking at the corners of the owner's mouth. My eyes widened as I recognised the man I'd shaken out of my head a few moments ago.

Could I be seeing things?

His smile faded. "Well, that's not the reaction I usually get when a woman wakes up."

Unless I was hearing things as well, he was real. I scrambled into a sitting position, clutching the dark-purple quilt in front of me like a shield.

"How did you get here? Why are you in my bed?"

He rubbed his stubbly chin and blinked a couple of times. Finally, he shook his head. "Honestly? I have no idea *how* I got here, but I can take a fair guess as to why."

I wriggled sideways, putting some space between us. Unfortunately, I didn't think that move through because it pulled the quilt off him completely, and I quickly realised that his body matched up to the picture in my dirty mind as well. Every single inch. Nope, he wasn't wearing a stitch of clothing, and his muscles weren't the only things that were big. Hot damn—it was pointing right at me. I squeezed my eyes shut again, wishing this would all go away.

The stranger chuckled. "Looks like someone's happy to see you."

I tried to think again, and the bowling ball careening around inside my skull shook something loose. The bar. This had all started in the bar last night.

I'd travelled to Vegas with my mother, my stepdaddy Clayton, and Wade. Clayton owned a car dealership in Norsville, and Wade worked for him as a salesman. They'd dressed this up as work trip—some conference to learn how to sell even more clunkers to unsuspecting schmucks—when in reality they spent their days drinking and their evenings drinking even more. I'd rather have taken an adventure vacation in Iraq than come with them, but wives and girlfriends were expected to attend the two formal evening events, so as Wade's fiancée designate, I'd been dragged along too.

Last night, I'd pulled on the hideous dress Wade had picked out for me and headed to the second event, a three-course sit-down meal with cabaret. And wine. Yes, the wine had been my downfall.

After the anger and humiliation of the first event, I'd decided getting drunk early would be the best strategy. That way, I rationalised, perhaps I wouldn't feel so upset when my stepdaddy introduced me as the daughter he'd been forced to take on at the age of seven —*forced*, as if I was an employee rather than a child. And when a pudgy stranger groped me on the dance floor, maybe I wouldn't remember the touch of his hands quite so vividly.

Only I must have drunk more alcohol than I'd intended. Another memory flitted back, this time of me sneaking away from our table after Wade upset me yet again. Of course, he didn't notice because he was dancing with a brunette who wore a skirt so short I'd class it as a belt, his sweaty body pressed up against her like they were Siamese twins. But that wasn't what had driven me to the bar. The brunette was welcome to him. If Wade had taken her off to the Little White Wedding Chapel after the song ended, I'd have celebrated with a dance of my own.

No, he'd upset me in the elevator before we even made it to dinner. We'd been alone when he pressed me up against the mirrored wall and shoved his hand between my legs.

"Three weeks and this'll be mine, sweet thing."

I'd had nowhere to go. Wade was six inches taller and a whole lot heavier than me. I couldn't even look him in the eye without craning my neck back. I was trapped in every way.

When I didn't answer, he'd grinned, but his eyes shone with lust.

"I hope you like it rough."

Two hours later, I'd still felt ill at the thought of it, not to mention scared. The prospect of him forcing himself inside me left me contemplating a leap off the balcony. I'd never slept with any man, let alone a sadistic asshole who got off on my pain. I had, however, googled the details and terrified myself by reading others' tales of how much it hurt the first time.

When we exited the elevator, I'd been shaking, and Wade must have noticed. Not that he cared. This was all a game to him. I was the mouse to his cat—a toy to be played with until he went in for the kill. And the clock was counting down.

Tick, tick, tick.

That was why I'd found myself sitting on a bar stool yesterday evening, throwing back a vile cocktail the bartender had pushed in front of me—whether out of generosity or pity, I wasn't sure. And fuelled by vodka, gin, and who knew what else, I'd come up with a plan. At the time, the idea had made perfect sense, but now, with the aftermath lying in bed beside me, not so much.

All I needed to do, drunk me had reasoned, was go out that very night and find myself a nicer man than Wade—which let's face it, wasn't a difficult task—and lose my virginity to him. Not only would I have the satisfaction of giving what Wade wanted to somebody else, but I'd also know what to expect on my wedding night.

So, the question was, had my plan come to fruition? The strangely exquisite throbbing between my legs suggested that was a definite possibility, and I half moaned, half groaned. What the hell had I been thinking?

Oh, that's right, I hadn't.

And now I had a problem to deal with. A big one.

Even with my eyes closed, I could still see him. His perfectly proportioned face, his straight nose, his strong jaw. Piercing blue eyes and that messy shoulder-length hair I wanted to tangle my fingers in. Wide, powerful shoulders leading to a tanned chest and chiselled abs. Then his... No! I shouldn't even be thinking about that.

But at least drunk me hadn't been blind as well.

His voice broke into my thoughts, hoarse and deep. "Are you going to open your eyes again, or am I that bad to look at?"

Open my eyes? No, I didn't want to do that. How far was the balcony? Six steps? Seven? One swift leap, a few seconds of exhilaration, and it would all be over. Only the thought of Lottie, my sister, kept me from running to the window. Which meant I needed to apologise. I wasn't sure exactly what for, but I very much suspected I'd taken advantage of the poor man next to me yesterday evening and possibly part of this morning too.

"I'm so sorry."

That got me an amused chuckle. "Sorry that I'm bad to look at?"

"No, no, of course not. You're very pleasant to look at." How did other women thrive on hookups? This morning would fuel my nightmares for years, the kindling to Wade's gasoline. "I meant, I'm sorry for whatever it was we did last night."

I forced myself to woman-up and look at my companion. His smile was back. And he was still very much under-dressed. *Keep your eyes on his face, Chess.*

"Why?" he asked. "I'm not sorry. At least, I'm pretty sure I'm not. Can you remember what happened? Things are kinda...hazy."

So it wasn't only *my* memory that was acting up. Should I be relieved or upset by that?

"Uh, not really. Do you think we did it?"

"It?"

"You know..." My cheeks heated, and I was sure they'd gone quite pink. "*It.*"

"You mean did we fuck?"

Well, I wouldn't have put it quite so crudely.

"Yes." The word came out as a whisper.

He leaned to the side and peered over the edge of the bed. Curiosity got the better of me, and I shuffled sideways on my butt to look too. A condom lay on the floor, the shrivelled evidence of alcohol and bad decisions, and the white gloop leaking from the end of it gave me my answer.

The blond guy came to the same conclusion. "Yeah, I'd say we did."

CHAPTER 2

THUNKING MY HEAD back against the headboard only made it hurt more. Well, that was it—virginity gone. The most precious gift I'd had to give a man, and I didn't remember a thing about handing it over. Surely if it had been painful, I'd have some recollection?

The man's watch beeped, and he glanced at the screen.

"Hungry?" he asked.

My heart seized. "What time is it?"

"Nine thirty."

"Oh, hell."

I'd promised to meet Wade in the lobby at ten. We were due to have a fun-filled family breakfast before we headed for the airport. Our flight was scheduled to take off at ten past two, and my stepdaddy always insisted on being early for check-in.

I sprang out of bed, realising too late that I was as naked as the stranger. Yes, he might have seen it all already, but in the harsh light of day, awkwardness ruled. I snatched up the quilt and covered myself again.

"Could you stop looking? I need to get dressed."

"Why the hurry?"

"I'm late for breakfast."

"I've got something you could eat right here."

Ugh. What a manwhore! I'd lost my damn marbles

last night, hadn't I?

"You've got a filthy mind."

"It's more fun than a clean one."

"Well, I'm not interested in what you're offering. Not anymore. And would you cover yourself up? It's very distracting."

"Darlin', I'm pretty sure we saw everything there was to see last night. You might as well enjoy the view."

I added arrogant to his list of attributes. But he was right—I couldn't help sneaking another look, and from his lopsided grin, he saw me do it. I wanted to sink into the floor. How did other women do this? Have one-night stands, I mean. This was without a doubt the most awkward moment of my life, and with a family like mine, that was saying something.

"Please," I begged.

"Only if you stop biting your lip. It's doing bad things to me."

I hadn't noticed I was, but I sure stopped quickly. "Fine."

He sighed and put a pillow over his lap. "You drive a hard bargain, lady."

I gripped the quilt with one hand, knuckles white as I threw my belongings haphazardly into my suitcase. Shoes, a novel, my hairbrush. Then I caught sight of myself in the mirror—flushed, with bruised lips and hair the size of Texas. I retrieved the brush and put it on the dressing table. Right next to... What was that?

I picked up a photo of the mystery man and me, stuffed wonkily into a cardboard frame. It could only have been taken last night. I looked far happier in the photo than I felt now. Maybe that was because of the flowers? I loved roses, and I was holding a huge bouquet of them. Where were they now? I couldn't see any sign of them in my bedroom. Had Elvis kept them? He was standing in the background of the picture in a shiny white suit.

Oh, what did it matter? I had more important things to worry about than a bunch of damn flowers. Like getting to breakfast.

Or so I thought. When I dropped the frame back onto the table, I caught sight of the piece of paper underneath. Pale cream, with *State of Nevada* emblazoned across the top. Right above the words *Marriage Certificate.* My stomach lurched halfway up my throat as I read the small print.

This is to certify that the Reverend Elvis Priestly did on the 15th day of June at The Little Chapel of the Flowers, Las Vegas, Nevada, join in lawful wedlock Jared Harker of Richmond, Virginia and Francesca Lane of Galveston, Texas... I couldn't read any farther.

I turned to the blond guy, whose eyes had dropped to my ass. "Is your name Jared Harker?"

"Sure is. I thought you didn't remember anything about last night?"

"I don't." Beads of sweat popped out on my forehead as I waved the certificate at him. "I certainly don't remember getting married, do you?" My voice rang in my ears, high enough to attract passing dogs.

His face paled a few shades. "You're kidding, right?"

I sat down hard on the stool next to the dressing table. "I don't think so. I don't know. There's a marriage certificate here and a photo of us with Reverend Elvis."

Jared leapt out of bed, forgetting the pillow. This time, I barely noticed his goods, not when my world had just caved in.

He grabbed the paper out of my hands and skimmed down it. "And I take it you're Francesca Lane?"

"That's me."

He swore under his breath and grabbed my left hand. A thin silver band twinkled in the sun. How had I not noticed that before? I peered at the fingers wrapped around mine. Sure enough, there was a matching ring.

Jared stared for a few seconds and lost the last of his colour. "I'll make some calls. This has to be a joke."

"Okay," I whispered, although I had an awful suspicion it wasn't a prank. The certificate was signed, numbered and had a seal for Clark County, Nevada in the bottom left-hand corner.

Jared fished a phone out of a pair of jeans lying on the floor and punched in a number. At least I wasn't the only one unhappy with the situation.

What on earth was I supposed to do? I was getting married in less than three weeks. My stepdaddy and Wade would make my life a living hell if they found out I'd accidentally gotten hitched to another man.

In front of me, Jared paced up and down the room, still naked as he muttered at somebody on the other end of the line. I'd gone numb, apart from my head, which felt like a freight train was doing a wall-of-death around the inside. I stumbled over to my purse in search of the painkillers I'd wanted earlier. That seemed so long ago now. It took me three goes to get the lid off the bottle, and I swallowed a handful without counting. Who cared about an overdose? Oblivion would be welcome.

Jared paused and covered the phone with his hand.

"Don't suppose I could have a couple of those?"

I handed him the bottle, and he tipped two tablets out into his hand, swallowed them dry, and resumed pacing. My eyes followed him unconsciously until I realised and forced myself to stop. He sure was pretty to look at, but he'd brought me a whole world of trouble.

After a couple of minutes, he tossed the phone down on the bed. "Right, I've got somebody checking whether this is a legal marriage. Apparently, we should have had a marriage licence first if it was. Do you remember getting one?"

I spotted another piece of paper on the floor, sticking out from under the dress I'd been wearing last night.

"You mean this marriage licence?"

He leaned over my shoulder and read the words I was trying to block out.

"Shit."

His hair got even messier as he ran his fingers through it, and my throat went dry. I absolutely did not need to get distracted by his sexy-ass hair when we were in the midst of a disaster of epic proportions. *Snap out of it, Chess.*

"Now what do we do? Can't we just cancel this?" I asked.

"Worst case scenario is that we need to get an annulment. I've got a lawyer looking into the process."

An annulment? This was getting more complicated by the second. I put my throbbing head in my hands.

"How long do you think it'll take? I'm supposed to be getting married next month."

He stopped and stared at me. Heck, even when he

was angry he looked hot.

"Fuck me. You don't do things by halves, do you? Without wanting to sound judgmental, why the hell did you sleep with me if you've already got a man?"

He didn't want to sound judgmental? Yeah, right. I jumped up, past caring about my lack of clothes.

"It's not as if I want to get married, okay? I hate my fiancé. I just don't have a choice in the matter."

Shouting made my head pound harder, but by that point I was in so much pain it didn't make a difference. Jared took a step backwards as I jabbed him in the chest with my ring finger. "If you must know, I wanted my first time to be with someone other than my future husband, because I know he's planning to make it hurt."

Then the tears came. Why did I just tell Jared that? To all intents and purposes, he was a perfect stranger—emphasis on the perfect—albeit one I was now legally joined to until a lawyer worked a miracle, probably at the cost of thousands of dollars I didn't have. I sat on the bed, drew my knees up to my chest, and wrapped my arms around my legs. Maybe if I made myself small enough, this would all disappear. The room, the ring, Jared...

Perhaps if I wished hard enough, *I* could disappear too?

CHAPTER 3

I DREW IN a ragged breath and looked away. Jared's anger had turned to pity, which made me feel even worse. The bed dipped as he sat down next to me.

"Go away. I'm fine."

"No, darlin', you're not fine. You just told me you're being forced to marry a man you hate."

When my mother sobbed, she dabbed at her dainty tears with a handkerchief and garnered sympathy from everyone who saw her. Lottie too. But not me. I'd always been an ugly crier. Big, nasty tears leaked down my cheeks as I snuffled to stop them from running. On the rare occasions I let emotion get the better of me, people usually scattered like deer at an alligator party.

Jared was the first person I'd told about the situation with Wade. My friends were all lab rats—emotion was something they studied, measured and wrote a paper on, not empathised with and tamed with candy. And I certainly couldn't tell my sister, even though she knew the rest of my secrets. In an odd way, it felt good to get it off my chest, and the lead weight that had filled my ribcage for the last few months grew a tiny bit lighter. Now I understood why Catholics went to confession—there was something cathartic about unloading your worries and fears and sins onto a stranger.

So, I kept talking. Seeing as I didn't know any priests, I figured I might not get another chance.

"When I was fourteen, Wade asked me out on a date. I mean, I should have been flattered, with him being two years older and on the football team, but there was something off about him."

"Like what?"

"I don't know. Just the way he looked at me, I guess. Like he thought he owned me. Being in the same room as him made my skin crawl." I shuddered. "Still does."

"So you said no?"

"He didn't take it well. You know what he said to me? 'Chess, you'll be mine in the end.' Word for word, he actually said that."

Together with the words, more tears cascaded out of me. Now the floodgates were open, I couldn't close them again. Jared passed me a tissue.

"Thanks."

"Better out than in. My grandmother always told me that."

The thought of that living god having a grandmother seemed so...normal. Not like today in Vegas.

"I thought they were just words, but every few weeks he'd remind me of his promise. Taunting me. I don't even know why he was interested. I mean, he had all the football groupies throwing themselves at him."

"Wanted what he couldn't have, probably."

"Maybe. I thought he'd finally given up when he went away to college."

"But he came back?"

"Right after he graduated. I walked into my

stepdaddy's car dealership to drop off some paperwork and there was Wade, polishing a Ford Taurus." And when Clayton stopped to speak to him, he'd patted him on the shoulder and called him "son." Two assholes, new best buddies. "And he reminded me of his promise again."

"Did you tell your stepfather? Or your mother?"

I choked back a laugh. "They wouldn't have believed me."

"Known you five minutes, darlin', and I believe you."

"Then you don't know me very well, do you?"

He blew out a thin breath. "No, I don't. But I know a girl doesn't get this upset over something trivial."

Why did he have to be so sweet? I didn't know how to act when a man was sweet. I didn't have any male friends outside of my studies, and the idea of one having an attitude outside of geek or asshole confused me. I tried a tiny smile.

"They like Wade better than me. He's part of the family now."

"I'm sure that's not true."

"That he's part of the family? It is! He's invited to dinner every single night."

"No, that they like him better than you."

"They do. Wade didn't even ask me to marry him—he asked Clayton."

"Isn't that tradition?"

"Not when they arrange the entire wedding without even telling you, then inform you of the date to show up. I mean, what kind of psycho expects to marry a woman he hasn't even been on a date with?"

Jared gave me a wry smile. "Yeah, what kind of

psycho?"

I realised what I'd said. "Oh heck, I'm so sorry. I didn't mean you. You're not a psycho. At least, I don't think so. I mean, I hardly know you."

He narrowed his eyes as I carried on babbling.

"You were just drunk, right? Not drunk like an alcoholic, although I guess you could be one, and maybe you missed some meetings and then this happened and... I'll be quiet now."

Please, somebody shoot me.

A smile tugged at the corners of his mouth. "Let me know how Australia is when you finish digging that hole of yours."

"You're not an alcoholic, are you?"

He shook his head and rubbed his temples. "After what happened last night, I'm not sure I'll ever drink again."

No, of course he wouldn't. When he was sober, he'd pick a far more appropriate girl—someone pretty and interesting. Not an idiot who knew more about the immune response in non-human primates than she did about sex and shopping. I held up an imaginary wine glass. "Here's to sobriety."

He chuckled and held his own hand up in a pretend toast. "No changing the subject. You were telling me about the other man you don't want to marry."

"Well, obviously I said no to the arrangement." Said no? My knees had given way and I'd collapsed. "But they convinced me."

"How?"

"I say convinced, but it was more blackmail. Clayton did a deal with Wade's father over a piece of land to expand his car showroom, and I'm the payment." Not content with being the car king of Norsville, Clayton wanted the biggest dealership in all of Texas.

"What did Wade say to that?"

"It was his idea. Truly? I'm not sure he even likes me that much. I'm just part of a game he wants to win."

The AC wasn't turned up high in my room, but even in the Nevada heat, I gave a shudder.

That didn't go unnoticed by Jared. "Stating the obvious..." His eyes flicked down my body, and I clutched the quilt tighter. "You're a grown woman. Why don't you leave?"

A question I'd asked myself a thousand times over. "Because of my sister. She's sick. If I don't do as Clayton says, he won't pay her medical bills."

He let out a low whistle. "That's cold."

"Tell me about it." Funny how a stranger in Vegas understood what nobody back home ever would. I shrugged. "But everyone in town loves Clayton."

"They don't see through him?"

"Want a car in the west, then come to the best." I read out his marketing slogan. "He donates to charity and judges the annual talent show. Just an all-around great guy. And Wade's family's rich. Everyone thinks I've made a good catch."

Even my own sister. I saw it in her eyes every time the wedding was mentioned.

She thought I was living the freaking dream.

CHAPTER 4

JARED PUT HIS arm around my shoulders and squeezed me close. "Darlin', there must be something you can do."

Something I could do?

"Believe me, I've thought of little else for the last six months. Clayton won't budge. When I threatened to veto the honeymoon, he promised I could stay at college for the next year to finish my PhD. That was the best I could do."

Jared gently kissed the top of my head, and I leaned into him. His body heat seeped into me even through the quilt. Logic told me I should feel scared, or at the very least, disgusted. After all, I barely knew him and he'd clearly had his hands all over me last night. But I shoved logic into a cage, locked it, and snuggled closer.

"What's your thesis on?" he asked, his tone light.

I gave a hollow laugh. "My stepdaddy thinks I'm studying nineteenth-century literary heroines. I leave copies of Jane Austen and Charlotte Brontë around the house to keep up the act."

"So, what are you studying?"

"Science. Which is not a woman's job, according to Clayton."

"Does he know what century it is?"

"He's a relic from the last one."

"Maybe you could build him a time machine and send him back there."

A giggle escaped. "It's not that kind of science."

"What kind, then?"

"It doesn't matter. If Wade gets his way, I'll wind up serving coffee."

He chuckled and tightened his arm around me. Why did his smile do funny things to my insides?

"You need to have more confidence in yourself. You're clearly smart as well as pretty, and you need to make sure the world sees it."

Words. They were only words. But my heart pounded harder as those words left his lips. *Stop it, Chess. He's just being kind.* Probably to stop you from crying again. After all, Jared was just a stranger I'd bumped into by accident and done something outrageously stupid with.

His phone rang, making me jump. He snatched it up and resumed pacing. Was that his lawyer? Could he fix the problem? All I heard were a series of yeahs and okays from Jared's end.

Then he clicked off and stood in front of me. Awkward, because that put certain parts of his anatomy right at my eye level, and they were very...distracting. Clearly, the man didn't have a problem with nudity. Mind you, if I was a man and looked like Jared, I wouldn't wear many clothes either.

"...agreeing to the marriage."

I cleared my throat. "Sorry, what was that?"

He looked down, realised what the problem was, and then smirked.

"Mind on other things, darlin'?"

"Er, I was just thinking about breakfast." I clapped

a hand over my mouth as his eyes widened. "I meant the hotel breakfast."

"Sure you did. Anyway, my lawyer figures we'll get an annulment on the grounds of lack of understanding. All we have to do is prove that at least one of us was incapable of agreeing to the marriage."

"How do we do that? How do we prove that we were so drunk we can't remember anything? Isn't that the point? We can't remember?"

"I was with a group of friends. Bachelor party." He grimaced. "I'm never going to live this one down. But don't worry—they'll all confirm I was incoherent and had no clue about anything. We submit their statements to the court, and bingo, we get an annulment."

"How long will that take? I'm supposed to leave in..." I peered at his watch. "Twenty minutes."

He shrugged. "A few days. Look, I'll take care of it. Just give me your address, and I'll send you the papers to sign."

Oh, no. No way. "You can't send the papers to my house. Clayton opens all the mail." Twenty-five years old and I had no privacy whatsoever.

"Okay." Jared's lip twitched as he thought. Cute. "I'll get a courier to bring the papers to you at college, wait while you sign them, then bring them back. That work for you?"

My shoulders sagged with relief. "Perfect. Thank you."

At least it looked like we'd found a solution to this whole mess. Well, Jared found a solution. What did I do apart from fall apart? I carefully jotted down my details on a piece of hotel stationery. Name, department, a map of how to find the lab. For a moment, I got so frazzled I couldn't remember the name of the damn building. Jared lay back in the bed while I wrote, and more than once I caught myself glancing in his direction.

Despite what had happened last night, he seemed like a mostly decent guy. Not just his looks—he'd considered my feelings and treated me like a human being. For one crazy moment, I wondered what would have happened if we'd met under different circumstances.

Then I gave myself a mental slap. *I absolutely should not be thinking that way.* No, I needed to get rid of Jared, pack, and go home.

I folded the piece of paper and handed it over, but Jared didn't move.

"Uh, I need to get dressed."

He stayed still, but his lips quirked upwards.

"Alone."

"Aw, I was hoping for a final show."

Okay, maybe I'd misjudged him. He really could be an asshole like the other men in my life. "You're not getting one. Would you please leave?"

He smiled wider and swung his legs onto the floor. "You're cute when you get pissed. And so damned polite."

"And you're..." Naked. Again.

He'd dropped the pillow when he got up. I closed my eyes to block out the sight of his golden abs, with that little trail of blonde hair leading down to... *No! Don't think about it!* In three weeks, I'd have to get used to Wade's fledgling paunch and that was that.

"And I'm what?" His tone was light, teasing.

"You're annoying."

He sighed. "Fine. Just let me get my clothes on. Wouldn't want to give any other ladies an eyeful, would I?"

They'd probably disagree. In fact, ladies from Texas to Toronto would pay good money for an eyeful of what Jared had to offer. He began sorting through the mess on the floor, and I breathed a sigh of relief when he picked the condom up and flushed it. I wasn't sure I'd have dared to touch that.

A hammering at the door made my eyes widen, and I stifled a scream. Jared paused mid-hop, one leg in his jeans.

"You expecting anyone?" he whispered?

I shook my head. Unless...

"Francesca? Are you in there?"

Oh, hell. A shiver ran through me and beads of sweat popped out on my back. Jared raised an eyebrow.

"Wade," I mouthed. And he didn't sound happy. "Hide. Please, hide."

Jared buttoned his jeans, and I couldn't help sneaking one last glance at what lay inside. Then he pulled on his shoes, grabbed the paperwork and his jacket, and scuttled out onto the balcony. Heart hammering, I pulled the drapes tightly shut.

"I'm here," I called.

"What are you doing in there?"

At that moment? Hastily pulling on a bathrobe and doing one last check for evidence. I cracked open the door. "Sorry, I overslept."

He shouldered his way inside. "Where the hell did you go last night?"

Wade was a good-looking man, but at that moment,

with his face all scrunched up in anger, he displayed his ugly soul. I followed him inside, my toes scrunching in the deep pile of the carpet, praying he wouldn't notice the room smelled of sex and another man. I needn't have worried. As usual, Wade was only interested in himself.

He didn't even wait for my answer before launching into a tirade.

"You disappeared, Francesca. When we sat down for the speeches, I was the only man with an empty seat beside him. Do realise how embarrassing that was?" He thumped the wall for emphasis, and I hoped it hurt. "Do you?"

I nodded, afraid to speak.

"So you just don't care then, is that it? Everyone looked at me like I was a loser. Don't you dare do that again, you hear me?"

"I'm sorry," I whispered.

His eyes flashed. Apology not accepted. "You'd better be downstairs in ten minutes or your father'll be even angrier than he is already."

Still furious, he stormed off, slamming the door behind him.

I sank to the floor, sliding my back down the closed door and biting back tears. I had a lifetime of that to look forward to. At that moment, I understood why my sister had tried to kill herself. Death was the easy way out. If it wasn't for Lottie, I'd do it.

The drapes caught my eye as a breeze tugged at one corner. Shoot! Jared was still on the darn balcony. Wade had a way of making me forget everything, even my own mind. I hauled myself up and crossed the room on shaky legs.

"It's okay. He's gone. You can—"

I whipped the drapes back and found empty air. Huh? Where did he go? I stepped out onto the balcony, but at only a few feet wide, there wasn't anywhere for a mouse to hide, let alone a man, and Jared hadn't been small. No, he'd been big all over, especially his... *Snap out of it!*

I peered down over the railing, just in case he'd fallen off, but everything was quiet on the sidewalk as tourists ambled along and the last few all-night gamblers staggered home to drown their sorrows. The balconies either side were empty too, not that I expected him to have jumped the four-foot gap between them. Where did he go?

Could I have dreamed him up? A brain's rebellion over my imminent nuptials? Only the delicious ache between my legs told me otherwise.

CHAPTER 5

WITH WADE, CLAYTON, and my mother waiting downstairs, I didn't have time to worry about Jared and his disappearing act, especially with Wade so angry he was hitting things. At least it had only been the wall today—with his temper, I had a horrible feeling in time it would end up being me.

A part of me wanted to flee back to Galveston, snatch Lottie from the rehab centre she was staying in, and run to the end of the earth. But I couldn't, not if we wanted any sort of future. No, I'd come up with a long-term plan, one that meant I'd have to go through with marriage number two in as many weeks to secure a better life for Lottie and me. I'd spend the next year finishing my studies and do everything in my power to help her get well. Then we'd run. With a PhD, I had a chance of working a job that paid better than waiting tables.

A year, that was all.

I just had to stick it out for twelve months. Fifty-two weeks. Three hundred and sixty-five days. Not that long really, at least that was what I kept telling myself. Less than two percent of my life. Then Lottie and I could start over.

Goosebumps popped out as I stepped into the freezing shower. I didn't have the luxury of waiting even a few seconds for the water to warm up. A twinge of regret ran through me as I lathered up with complimentary shower gel, the fruity scent erasing the last traces of Jared from my body and leaving me with only memories.

Shoot, even thinking about the man caused heat to pool between my thighs. What was wrong with me? Okay, so he had the body of a Hollywood hotshot and mussed-up hair it would be a crime to comb, but surely that shouldn't warrant such a reaction? Yes, he'd been kind, but any man seemed like an angel beside Wade.

My heart sank at the thought of eating breakfast with the two people I disliked most in the world, three if you counted my mother, which half of the time I did. My daddy's passing changed her. Once, she'd been a loving mom, but now her affections revolved around material things rather than her children. Three years ago, on the anniversary of the accident, too much wine led her to confess that she found it easier to love diamonds now because they couldn't die. While I understood her sentiment, it made her difficult to live with.

But with no choice, I hopped out of the shower and narrowly avoided ending up on my behind as I slipped on a patch of water. The brush snagged in my hair as I dragged it to the ends, splitting now as I was long overdue for a cut. I longed to colour it as well. Not just because my natural platinum was too noticeable but because Wade loved it and refused to let me change.

Back in the bedroom, I blasted my hair with the dryer for thirty seconds, then stuck my toe straight through one pair of pantyhose before forcing myself to be more careful with a second. Before I met Wade, I'd been a jeans and shirt girl, but he liked me in dresses so that was what I had to wear. He bought them for me too, no consultation involved. Today's was too tight, too short, and too red.

One minute left. I grabbed the little bottles of toiletries from the bathroom vanity and stuffed them in my suitcase. I didn't have much money of my own so I couldn't pass up the chance of some nice things.

Thirty seconds, and I slid my purse over my arm and pulled out the handle of my wheeled case. But before I left the room, I took one last good look around, committing it to memory. That mid-market hotel room in Vegas, had, after all, hosted a momentous event in my life even if I didn't remember it. If the way Jared moved—smoothly and with a graceful power—was any indication, then it had most likely been spectacular.

Shit!

I hopped up on the bed and retrieved last night's panties from the light fitting. Yes—spectacular.

By the time I'd waited for the elevator, which stopped on every darn floor, I was five minutes late to the dining room. Clayton's look made me wither, and I willed my heart to slow down as I helped myself to a bowl of fruit and yoghurt from the buffet and then sat next to Wade. My self-proclaimed beau was halfway through a mountain of fried food, shovelling it into his mouth as he chewed it noisily. Watching him eat made me nauseous under normal circumstances, and today was far from normal.

Mother sat opposite me, perfectly turned out as

usual. I caught the vague whiff of hairspray mixed with Chanel No.5 as she turned her head towards me. Never in my life had I seen her without a full face of make-up, even first thing in the morning, and she'd never dream of stepping outside the house without looking runway-ready.

"Francesca, your hair's a mess." Her voice had gotten higher in pitch over the years as she turned herself into the caricature of a perfect southern belle. "Is it still wet? Did you look in the mirror this morning?"

"Sorry," I mumbled.

I wasn't about to explain I'd had far bigger things on my mind this morning, like Jared and his...ability to get an annulment sorted in time for my next wedding. My knee bounced under the table of its own accord, and I earned a disapproving glare from my stepdaddy as my spoon slipped out of my hand.

"Francesca, be more careful."

"Yes, Clayton."

I couldn't help emphasising his name a touch. I'd always refused to call him daddy, and it irritated him to no end. I had a daddy, and even if he no longer walked this earth, Clayton would never replace him.

Every day, memories of my daddy faded a little, never to be extinguished but never to blaze again. The only evidence of his existence was a tombstone in Norsville and a single photo I'd salvaged from Clayton's cull when we first moved in with him. After a few fingers of Jack Daniels and a tiff with my mother, he'd burned all the others. We weren't even allowed to mention his name.

But I had that photo, hidden at the back of my

wallet. Me, my daddy, and baby Lottie, so tiny in his arms. The picture had been taken in the yard at our old house. We'd been laughing about something, and no matter how hard I tried, I couldn't remember what. Funny how inconsequential things become so important later on, isn't it? But that day, my daddy wore his dimples and his eyes sparkled in that magical way of his.

Seven years old and that was the last day I'd seen my father.

Six hours later, the police knocked on the door. I'd hidden in the hallway as they spoke to Mom in the living room, and while my father had faded from memory, the sound of her cries when she found out he'd died never would. An accident, they said. The wrong place at the wrong time, they said. But I knew better. Daddy died going to the 7-Eleven to get me ice cream, and if I hadn't begged he'd still be here.

And how different life would be.

"Is that low-fat yoghurt on your fruit?" my mother asked.

"Yes."

I didn't know whether it was or it wasn't, nor did I care. Mother's obsession with counting calories nearly destroyed my sister, and I wanted no part of it.

Next to me, Wade shoved his chair back and headed back to the food counter. Mother stayed silent—in her book, having a stomach that bulged over your belt was acceptable if you were male and wealthy. But it wasn't her who'd have to look at it every day. It was me. I thought again about running, just jumping on a plane and flying to New York, or Chicago, or Los Angeles. Somewhere big enough to get lost.

The crack of Clayton slamming his coffee cup on the table made me jump. "Girl, are you listening?"

"Sorry, what did you say?"

"I said, I want more coffee." He enunciated each word slowly as if speaking to a child.

I leapt up, not because I wanted to wait on Clayton, but because I could escape from the table for a minute or two. "Mom, do you want a drink?"

She patted her tiny stomach. "Just iced water. You know how many calories coffee has."

I dithered over their requests, and when I got back to the table Wade decided he wanted a cup of English breakfast tea, which made him sound far more refined than he actually was. If I played my cards right, by the time I'd messed around with the teabag, breakfast would be half over.

When I slid back into my seat beside Wade, I picked at another piece of mango, but even the sweet smell made me feel ill. I wasn't hungry—far from it. Instead, I was kicking myself for not getting Jared's number, or at least his address. What if he didn't do as he promised and sort out the annulment? Should I confess to Wade and hope he dumped me? Or get married anyway and pray nobody noticed? What was the penalty for bigamy in the state of Texas? Could I go to jail?

Actually, compared to a life with Wade, jail looked the more attractive option. Sure, the food sucked and I'd heard showering could get a bit awkward, but that beat going to sleep every night next to a man who made me want to drink bleach.

Speaking of Wade, he belched loudly enough for a woman two tables over to purse her lips, then stood up, followed by Mom and Clayton.

"Time to go."

I trailed him to the lobby, wheeling my little case behind me.

"I just need to visit the bathroom."

The asshole blocked my way. Why? Because he could.

"You'll have to wait. It was you who didn't show up to breakfast on time, and now we're late for our flight."

I almost pointed out it was him who'd been eating for the last twenty minutes rather than me, but I knew from experience it wouldn't end well. Even so, he still grabbed my arm, nails digging into my skin, and dragged me across the lobby.

Caught by surprise, I tripped over my case and his grip tightened.

"Francesca, for goodness' sake, walk properly."

"You're hurting me."

His only response was to hold tighter and walk faster. Until he stopped.

Over six feet of toned muscle blocked Wade's way, arms folded. Jared's scowl was a far cry from the sweet smiles he'd given me earlier, but the sight of him still made my heart thump. His messy hair was damp, and I could count his abs through his "I heart Vegas" T-shirt. Wade's un-toned bulk was no match.

"Let go of her." Jared's voice matched his expression, and the row of equally large men lined up behind him didn't look thrilled either.

Never one to heed a warning, Wade met his stare. "Butt out. We're having a private conversation, and it's none of your business."

"You made it my business when you hurt the

woman by your side." Jared spoke quietly but firmly. "And it's hardly a private conversation when you're raising your voice in the middle of a hotel lobby."

Jared's attention flicked in my direction, and for a fraction of a second I caught his gaze. And in that fraction of a second, his eyes softened and so did something inside me. Nobody apart from my daddy had ever defended me like that, and his stand against the kid from three doors up who stole my tricycle was hardly comparable.

But as soon as I felt it, the happiness fluttered away, replaced by guilt at putting Jared into a situation where he felt the need to defend me in the first place.

"It's o..." My voice came out as a croak, and I cleared my throat. "It's okay. I'll be okay."

He looked at me, then Wade, then back to me, but before Jared could speak, Clayton's voice boomed over my shoulder.

"What's the hold-up? What have you done this time, Francesca?"

"She hasn't done anything. This asshole was hauling her across the lobby."

Clayton stepped forward, level with my elbow. "How dare you speak about my son-in-law like that?"

Son-in-law? Talk about jumping the gun. There were still two blessed weeks left until he could call Wade that. I took in Jared's clouded face and knew he'd had the same thought. *Please don't say anything.* I tried to convey my plea through my eyes.

Wade's anger rolled off him in waves, but Jared remained calm.

"Because somebody has to educate the little prick. It's a father's job, but you seem to have fucked it up so far."

Oh, Jared, Jared, Jared.

Clayton began spluttering, garbling something about hotel security and manners. Wade let go of me and balled his fists up, advancing slowly, but Jared shook his head and backed away. I had no doubt he could have flattened Wade, but he was too much of a gentleman to do so.

And that was it—my moment to escape. I flashed Jared a smile, abandoned my suitcase, and dashed past, heading for the bathrooms on the far side of the lobby.

A temporary sanctuary, but a sanctuary nonetheless.

CHAPTER 6

I DIDN'T CARE who turned their heads as I ran across the lobby. Dignity? What dignity? A twinge of pain shot through my wrist as I smacked into the bathroom door, but I barely noticed. Was anyone else in there? I did a quick recon, relieved to find myself alone in a fancy bathroom complete with rolled towels and a basket full of make-up samples. At least that meant when I locked myself in the furthest stall, put the toilet lid down, sat on it, and burst into tears, there was nobody else to hear me.

Why was I even crying? What just happened with Wade was hardly an isolated incident. All the other times he'd manhandled me I'd coped without flipping out and running across the lobby of the Black Diamond Hotel. A reaction to Jared—that was what it was. Not just my accidental marriage but the way he'd charged in, a knight in denim rather than shining armour, and given me the illusion of hope when, deep down, I knew there wasn't any.

I noisily blew my nose on a piece of toilet tissue, then grabbed a fresh handful and tried to wipe away my tears. Failed. The darn things wouldn't stop. Or they wouldn't until the bathroom door opened and I held my breath mid-sniffle. No point in the newcomer thinking there was a hysterical lunatic in the next stall, even if there in fact was.

"Francesca?"

Oh, shoot! Jared? He'd come into the ladies' room?

"Chess? I know you're in there."

Why was he here? Hadn't I caused him enough drama for one day?

"I also know you're upset."

I took one deep, shaky breath. "Thank you for helping with Wade, but I'm fine." Oh heck, I'd tried to hold back my sobs and now I sounded as if I was being strangled.

"Fine doesn't sprint across the lobby like her heels are on fire."

"Honestly, I'm okay."

"The hell you are. Open the door."

And let him see me like this? No way. I tried again. "I just got a bit emotional. It's been one heck of a morning."

Lost my virginity? Check. Accidentally married a stranger? Check. Made a fool of myself in public? Check. Surely I deserved a few tears? Any girl would cry at that, right?

"I'm counting to three, and if the door isn't open, I'm taking it down."

I stiffened. He wouldn't, would he? I swiped at my face with the tissue, trying to wipe away the mess around my eyes, but when I peered into the shiny surface of the tissue-holder, it seemed it was there to stay. Jared might not have great memories of me, but I didn't want to make them worse.

"I'm not opening the door."

"One."

He wasn't serious, surely? What kind of man broke

into a bathroom stall? "Please, don't."

"Two."

In the silence that fell over the room, I heard the squeak of rubber on tile as he took a couple of steps back. What if he wasn't bluffing? What if he really did intend to destroy a darn door?

"Three."

Coward that I was, I lost my nerve, leapt forward, and unlocked the door. Just as Jared charged. The door missed me by an inch as it flew open and crashed against the marble, Jared barrelled into me, and we ended up stuck in the tiny gap between the toilet bowl and the wall. That positioning gave a whole new meaning to the phrase "my life is in the toilet."

And my hand was in a whole other place. Could this get any more embarrassing?

Jared levered himself up, shaking his head. "Shit, darlin', give me some warning next time you do that." His frown turned into a cocky smile. "And next time you want to feel up my junk, you only need to ask."

My cheeks burned as he held out a hand to help me up, but wedged as I was I had little choice other than to take it. He pulled me to my feet, leaving us inches apart in a space that suddenly felt very warm. I tried to snatch my hand back, but he twined his fingers with mine instead.

"Chess?"

I leaned forward and buried my head in the crook of his neck. Mortification: complete. "I don't want to talk about it."

He wrapped his spare arm around my back, pulling me closer. For the first time in years I felt safe, drawing some strength from a man who was everything I wasn't. Tough. Confident. Brave. Oh, and he smelled really good.

For a minute or two we just stood there, motionless as time ticked by around us. Then Jared let go of my hand and tilted my chin up to look at him. Seeing as he had ten inches on me, that meant craning my neck back to meet his eyes. He used his thumb to brush away the last of my tears.

"At least you've stopped crying now."

I detected a hint of relief in his voice, and a tiny giggle escaped. In return, he rewarded me with a smile.

"That's better. Now, what was that all about?"

"Things. Life." I shrugged, going for nonchalant, difficult when he'd seen me broken just minutes before. "The wedding, mainly."

His eyes really were a strange colour. Sea blue with pale flecks, like the foam cresting a wave. The kind of eyes a girl could lose her heart in if she didn't protect it.

"Don't worry about the wedding, darlin'. I promised you I'd fix it and I will."

"Not that wedding. The other one."

He squeezed me tighter but stayed quiet. What could he say? Offer condolences? A handful of vague platitudes about everything working out okay in the end? I took his silence as a gift, a precious few minutes in my life where someone cared enough to comfort me. To make me feel protected.

"Chess?"

"Mmm?"

"Don't get married again. Come with me instead."

My head jerked back. "Did you just say what I think you said?"

If Jared's expression was anything to go by, he was

as surprised as me by what had just come out of his mouth. But he blew out a long breath and then nodded.

"Whatever needs fixing, I'll help you fix it. I never like to see a girl unhappy."

Pressed against me, Jared's chest hammered in time with my own. Thoughts flew through my head, a jumble of reasons why leaving with him was an insane idea.

First and foremost, Lottie. Her care bills ran to thousands each month, and Clayton would cut off the payments the instant I went. Not only that, we needed each other. Lottie didn't make friends easily, and without me near Galveston to visit her I feared she'd relapse.

Secondly, my research was based at the Galveston National Laboratory. Facilities rated at Biosafety Level 4 were few and far between, and even if I found another lab to work at, shipping my equipment and samples with the amount of funding I didn't have would be impossible.

And then there was the not-so-small matter of Jared himself. I'd only met the man this morning, and while he'd been nothing but kind, what if he was a wolf disguised as a pussycat? Throwing away what little I had on an unknown future would be crazy. Wouldn't it?

The dreamer in me made her presence known, teasing me with visions of a perfect future. As a little girl, I'd believed in Santa Claus, the Tooth Fairy, and the Easter Bunny. And fairy tales. I'd believed in fairy tales. Before Daddy died, I always thought a charming prince would arrive and sweep me off my feet, then take me to live in his castle, complete with a carriage, white horses, and a pink dress. Well, Jared swept me off my feet all right, but not quite in the romantic way I'd imagined.

But what if he was my Prince Charming? What if he was my only chance to escape my wicked stepdaddy?

Hammering at the door brought me crashing back to reality.

"Francesca? What are you doing in there?" Momma's voice lost its practised sweetness when she got angry.

The dream faded as my head defeated my heart. "I can't," I whispered. "I wish I could, but I can't."

Jared's eyes turned a shade darker as he nodded, his mouth set in a hard line. "I understand. I don't like you going back to that asshole, but I understand."

I buried my head against his chest one last time. "Thank you for making me feel special, even just for a few minutes."

"You deserve to feel special your whole life. Don't ever forget that."

I sighed. Happiness just wasn't in my stars. "I need to go. My mother's waiting for me."

"Give me your phone."

Silently, I handed it over. Jared tapped on the screen and his own phone vibrated between us. "Now you've got my number. Call me any time if you need help, day or night." He gave me a sad smile. "Or even if you only want someone to talk to."

An overwhelming sense of loss swept through me as I pocketed my phone again. I'd rarely needed to say goodbye to anyone I cared about, and as I breathed in Jared's musky scent, it hit me that I did—care about him, that is. In only one short night, he'd come to mean something.

Momma thumped the door again. "Francesca, get out here this instant. We're late for check-in."

Jared bent his head and pressed a sweet but chaste kiss to my lips, then with his touch still burning on my skin, I backed out of the stall and planned my apology. Time to grovel.

"I'm sorry, Momma. I wasn't feeling well."

"You'll be feeling even worse if we miss our flight. Now get a move on and stop causing problems for Clayton and Wade."

She ushered me back to the lobby, but even as my bladder reminded me I'd forgotten to use the toilet in the manner I'd intended, I couldn't keep from smiling inside. With Jared's number in my phone, I had a lifeline now.

CHAPTER 7

THE ENGINE IN Jed's vintage Porsche 911 grumbled as he steered through traffic and hit the brakes for a red light. He caressed the steering wheel sympathetically. This car wasn't designed for city driving. He'd spent two years restoring the silver beast, and normally he'd take any excuse to get behind the wheel, but today he was on autopilot. Good thing he'd made the journey to Washington, DC so many times.

Beside him, Emmy, a friend, colleague, ex, and occasional irritation, shifted her stocking-clad feet on the dashboard. The high-heeled pumps she'd kicked off lay in the footwell. "Why'd you stop?"

"Because the light was red?"

"Barely. You could've made it."

And she undoubtedly would have, but today Jed was the one in the driver's seat. They'd begun the trip arguing about whose car to take and ended up flipping for it. Jed called heads and won, so now Emmy was driving from the passenger seat, coffee in one hand and phone in the other. If she kept it up, one of them would be coming home in a cab. Jed scowled because he knew it wouldn't be her.

"Look, I don't have the tits to get me out of a ticket, so unless you want to oblige, today we're stopping at red lights."

"What if we got pulled over by a female cop?" Emmy glanced down at his crotch. "No woman with a pulse can resist the Harker charm."

"It's irrelevant because we're not getting pulled over."

"You're no fun. You need to do something crazy every so often."

The light was still red, so Jed turned to stare at her.

She grinned back, unrepentant as always. "Oh, yeah, I forgot. How is the old ball and chain, anyway?"

"Fuck off."

Emmy threw her head back and laughed. "Defensive much? You actually liked her, didn't you?"

Truthfully? Jed was confused. Usually a woman leaving a toothbrush at his place was enough to call things off on the spot. Yet, with Chess, even when he saw the damn marriage certificate he hadn't felt the panic he expected. Although that could have been because she shared his horror. Yes, that must have been it.

Still, he hadn't been able to get her out of his head since he got back home. Usually, he was a fuck-and-forget man, but she'd paraded through his mind at every opportunity for the last twenty-four hours. That sweet face. The sweeter body. He pinched the bridge of his nose, trying once more to recall what happened that night. She'd been a virgin, for fuck's sake, and he'd taken that from her like an asshole. If only he could turn the clock back and make it special. His pants stirred just thinking about it, despite him rubbing one out right before he left home. Clearly, his body hadn't gotten his head's memo.

The light went green, and he gave himself a mental

slap. *Forget it, Harker.* Go out tonight, find yourself a hot piece of entertainment, and move on.

When he didn't answer Emmy's question, she decided to fill in the blanks. "Admit it—I'm right. Jed Harker, the man who can't spell the word *commitment*, finally bought a dictionary."

He was admitting nothing. Not to Emmy, and certainly not to himself. "It was a stupid accident, that's all. Oliver's working on an annulment right now, and in a week, it'll be over."

"An accident, huh? How do you accidentally get married?"

"I don't know, exactly." He grimaced. "There was alcohol involved. Chess couldn't remember either."

"Chess? That's her name?"

"Yeah. Well, Francesca."

"So did you...?"

"Oh yeah, we definitely did that."

Jed wished he could smile at the memory, but it still fucking eluded him.

"How did you meet her?"

He gritted his teeth in frustration. "Not sure of that either."

"Stripper?"

For many men, that would have been an insult, but normally with Jed she'd have been right on the money. He tended to go for pretty girls interested in the same thing he was—one night, no strings. No G-strings, either.

But that sure as hell wasn't Chess. "No, a student. Some kind of scientist. Anyhow, I remember the strip club. We got bored, left early, and went back to the hotel. Nick said I disappeared after we stopped off in the bar." And Jed could only imagine what had happened next. A pretty girl, his black Amex, a few drinks...

"Hold on—the strip club was boring? What happened to your crazy bachelor party weekend full of debauchery?"

"We must be getting old." Jed glanced in the rearview mirror, checking his forehead for lines. Two, still faint.

"Or sick. Are you feeling okay? What did the rest of the guys think?"

"Nick kept looking at his watch while a couple of the girls licked whipped cream off each other in front of him and Black was answering emails in the middle of a lap dance."

Most women would be upset at hearing their husband got a lap dance, but Emmy wasn't most women. She grinned instead. "I'd bury him if he did that with me."

She wasn't joking, either, but no man would look away if Emmy danced naked in front of him. Her husband was a lucky bastard. The pair of them hadn't been exclusive for the first twelve years of their marriage, and although that had changed now, Emmy still gave Black a long leash. The trust they shared sometimes made Jed wish he could meet "the One."

He'd always hated the idea of being tied down, and in any case, the amount of time he'd spent travelling in his twenties had hardly been conducive to a healthy relationship. What kind of woman stayed loyal to a man who spent half his time abroad? Not his colleagues' wives, that was for sure. One by one they'd lost interest and strayed, costing most of the men he worked with their hearts as well as their money.

Like last year, when Blaine returned from a three-month stint in Afghanistan and found his pretty young wife in bed with not only the female babysitter but the pool boy as well. No way was that happening to Jed, unless he got invited to make it into a foursome, of course. Then there was his old army buddy, Quinn. He'd gotten screwed over by a woman in Moscow, and to this day he refused to talk about it. But he didn't need to. The mere mention of Russia sent him straight to the vodka bottle and those depressions lasted for days.

Jed studied Emmy's legs, resting mere inches from where his hand gripped the steering wheel. It was a sad day in his life when she went monogamous. That bitch had been the most uncomplicated lay of his life, and the hottest too. But he respected her decision, and above all they were friends.

As were he and her husband. "Rest assured Black behaved himself the entire weekend. Well, apart from driving a golf cart into a lake, but that was partly Nate's fault."

She laughed, deep and throaty. "What were they doing? Racing?"

"Yeah. After that, we got banned from the golf course so we came home. How was the bachelorette's spa trip? I can't picture you girls sitting around drinking smoothies for three days."

"That was more Bradley's vision than ours." Emmy referred to her personal assistant who had made all the arrangements. "We lasted the first day and most of the second."

"Is that when your hair happened?" She'd gone

from her natural honey blonde to almost white.

"No, that was Bradley too. He's been watching *Frozen.*"

"So, do I dare ask what day two of the spa brought?"

"There might have been a teeny incident."

"Someone put the wrong dressing on the salad? A broken nail?"

"More a kidnapping, a trek through the woods, and Bradley scuffed the knee out of his new jeans and he won't shut up about it. But none of us got arrested, so it was all good. Anyway, stop changing the subject—I want to hear more about your fuck-up. The shit we did pales into insignificance beside that."

The details were for him and him alone. "Not much to tell. It's over. You know I don't do long-term."

"Really? So you're just going to get un-married and carry on as before?"

"Yeah, that's exactly what I'm going to do."

Emmy went quiet for a long minute, the silence in the car broken only by bad-tempered drivers laying on their horns as they hit traffic on the outskirts of Washington, DC. Up ahead, an ancient Chevy blocked the inside lane, and far from being sympathetic, most vehicles carried on by without their passengers giving a second glance.

"We stopping?" Jed asked Emmy.

She glanced at her watch. "Why not? It's only the White House."

Despite Emmy's sniping about his driving speed, they'd hit the capital early, so Jed signalled and pulled over in front of the vehicle. Its elderly owner looked shell-shocked as the traffic barged past. Emmy hopped out and slid in next to the white-haired man while Jed leaned over her shoulder.

"You okay, sir?" she asked.

"Darn car just stopped. Meant to be visitin' my daughter."

"Aw, that sucks. Let's see if we can help. What's your name?"

"Jimmy."

"Your parents named you well—my daddy's called Jimmy. Can you pop the hood? I'll take a look."

"You?" The man's eyes betrayed his confusion but Emmy patted him on the hand.

"My godfather ran an auto shop." She grinned. "Taught me everything he knew."

Jed stopped his eyes from rolling at the lies that tripped off Emmy's tongue. Her acquaintance, not her godfather, ran a chop shop, not a repair shop, although the part about him teaching her auto mechanics was true.

Still, Jimmy did as she asked and flipped the catch, and seconds later Emmy had her head buried under the hood.

Two minutes after that, the sound of crunching metal made Jed realise their mistake. Mind you, if he'd been driving that BMW, he'd have slowed down to stare at Emmy's ass too.

"Are you done there yet?"

She poked her head out. "Just about. Can you call a tow truck? The timing belt's snapped, so this car isn't going anywhere."

"Yeah, I'll call."

Twenty minutes later, they'd heard all about Jimmy's new granddaughter, and the tow truck driver was winching the old car onto a flatbed.

"At least he'll get to his family in time for lunch," Emmy said.

"And you've done your good deed for the day."

"I do so much shit, I need to build up the karma when I can."

Jed hoped their untimely interlude would have made Emmy forget their earlier conversation, but damn her and her computer-like memory. She picked up exactly where they'd left off.

"You may not want to say it out loud, but I know you well enough to see you feel something for Chess. Why don't you take her out a few times? At least then you'd know if there was a spark. Maybe she's sitting in who-the-fuck-knows-where moping around as well?"

"Texas. She's in Texas. And I can't, okay?"

"Why not? Texas isn't that far by air, and I'll even lend you a plane. All it would take is a phone call."

Chapter 8

"I COULDN'T TAKE Chess on a date, even if I wanted to, and I'm not saying I do."

"Why? Don't tell me she knocked you back?"

Jed had no desire to tell Emmy Chess's secrets, but if nothing else, he was a realist. If he didn't spill, Emmy would find out everything she wanted to know by the time the White House minions served coffee.

"Only because she's engaged."

Emmy choked, then began coughing. "Shit. I just swallowed my gum." Jed thumped her on the back, and she glared at him. "You know I have a gun, right?"

"I'm too sexy to shoot."

"Don't test me." She grabbed a bottle of water from behind the seat and took a gulp. "So, engaged? As in, she's getting married?"

"How many other kinds of engaged do you know?"

"Fuck. And people call me cold? Still, if she's screwing around on her fiancé, you're better off without her."

Knowing how many years Emmy spent fucking men who weren't her husband, including him, Jed wasn't worried about her judging. She'd make fun, but she wouldn't judge. "It's not like that. She's marrying some asshole because her family's making her."

"So she says."

"It's true. I ran into him in the hotel lobby, and it took all my self-control to let him walk out of there with his teeth intact."

"Do you want me to kill him?"

He glanced across to check whether she was serious or not. He never quite knew with Emmy, but the quirk of her lips suggested not this time.

"That won't be necessary, but thanks for the offer." *And please, stop talking about it.* The last thing he wanted was another rehash of events. The guys had spent the entire flight back taking the piss out of him, and Nate had already photoshopped his head into an entire wedding album. "So, why are you coming to the meeting today?"

Emmy's smug smile said she knew exactly why he'd changed the subject, but she gave him a pass. "James's request. I don't know the exact reason, but he's paying me so here I am."

Jed would put money on knowing the reason, and it was nothing to do with America's foreign policy. President James Harrison may be the leader of a world superpower, but he still thought with his dick on occasion. Inaugurated two years ago, and now forty-two, Harrison was the youngest man to hold the job, and since he took office, Emmy had become a regular visitor to the White House.

Like today. As the CIA Special Operations Group's head of section for the Middle East, it was obvious why Jed needed to attend the president's bi-weekly briefing on Middle Eastern affairs, but as a private contractor, Emmy's role wasn't quite so clear-cut.

Jed had often wondered about the relationship between his ex and the president. She made no secret of the fact that she and her husband had donated heavily to Harrison's campaign, but was there something more? Although Emmy's marriage was now tight, Jed had a sneaking suspicion that during the looser years, her relationship with then-Senator Harrison may have crossed the line into something more. Not that he'd ever asked her—she lied as often as she told the truth, so it would have been a pointless question, anyway.

Jed cursed as he cut past a slower car driving in the wrong lane, ignoring the man's blast on the horn. "Get out of the damn way."

"That's more like it," Emmy muttered.

Whatever the real reason for her presence today, Jed viewed it as a good thing. Unlike many of the men on Capitol Hill, her job didn't depend on kissing ass or garnering votes, so she said what she thought and voiced the questions nobody else dared ask. Courting controversy was a sport for her, even if she pretended otherwise.

Another advantage of having Emmy by his side was the apartment she owned within spitting distance of the White House. She rarely stayed there, but its private parking garage saved them the trouble of hunting for a space.

"Ready?" he asked.

"Two seconds."

She flipped down the mirror and applied a layer of bright red lipstick. Not because she habitually wore make-up, but because it scared people. She'd confessed as much once.

A short walk took them to the back entrance of 1600 Pennsylvania Avenue, where as established visitors, they quickly cleared security.

"How are you, Murphy?" Emmy greeted the guard who searched them.

"Good, thank you, ma'am."

The man smiled nervously as he waved her through. If she wasn't carrying some kind of weapon, Jed would have been surprised.

He trailed her along the hallway, the click-click-click of her heels muffled as they stepped onto carpet. She didn't hesitate as she navigated the maze to the room they regularly met in, and a member of the secret service scrambled to hold the door open as she headed towards it.

"Thank you, Mike."

"Yeah, thanks," Jed added as they walked inside.

Three men were already seated as they took their places at the table, and five more filtered in while Jed read over the agenda in front of him.

"Coffee, sir?"

He glanced up at the blonde assistant looking down at him. Not bad, but Chess was prettier. "White, one sugar, with a touch of cream." Normally, his grin came easily, but today he had to force it. "And could you bring some of those cookies with the chocolate?"

Her genuine smile made him feel guilty. "Of course." Her expression faltered as she turned to Emmy. "Mrs. Black? Would you like a drink?"

"Double espresso, no sugar. Thanks."

Heads turned as the double doors opened once more. Mr. President, right on time.

James circulated briefly like the seasoned statesman he was, greeting each attendee by name and murmuring a few words. The man always did know how to work a room.

"Jed, how are you?"

"Good, thanks. You?"

James ran a hand through his light brown hair and gave a lopsided smile. "Nobody said this job would be easy."

"Well, you wanted it."

"Yeah. Kind of miss the old days, though." Out of the public eye, Senator Harrison had been a regular guest at Riverley Hall, the home Emmy shared with her husband. The ex-Navy helicopter pilot had liked Friday-night beers as much as the rest of them. "But I hear you've changed. Marriage?"

Jed sliced his eyes to Emmy, talking to one of the Joint Chiefs. "Is there anyone she didn't tell?"

"Don't worry—I talked her out of hiring the skywriter. So, who's the lucky lady?"

"It doesn't matter. We got an annulment as soon as we regained consciousness." Well, not quite, but according to Oliver it was practically a done deal.

James's lip quirked as he tamped down a smile. "I'll hold off on the congratulations then."

Emmy meandered over, coffee in hand. "Mr. President."

Coming from anybody else, the words would have been a mark of respect, but Emmy made them sound playful. Mocking, almost.

"Mrs. Black. Delightful as always."

"Practising your politician skills? Telling fibs will get you everywhere."

He leaned down and whispered something too quiet for Jed to hear, and Emmy gave Harrison a tiny smile. "Yeah, I remember," she murmured. Then louder, "We should get started."

This morning's meeting wasn't as eventful as some. Frank, the chairman of the Joint Chiefs, a man who looked like everyone's favourite grandfather but had a mean bite when needed, led the proceedings, beginning with an update on activity in the region. Car bombings, suicide bombings, terrorists-getting-it-wrong-and-blowing-their-own-arms-off bombings. Business as usual, sadly.

Jed tried to concentrate, but as the discussion drifted onto a review of long-term plans, his attention wandered. All the way to a bathroom stall where he'd spent too long and not long enough squashed next to a petite blonde. One he couldn't get out of his mind no matter what he did.

The thought of her marrying the asshole from the hotel lobby made him want to break something. Preferably the guy's nose or maybe his jaw. Why did Jed feel so possessive over Chess? He didn't understand it and wasn't sure he wanted to. He'd known the girl less than twenty-four hours and most of that time was blank. But the bits he did remember? Those curves... He heard a crack, and ten faces turned in his direction. Emmy's gaze dropped, and he followed it to the broken pencil in his hand. Shit.

He really needed to forget this woman.

And he had every reason to. Hadn't she knocked him back? He'd broken every one of his rules and asked her to come home with him, and she'd declined. What was he supposed to do? Beg? Plead? Go full stalker?

He dropped the remains of the pencil and forced himself to tune into the discussion. Frank was still talking, and James was doodling a picture of a

Doberman that looked remarkably like Emmy's. At least Jed wasn't the only one struggling to stay focused.

"So, our last item on the agenda. Bit of a strange one." Frank fiddled with his laptop, and a small town appeared on the screen. "This is Al Bidaya. Located two-hundred miles south of Baghdad, west of Najaf. Local doctors have reported an unusual number of deaths there recently, and the International Red Cross went in to assist. Two of their team died and three are in a critical condition."

Jed sat up a little straighter. This made a change from their usual discussions. The representative from the US Army grabbed his laser pointer and took over.

"We sent in a team to assess the situation, but the details coming back are confusing to say the least. One of them is currently hospitalised."

James dropped his pen and spoke up. "So, what's the problem? Have they been attacked? Are they ill?"

"At the moment, it seems to be a sort of fever. Some reports say the victims are vomiting, others say they're coughing. They've been experiencing blisters, rashes, fatigue, stomach pains, and diarrhoea. The only thing all the sources agree on is that a hell of a lot of people have died."

"Is it just in Al Bidaya? Or the region as a whole?"

"So far, it's only affected the town. At least, that we know of. I can't emphasise how sketchy this information is, but there's enough to warrant a further look."

James raised an eyebrow. "You think there's a risk of it spreading?"

The guy shrugged and held out his hands. So much for the US's superior intelligence gathering capabilities.

One of the other committee members spoke up. "Let's not get too excited. Stomach pains? It could be food poisoning."

Emmy fixed him with a stare. "Or something could have escaped from one of those chemical weapons stores Saddam claimed he didn't have."

"We found no evidence of—"

James waved a hand. "I'll agree to take a look as long as we can get the local authorities to cooperate. What are you proposing?"

"A small team," Frank suggested. "Say, a couple of doctors, somebody from the CDC, bodyguards, and someone with the experience to coordinate it."

Jed sighed. The last time the Centre for Disease Control and Prevention sent an advisor to brief the committee, she'd talked for so long James faked an emergency to get them out of there. Fierce, too. If ever she got bored with staring into microscopes, the bitch could have made good money as a dominatrix.

At the thought of microscopes, Chess popped into Jed's head again as proof that scientists could be sexy. And sweet. And incredibly distracting.

"Any suggestions as to who we could use to coordinate?" James asked.

"I'll go." Jed's words surprised even him. But it made sense. A little field trip would take his mind off events in Vegas once and for all, and his tan could use a top-up. Since his promotion to head of section six months ago, he'd spent most of his time behind a desk. "As long as the CDC doesn't send that woman who kept whacking her thigh with the ruler."

The whole table snickered at that.

"You sure about this?" James asked. "It's low-level

for you."

"Don't want to get rusty in the field, and I could do with brushing up on my Arabic. Besides, a review won't take more than two or three weeks." Enough time for Chess to have married the prick with the attitude problem.

James glanced at Emmy, who gave him a barely perceptible nod. "Then okay. It'd be good to get your eyes on this."

The meeting wrapped up on schedule, and yep, there it was—Harrison holding onto Emmy just a beat too long when he politely kissed her goodbye on both cheeks. Emmy's face betrayed nothing, a cool mask as always, before she drew back and walked to the door.

Back at the car, Emmy threw her leather purse onto the tiny backseat. "You gonna let me drive this time?"

"Nope. I want to get home in one piece."

Jed opened the driver's door and climbed in, leaving her to get her ass into the passenger seat.

"And I want to get home in one piece and do it quickly. Time is money, Jed."

"You don't give a fuck about money."

Emmy had more cash than she could ever spend, but it hadn't changed her. She still displayed the same acerbic personality she'd had a decade ago before she got rich.

"Okay, you got me. How about 'fast is fun?'"

"Now that, babe, depends on what you're talking about."

"You're such a whore, Jed. Do you ever think of

anything except sex?"

"Not often," he admitted. "Especially when you're sitting next to me rockin' the slutty secretary look."

"You don't like it?" She batted her eyelashes in mock-innocence.

"Oh, I like it. Everyone at the meeting liked it, including Mr. President."

"The president is married. Now shut up and keep your eyes on the road."

Her red lips pursed into a thin line, and Jed grinned. Score one to him.

Emmy stayed quiet most of the way home, which made a change from the morning's journey. It was hard to know whether she was tired, grumpy, or plotting something. Over the years, Jed had gotten used to her mercurial nature, but he didn't claim to understand her.

When he turned into the driveway at Riverley Hall, she smiled and waved at the guards in the gatehouse, then patted Jed on the thigh.

"I'd say thanks for driving, but you know how I felt about it."

"Next time, I'll let you take your car while I follow behind."

She chuckled. "The meeting would be done before you got there. Are you staying tonight?"

Jed spent half his life staying at Riverley. The house was a grown-up's playground, and neither Emmy nor her husband minded when their friends crashed there. He took a mental inventory of the contents of the refrigerator in his apartment—a six-pack of beer, condiments, and a loaf of bread.

"I'll grab dinner, but I'm planning to head out with

Quinn."

"Anywhere special?"

"A bar. A club. Somewhere."

Anywhere to take his mind off Chess. He needed to find a new girl, one he could use to fuck away the memories. Preferably a brunette. A tall, skinny brunette.

Did he have wine in his kitchen? A bottle of red if he remembered right. With any luck, he'd need it later, as well as the economy-sized pack of Trojans stashed in his nightstand.

"When are you heading to Iraq?" Emmy asked.

"As soon as I can. Tomorrow, if I can get a team together and there's a flight leaving."

Jed parked the car, and before he could get out, she gripped his hand. "Be careful out there."

"I'll be fine. It's not my first rodeo." Ah, rodeos. They'd tried that together too, with Emmy as the cowgirl. He blocked that thought from his head as he covered her hand with his. "I'll make sure I wear one of those hazard suits when I go near the hospital."

"I've got a bad feeling about this."

"We've had scares before."

She looked past him, into the distance. "But this is *al bidaya*. The beginning."

CHAPTER 9

THREE DAYS HAD passed since I arrived home from Vegas, three days where Jared had tried to insert himself into every waking thought. And my sleeping ones too.

Why had he made that offer? Was he genuine? Every time Clayton barked an instruction at me, the ache in my chest that had started when I walked out of the Black Diamond hotel grew a little stronger. Right now, it pressed on the inside of my ribs, well on its way to doing permanent damage.

"I made the right decision," I whispered to myself, as if saying it out loud would somehow make it true. I'd done the sensible thing, followed the best path for my future. After all, I had a plan, didn't I?

A plan that didn't involve having a tower of blond hair and muscles sweep me off my feet. I shook my head and caught movement in the vehicle next to mine. An old lady scowled. Yes, ma'am, I have gone crazy, okay?

Ahead, the traffic inched forward, and I pulled away from her disapproval.

Where would I be now if I'd left with Jared? Not stuck in a Galveston traffic jam with broken air conditioning. I let out a thin breath as I lifted my top away from my stomach, but as soon as I let it go, it stuck to my skin again.

Would Jared really have helped Lottie and me? Or would he have given up once he found our problems weren't as easy to solve as he thought? What did I know? Up until three days ago, I'd never done more than make out with a man—well, two men, and neither of those had been a pleasant experience. Kissing Wade was less pleasurable than sucking a wet fish, and the guy in my junior year of high school? I couldn't even remember his name.

But Jared... I bet Jared knew how to make a woman's toes curl.

Darn it, Chess, Jared's out of your league. So far out of my league we weren't playing the same sport. Jared was skydiving, surfing, and downhill skiing. I was more lawn bowls. And I bet Jared wasn't poor either. Rooms in the Black Diamond started at $300 a night, as Wade told me over and over, and Jared hadn't even cared about sleeping in his. No, if we hadn't been so drunk we didn't know our own minds, he wouldn't have given me a second glance.

But he wasn't drunk the next morning when he asked you to leave with him. Maybe not, but he felt sorry for me, that was all. Pitied me after I told him about Wade.

For three days, my head and heart had been waging war—the cold light of days versus my hopes and dreams. Reality against fantasy. All that darn thinking made me so exhausted I just wanted to sleep.

Except when I did sleep, Jared invaded my dreams too. Alone in the attic room I shared with Lottie when she was well enough to stay home, I tossed and turned until I woke up sweating in tangled sheets.

Each time I closed my eyes, Jared kissed me, caressed me, touched me in places I didn't want to admit. Sleeping me felt his tongue clash with mine, the heat of his body as he covered me, and the delicious violation as he pushed himself inside. Last night, I came in my sleep for goodness' sake! I'd lost my darn mind.

I'd tried to deal with it by throwing myself into my research. Apart from dinner with Mom, Clayton, and Wade, I'd spent the last three days studying, although I'd only been into the lab itself twice. If I didn't concentrate there, dying was a very real possibility, and on Monday I'd made a huge mistake and forgotten to connect my air supply to my hazmat suit. Two minutes in, only some frantic hand signals and the quick thinking of my lab assistant saved me from passing out.

But this morning I hadn't been able to put it off any longer. I'd banished Jared from my thoughts, suited up, and done what I needed to do. And as a reward, now I was on my way to visit Lottie. Maybe spending some time with her would take my mind off the car crash the rest of my life had turned into?

The driver behind blasted his horn, and I realised the light had turned green. Darn it—I'd zoned out again. I gritted my teeth, stomped on the gas and shot off. Well, as much as a 1996 Toyota Corolla can shoot off, which is to say I pulled away at slightly more than walking pace.

Twenty minutes later I turned into the parking lot of the Bayview Centre, a misnomer if ever there was one. There was no bay, and when Lottie looked out of her window, she only saw the delights of the industrial complex next door.

Before I headed inside, I made sure my sleeve was pulled down over the bruises left on my arm in Vegas. Wade's fingermarks, now a yellowish-green, would only invite questions, although Mom and Clayton either hadn't noticed or hadn't cared.

Lottie's door was propped open as the air conditioning fought a losing battle against the June heat. She'd slid the window up too, and the noise from the auto repair shop opposite drowned out the TV. Not that Lottie was looking at the screen—as usual, she was curled up on the bed with a book. Another romance, judging by the guy on the cover. I couldn't help comparing him to Jared, and Jared easily came on top. Quite literally, if my dreams were anything to go by.

"Hey," I said from the doorway.

Lottie dropped the book, then leapt up and flung her arms around me. "Chess! You're early today."

"Just wanted to spend a bit more time with my favourite sister."

She poked me in the arm. "I'm your only sister."

"And still my favourite. I brought you more books." I held up the bag of paperbacks I'd picked up from the thrift store on my way over.

She grabbed it off me like it contained treasure and tipped the contents onto the bed. "Awesome—I haven't read any of these."

Before I sat down, I took a moment to study her. She still looked so thin. Lottie always refused to discuss her weight, but in my phone catch-up yesterday, her nurse told me Lottie weighed ninety-nine pounds. Only one to go until she'd hit triple figures. When she got admitted three months ago, she'd been seventy, which at five feet eight wasn't much more than a skeleton.

Just thinking of those days made marrying Wade worth it.

Because Lottie still had a long way to go. Her hair didn't shine like it used to, and her papery skin highlighted every blemish. The nurse said they still struggled daily to make sure she ate, and she refused to socialise with the other patients. If not for my visits, her only company apart from the staff would be the characters she loved to read about so much.

But I couldn't tell her any of that. The psychologist she saw twice a week emphasised the importance of staying positive, so I pasted on a smile as I sat beside her on the bed.

"They should keep you going to the weekend, then?"

Lottie read so fast, and I'd struggled to feed her habit until I'd found the thrift store six blocks from the university. After a month, I'd become friendly with the manager, and now she set aside all the books she thought Lottie might like. Twice a week I stopped by to pick them up in return for a donation to the local animal shelter.

My sister eyed the pile critically. "I might finish them by Friday, but I can always watch TV after that."

"How are you feeling?"

We always followed the same ritual. I'd ask Lottie how she felt, and she'd tell me she was fine, when we both knew she was anything but. Today was no different.

"I'm good. Yeah, really good. And how are you? Is college okay? How are the wedding plans?"

Oh, the wedding. Between Jared and the lab, I'd managed to block it out of my mind for a few days, and

I certainly didn't want to think about it now.

"I started the next stage in the vaccine trial today."

She clapped her hands. "That's great! You've been working towards that for ages, haven't you?"

Yes, I had. And along the way, I'd celebrated the small victories and cried more times than I could remember. I envied my colleagues who could stay dispassionate as they recorded results and studied reactions. Too often I let the emotions get the better of me.

But with every setback, I reminded myself of my long-term goal—to save lives. Every experiment that failed, every funding application that got rejected, every animal that died in my lab—I pushed past them all. Because if watching a rat die from haemorrhagic fever hurt, seeing a whole family of humans succumb must be a million times worse. Every victim was somebody's son or daughter. They all had people who loved them. And many years ago, one of them had been my best friend.

CHAPTER 10

FILOVIRIDAE. ONE TINY word, a family of tiny viruses, but they could be oh-so-deadly. Ebola, Marburg, and the more recently discovered Cuevavirus, in all their terrifying variants. With a fatality rate as high as ninety percent of those infected, there was no organism more dangerous.

As long as the viruses stayed in the jungle where they came from, they didn't cause too many problems. But every so often, one of them would sneak out, usually into a remote village where a lack of modern healthcare and understanding of the symptoms meant an isolated case could turn into an epidemic. And a global crisis.

During the last outbreak, world governments went crazy for a couple of months, dishing out cash for research like candy at a birthday party. I'd managed to snag enough for my current project. But when the chaos died down and the bodies stopped piling up, they diverted their attention and their money to more important causes, like token tax breaks and buying lots of weapons.

Without government money, the urgency went out of finding a cure. The big pharmaceutical companies weren't interested. After all, who succumbed to the filoviruses? People in developing countries living hand to mouth, whose lives revolved around their families and the small communities they called home. People who couldn't afford to pay for medication.

So, while Ebola and its evil cousins slumbered, all but a small handful of researchers moved onto more profitable projects. But the filoviruses would come back. They always did.

Lottie's next question snapped me out of my thoughts. "Is the trial on the monkeys?"

"Yes."

"So, has anything happened yet?"

"Not yet—I only injected them this morning."

And even if something had happened, I'd spare Lottie the details, because no matter how high I got my hopes, for the last two years I'd lost most of the animals. I wished I could spare myself from the details too.

"Well, I'll keep my fingers crossed for you. And my toes. Everything crossed."

"I'll need all the luck I can get."

She chewed on her lip for a second. "Faith would be proud of you."

A tear escaped and rolled down my cheek. "I like to think so."

Faith Hillman had been my best friend in high school. I say that as if I'd had others, but really that wasn't the case. Faith was my only friend in high school. We sat next to each other in chemistry class from the age of twelve, and until we graduated nobody could prise us apart. Faith always used to kid that the bond between us was covalent. Apart from Lottie, she was the only person who knew about the hell I went through at home, and after I confided in her, she'd changed from a good friend into a lifeline.

I still remembered the day after my confession. As I snuck out of English class at the back of the crowd, Faith had been waiting for me in the hallway with a wide grin plastered across her face.

"You'll never guess what."

She was right. I wouldn't. I was hopeless at those games.

"What?"

"Mom accidentally gave me two packages of chips in my lunch, so you can have one of them."

My stomach grumbled at the thought. My mom had packed me cucumber sticks, carrot batons, two apples, and a package of low-fat crackers.

"Are you sure you don't want them?"

"Yeah. I ate loads for breakfast."

The next day, it happened again, only the "extra" was a chocolate bar. After a month or two, I began to suspect Mrs. Hill wasn't making mistakes at all.

"Did you tell your mom that my mom doesn't give me enough to eat?"

Faith went a little pink and studied her shoes—pale pink sneakers with orange laces. Funny how I still remembered that, wasn't it?

"I didn't mean to. But she saw me taking extra gummy bears from the cupboard and got all grumpy."

"Did you get in trouble?"

"Not after I told her. She said we should always help people who need it."

And so the gifts continued and my stomach didn't growl all night anymore. Extra lunch turned into dinner twice a week—a proper family dinner like we used to eat when Daddy was alive. Money had been short, but Mom was more normal back then. Daddy's death had affected her badly, and she'd only married Clayton out of desperation when our cash finally ran out. At least, that was what I suspected. I couldn't see how any woman would betroth herself to him willingly. Although Mom was sort of happy now, and maybe that was why she couldn't understand my problem with getting hitched to Wade.

When she realised how hungry I was, Faith's mom saved me by calling mine and telling her I was studying in the evenings. But that came at a price, and the price was my sister. While I hid out at Faith's, Lottie stayed at home with Mom. Twelve-year-old me didn't worry about my little sister—after all, she'd always been Mom's favourite, and she never liked to stray far from the apron strings. It was only as I got older I understood the pressure Mom heaped on Lottie over her looks. Eat this, don't eat that. Wear this dress. Ladies shouldn't be in trousers. By the time Lottie suffered her first collapse, and I realised how awful I'd been as a sister, it was too late.

Yet another reason I was trying to fix everything now.

Lottie reached over and gave me a hug. "Don't cry. It's a good thing you're doing."

"I just miss Faith; that's all."

I squeezed her back, trying not to wince as her bones pressed into me.

Darn it, I should have been cheering Lottie up, not getting all melancholy about the past. Nothing would bring Faith back.

I made an effort to smile and inject a little happiness into my voice. "So, how are things here? Did you do anything fun today?"

She shrugged. "Not really. Read another book." There was a long pause. "Maria got taken into intensive care again." Lottie's voice shook as she said the words, even though she attempted nonchalance.

I closed my eyes and leaned back against the wall. Maria was being treated for anorexia, the same as Lottie, only I'd watched her lose weight for weeks. The nurses tried their best, but Lottie's nurse said Maria's family stopped visiting so often, and without their support, she went downhill. I couldn't let Lottie travel down that same road.

"That's not going to happen to you; I promise. Just keep listening to the doctors, and you'll be out of here in no time."

All pretence at indifference stopped. "I hate it here. I hate being ill. I hate that it's so quiet and everything smells like death."

Now it was Lottie's turn to cry.

Oh hell, I hated when she got upset like this. "You won't be here for long, honey." I snuggled her into my side and kissed her hair, so dull and lifeless. "How about we watch a movie together?"

"Okay."

She gave a long sniffle and pulled a tissue from the box on the nightstand.

"So, what are we watching?"

"*Pretty Woman*?"

Again. Twice in the last month alone. "Sure, I love that movie too."

After the credits rolled, we watched *Bridget Jones: The Edge of Reason*. Lottie knew all the words by heart, and she mouthed them along with the characters. While she got happier as the movies played, my mood went the same way as Bridget when she decided to try skiing—rapidly downhill. It was my own fault entirely because while Bridget rejected the advances of Mr. Cleaver, my mind drifted to Jared. What if he was meant to be my Edward Lewis? Or my Mr. Darcy? Without me being a prostitute, obviously.

Chess! Stop it. Jared was gone, out of my life. All I had left was half a memory and his number, carefully stored in my phone. Okay, and I might have written it out on a piece of paper just in case my phone got stolen. And saved it in my computer. And memorised it. Oh, what did it matter? It wasn't like I planned to call it. I mean, I'd stared at the darn screen for two hours last night without plucking up the courage to send him a message.

Because what would I say?

Hi, Jared, how's the annulment going?

Thanks for helping me in the bathroom. How was your trip home?

Uh, I don't suppose you'd like to get a coffee one day?

Scratch all of those, especially the last one. Definitely the last one. I may not have remembered the sex, but it had sure turned me into a crazy woman. After all, the marriage certificate said he came from Richmond, clear across the country. Even if I did want to fly to the East Coast, which I absolutely didn't, I couldn't afford a ticket.

I sighed as Mr. Darcy finally kissed Bridget. What would it be like to have a man who cared enough to rescue me on the other side of the world? To find somebody other than Lottie who loved me just the way

I was?

As if to emphasise my destiny, Lottie turned off the TV as the movie ended. "How are the wedding plans going?"

I'd never told her the real reason I was marrying Wade. For sure, she'd try to stop me, and I needed to think of her health above everything else. So while I hid my feelings, she got excited about my special day along with everyone else.

"Mom and Mrs. Bruckman have done most of the organising already."

"I'm so jealous of you, meeting the man of your dreams like that. Wasn't it lucky Daddy gave him a job at the dealership?"

Lucky? More like bad lucky. "I couldn't believe it when I walked in and saw him there."

"Fate, that's what it was. Did you get the bridesmaid dresses sorted out?"

There was a hint of sadness in her voice as she asked, because she'd wanted to follow me down the aisle, but Wade had vetoed that idea.

"I don't want her skinny ass spoiling our wedding photos," I believe were his exact words.

So, I'd had to break it gently to her that his two cousins were already taking the role. Brats, both of them. I'd never met ruder children than those little girls.

Three weeks ago, one of them threw a fit because she wanted a pink dress and hers was peach. And what did Wade's mom do? Did she insist the child wore the dress, anyway? Did she heck. She changed the entire colour scheme—flowers, the cake, table settings, the lot.

"Yes, it's all sorted. We're having a pink wedding

now." Not even a strong pink, rather a washed-out salmon that looked like it had been left in the sun for too long.

"I love pink. Chess, you're gonna look so pretty. It sure will be a wedding to remember."

At least that would be an improvement on my first one, if nothing else. No way could I tell Lottie I'd gotten hitched already, and to a different man. She'd freak, and then the nurses would call Clayton.

"Wade always did have his heart set on something out of the ordinary."

Another tear trickled down Lottie's cheek, only this time she was smiling. "I can't wait to see my big sister get married. Only a couple of weeks now."

I could hardly forget. For the last month, I'd been marking off the days, sort of like a nuclear countdown. "I can't wait." Even to my own ears, my words sounded false.

"Are you coming back this weekend?"

"Saturday morning, just like always." I gave her one last hug. "I wouldn't miss seeing you for the world."

Only as things turned out, I did.

Chapter 11

ON WEDNESDAY, THREE days after his return from Vegas, Jed slung his green duffel bag over his shoulder as he climbed the steps onto the military transport plane he and his team were hitching a ride on, cursing when he saw the canvas seats lining the fuselage. As head of section he usually flew business class, but American Airlines didn't fly to Wadi Al Khirr airbase. Hardly surprising, seeing as the godforsaken sandpit lay on the edge of the An-Najaf province with nothing around but miles of desert and the occasional camel.

He dropped his bag in the centre aisle, sat down, and tried to get comfortable—an impossible task. Whoever designed those seats obviously held a grudge against anyone who wore camouflage. Thirteen hours he'd be stuck there with no wine, no complimentary peanuts, and only a tube to piss in. And once he arrived in Iraq, the seventy-mile journey to Al Bidaya was unlikely to be any more enjoyable.

Accompanying Jed were two army doctors, a pair of lackeys from the CDC, and a trio of privates to act as muscle. With the situation in the province still unstable, attack was a real possibility. More ominous still were the three pallets lashed down in the centre of the plane and their contents.

This morning, the CDC guys had given the team a

crash course in how to wear the Level 4 hazmat suits, complete with self-contained air supplies and cumbersome gloves. After they'd practised walking in what amounted to a giant condom, a CDC doctor video-conferenced in and scared the fuck out of the entire team with tales of contagious diseases that made body parts drop off.

Jed sincerely hoped they wouldn't need to wear the suits, but until the team worked out what they were dealing with, they weren't taking any chances. Especially after reading the report from the Red Cross that had fallen across his desk this morning. The bodies were stacking up.

His team settled into the surrounding seats, and Bert, one of the doctors, got out a jumbo-sized bag of pretzels and offered them round.

"Got anything to drink?" the taller of the three privates asked.

"Do I look like an air hostess?"

Jed looked him up and down. "You don't have the legs for it."

That got him a good-natured middle finger. "What's our plan, boss?"

Good question. "At the moment, we're eyes and ears. We assess the situation and report back to my superiors."

Bert stuffed another pretzel in his mouth and spoke around it. "So, we're not treating patients?"

"The Red Cross has the lead on that. I'm not planning to go over their heads, but if they need more resources, we'll assist with coordinating that. And if it turns out this is something contagious that needs containment, our secondary task is to liaise with the locals and convince them to follow procedures."

One of the privates piped up. "What are the chances of it being contagious?"

Bert finished chewing and answered. "Fifty-fifty, I'd say. We haven't confirmed the symptoms; nausea and vomiting are fairly generic. Could be a virus, could be something in the water, could be radiation poisoning."

The private's eyes went wide. "Radiation poisoning?"

Bert shrugged. "Don't worry. We've brought Geiger counters."

Why had Jed volunteered for this operation again? Oh, yeah. Chess. Fuck it, now she was in his head again.

He fished a bottle of aspirin from his bag, popped a couple, and then washed them down with half a bottle of water. Once the plane took off, the niggling headache he'd had since he woke up would explode. C-130s weren't exactly renowned for their soundproofing. As the engines roared to life, he rolled up a spare sweater and wedged it behind his head. The pain was entirely self-inflicted, he knew that, but it didn't change the fact he felt like shit.

Last night, he'd met up with an old friend of his from the Army Rangers. They'd been stationed together, first at Fort Benning and later at Fort Lewis, and fought alongside each other on their first trip to Iraq. Later, they'd made the move to the CIA at the same time, but after that Samuel Quinn, whose mother hailed from Russia, headed off to Moscow thanks to his ability to speak the local lingo fluently. Despite almost getting his head blown off near Bagdad in those early days, Jed developed an affection for the Middle East and its people, learned to speak Arabic, and spent the next few years living and working in the region.

Life hadn't gone smoothly for either of them. Jed had dodged more bullets than he cared to count while Quinn spent his time dodging diplomatic incidents. Twice he got caught out, leading to his expulsion first from his mother's country, then from Venezuela, where the CIA had sent him to cool his heels after the Russian fiasco. Quinn never normally spoke about either incident, but one night a bottle of Scotch had loosened his tongue.

"So, what happened in Moscow?" Jed asked.

"My girl told me it was over."

"Sucks, buddy. But how did that upset the suits?"

"It didn't. It upset me. Ever have a girl reach into your chest, pull out your heart, stomp on it, set it on fire, then put it through the waste disposal?"

Jed shuddered. "Can't say I have."

"Well, that's what happened. I couldn't think; I couldn't concentrate. Then I blew my cover, and the Russians tried to kill me."

And if that was what love did to a man, it was best avoided.

"Harsh. And Venezuela?"

Quinn had been deputy head of station at the embassy in Caracas—he didn't have a cover to blow.

"Rumour has it I got caught in a compromising position with the president's niece."

"And is it true?"

Quinn smirked, and his old smile came back for a second. "I'd do it again for a fuck like that one."

So, Quinn was back in Washington until the CIA worked out what to do with him next. For now, they'd put him on extended leave, which meant when Jed suggested visiting a club last night Quinn had dusted off clothes smart enough to satisfy the door policy at Black's and jumped in a cab.

Back in their army days, they'd spent their spare time partying, sharing everything from beer to women. What better way to forget Chess than an evening in Richmond's best nightclub with his old buddy? Black's always had a selection of quality girls ready for the picking.

Which they managed, quite successfully. By eleven, they were back at Jed's place, he with a brunette and Quinn with an eye-catching blonde.

That was when the problems started.

For the first time in his life, Jed had issues with performance.

He'd spent days with a constant semi just from thinking about Chess, but when the brunette got on her knees and sucked like a hoover, his dick refused to cooperate. Eventually, he'd gone down on the chick as a sort of apology, but even that had been a by-the-numbers exercise. When she came, he'd heaved a sigh of relief and fetched her coat.

And Quinn didn't fare much better with the blonde.

"She kept calling me daddy," he grumbled once she and her friend slammed the door behind them.

"That's...weird."

"Tell me about it. I felt like a fucking paedophile. The only good part was that she left quickly afterwards."

Jed flopped back on the couch. "You know what this calls for?"

"Bourbon."

At some point between their fourth and fifth shots

—no sipping from tumblers for them that night—they'd both sworn off women for the foreseeable future. Just as well. It wasn't like he'd meet one while working in Iraq, anyway.

And a few weeks with an ocean between him and Chess would at least remove the burning desire to visit her. He'd been sorely tempted to take the annulment papers in person, just to have the excuse to talk to her one more time, to see if she was as sweet as he remembered. But now that temptation had been banished, he could concentrate on getting on with his life.

Yes, this trip was an excellent idea.

With Iraq eight hours ahead of Washington, DC, it was well into the following day when they arrived at Wadi Al Khirr, and the trip to Al Bidaya was everything Jed expected. Jarring, long, and hot.

There was only one guest house in town, and a local contact had procured rooms for use by Jed's team. Apparently, they'd be the only ones staying there.

"Nobody comes to Al Bidaya at the moment," the driver told him.

As the jeep rumbled through deserted streets, Jed translated "at the moment" into "ever." It was hard to see what could attract visitors to the tiny town so far off the beaten track and on the edge of a recovering war zone. Half of the buildings looked derelict at first sight, but on further inspection some of them showed signs of life. Children's toys on the front steps. Washing hanging on a makeshift line. The smell of fresh bread baking. Jed had been in the US for months, but driving into Al Bidaya, unfamiliar yet like a hundred other towns he'd visited in Iraq, reminded him why he'd spent so much time in the area. It felt real. The bullshit that came from the Pentagon didn't reach this far. These people lived simply, loved simply, and now, it seemed, died simply.

Beside him, Bert fiddled with a Geiger counter.

"Anything?"

"Nope. All clear so far."

Well, that was some good news at least. But what else lurked beneath the layer of dust that covered everything?

The driver dropped them at a dirty white building, with *Hotel* painted on the outside in lopsided English and Arabic. Home, sweet home, at least for the next couple of weeks.

A wizened old lady stepped out and gave them a toothless grin before rattling off a string in her native language.

"Her name's Maram," Jed translated for those who didn't speak Arabic. "She welcomes us to Al Bidaya."

They all trooped inside, and Maram led them to the second floor. The eight bedrooms were small but clean as were the two bathrooms they'd share.

"Would you like food?" she asked once they'd agreed who'd be sleeping where.

Trent, Jed's second in command, had gotten the biggest room by virtue of being fastest to the far end of the hallway.

Jed glanced at his watch. The equipment was on its way via truck but wouldn't arrive for another hour or so. "Lunch sounds like a good idea." He turned to his colleagues. "Then we should pay a visit to the hospital."

CHAPTER **12**

ONCE JED GOT his first look inside the tiny hospital, he realised eating lunch hadn't been such a great idea after all. Either the initial reports had been played down, or the situation had escalated faster than anyone thought possible.

On the advice of the CDC team, they'd suited up in hazmat gear, a process that had taken them twenty minutes and Jed thirty due to his unfamiliarity with the process. Every bit of his skin had to be covered, and the yellow suit taped at the wrists and ankles. It had seemed so much easier in the US, where he'd practised with the benefit of air conditioning. In Iraq, sweat caused everything to stick, and the inside of his clear visor fogged up before they'd even gone into the hospital.

"We'll only have an hour," Bert said. "Otherwise we'll risk heatstroke. We need to allow twenty minutes to get these suits off too."

Dr. Abadi, who ran the facility, met them at the entrance. Fear showed in his eyes, although whether it was due to his visitors looking like spacemen or because of the horrors behind the doors, Jed wasn't sure. The man himself wore a more basic Tyvek suit with a simple face mask and a single pair of rubber gloves.

"We have beds for twenty patients, but forty lay sick here. Four more have come today alone."

As they followed him into a waiting room full of the sick and dying, a flash of blue under a chair caught Jed's eye. A blonde-haired doll, her turquoise dress stained with red. Fuck. What happened to the toy's owner?

Retching from the far side of the room made him look up in time to see a man vomit up blood so thick and clotted it was almost black.

Words...he didn't have any. This was worse than any war zone he'd been to.

"We've lost two more patients this afternoon."

He turned to find a woman standing behind him, her features hidden behind a mask similar to Abadi's. Only her eyes were visible—wide and a peculiar shade of sea-green.

"I'm sorry."

Now Jed had found some words, they seemed vastly inadequate.

"Flavia Scoletti, with the International Red Cross. Forgive me if I don't shake your hand." On any normal day, her Italian accent would have been music to Jed's loins.

"Jed Harker, attached to the CDC. Could you give me an overview?" Best to keep the CIA out of this.

"The first patients showed up a month ago. Dr. Abadi diagnosed food poisoning initially and advised them to rest and drink plenty of water. When the first lady died, he thought it was due to her age."

"How old was she?"

"He estimates around seventy. Around here, people don't keep track of things like that. But then her son died, and two of her grandchildren."

"And they all lived near each other?"

"In the same house. Meanwhile, more of the villagers began getting sick." She waved an arm around the room. "And now you see... This isn't even the worst of it. They're in the next room."

Jed didn't want to ask, but he had to. "Can we take a look?"

Flavia nodded, then walked away. Jed followed, along with Dr. Abadi and the five members of the US team who'd come inside. The three privates remained on the perimeter, keeping an eye on things.

"Welcome to hell," Flavia muttered as she pushed through the double doors.

No, that wasn't just hell. The ward was hell's inner sanctum. A few feet away, two nurses held down a teenage boy as his back arched upwards in a seizure. Even through Jed's respirator, the stench of faeces invaded his nose, overlying the tang of blood underneath. And the noise—that got to him more than anything. Coughing, retching, the soft sobs of a child, and above it all, the wails of a woman in the far corner holding the body of a little girl.

Flavia followed his gaze. "The whole family got sick. Her husband died yesterday and now her daughter."

"Are there any others left?"

"Just her."

Beside Jed, Clint, the senior member of the CDC team, began videoing the scene. They'd need to send a report back to Washington that evening. Ten minutes later they'd seen enough, and Jed knew he'd never unsee the images from that day.

Sweat dripped down his back as the team left the

hospital. Flavia and Dr. Abadi came with them, and together the locals stripped off their protective suits at the side of the building and threw them onto a pile of others. Around them, a ring of scorched earth showed where the disposable garments got burned at the end of each day.

Jed copied Clint as he disrobed, starting from the top and working down, careful not to touch the outside of anything he'd been wearing.

Clint tutted as he worked. "We need to get proper biosafety procedures in place. This is woefully inadequate."

Flavia nodded in agreement. "We don't have enough people or enough equipment. And the locals don't understand the seriousness of the situation." She nodded at Dr. Abadi. "With all due respect."

He didn't argue. "We have never seen anything like this before."

Back in the hotel, they commandeered the dining room for a conference. Maram served up sweet, spicy tea and fresh bread, although the team only picked at it.

"It's worse than the reports suggested," Clint said.

Flavia nodded. "Trying to send current information is difficult. We're reliant on cellphones and the signal is patchy at best. We need to drive halfway to Wadi Al Khirr to pick up anything stronger."

Out of her hazmat suit, Flavia proved to be a willowy brunette with olive skin and a tense smile. Jed figured it matched his own. Pretty, but Jed always obeyed rule number one: Don't fuck around on duty.

"We've brought our own satellite equipment with us."

"The electricity here only works half the time."

Jed stared up at the naked bulb glowing above the table. "We're in luck at the moment, so if you can run us through the situation in more detail, we can send an up-to-date report to the CDC."

She opened her hands wide. "I usually run the children's clinics. This? This is beyond me. We need all the help we can get."

"Clint, can you take the lead on the questions?"

For the next half hour, Flavia and Abadi walked the team through the symptoms in all their horrifying detail. Jed took copious notes while the medical professionals talked, and the three privates, looking greener by the minute, listened from the end of the table.

"So, what do you think?" Flavia asked.

"Lots of diseases cause vomiting and diarrhoea, but not so many show the red eyes, the rash, or all the blood," Clint said.

"What would? I've only seen malaria, but that doesn't transmit on this scale."

"Radiation poisoning, for one. But we've found no readings to substantiate that. I'd suspect some sort of haemorrhagic fever. There are four families of those—Bunyaviruses, Flavaviruses, Arenaviruses..." He shuddered. "And the Filoviruses."

Bert spoke up. "In the Middle East? I've spent years out here and never seen symptoms like this. And the blisters in the longer-lasting cases? Those are strange."

"CCHF is endemic to this region."

"In English," Jed reminded him.

"Sorry—Crimean-Congo Haemorrhagic Fever. But it's usually spread by ticks, and we normally see a case here, a case there. Nothing on this scale. What's the survival rate?"

Abadi's voice shook as he answered. "All except five."

"Five people died?"

"No, five people lived."

Jed closed his eyes for a second. What the fuck had he walked into? "This CCHF—is there a cure for that?"

"Not a specific one, although we've seen some success using ribavarin. That's an antiviral drug," Bert said.

"Can we get that in Iraq?"

Clint shook his head. "Maybe in Baghdad, but I suspect it'd need to be shipped in."

Jed made a note. "How do we find out for sure whether it is CCHF? We can't go pumping people full of drugs without knowing they're the right ones."

"We took samples while you were talking earlier. There's a flight leaving for Atlanta tomorrow, and we need to get them on it." He turned to Flavia. "Do we know where it started? Who was patient zero?"

Dr. Abadi answered for her again. "The first couple who came to me ran a café on Peace Road. That's why I thought it was food poisoning to start with. And when I asked people where they'd been, several of the other early patients ate there recently."

"Any other common patterns?"

"Mostly it's spread among families and neighbours. The school closed at the end of the first week. At the beginning, people wanted to help each other, but now they are scared."

Clint's assistant cleared his throat. "There was a minor outbreak of CCHF in Ninevah a while back. A goat got bitten by a tick, and voila, that was the host. It was served up for dinner and a couple of dozen people got sick."

"That could have happened," Abadi agreed.

Meanwhile, Jed had scribbled out a bullet-pointed list, "One—we need to confirm exactly what this disease is and where it came from. Two—we need medical and scientific help. Three—we should establish a perimeter around the town to contain this thing. If it reaches Najaf, or Ramadi, or Baghdad, I don't think I need to tell you what damage it could do."

He looked at each person in turn. Nine pairs of eyes stared back at him, and the horror etched on each face matched his own.

Yes, they needed help, and fast.

CHAPTER 13

JED ASSEMBLED THE satellite equipment while the medical team wrote up the report. By the time they'd sent it to the White House committee and the CDC, the evening had slipped by and part of the night too. Flavia and her team were guests of Dr. Abadi, and they headed to the other side of town while Jed crawled upstairs.

He snatched a few hours' sleep, only to be woken by ringing. With jet lag, his body had no idea what time it was, where he'd fallen asleep, or what language to speak when he snatched up the phone.

English was usually a safe bet. "Hello?"

"Well, Harker, you sure find trouble easily."

James. "Just one of my incredible number of skills."

"I've read the report. Is it as bad as it suggests?"

"Worse." Jed took a deep breath to compose himself. "The inside of that hospital...You know the places I've been. That's worse than all of them."

"Fuck." Off-duty James didn't sound like the president. He sounded exactly like the Marine Corps officer he used to be. "The committee's meeting first thing in the morning."

"Thanks for being so prompt."

"If I hadn't been, Emmy would have kicked my ass."

He laughed, and Jed joined in. Neither of them

relished being on the receiving end of her ire.

"Still... It won't be easy to deal with this. Al Bidaya's inaccessible, the facilities are primitive, and dealing with the locals will be a whole other challenge especially if we quarantine the town."

"You believe that's necessary?"

"Until we ascertain what we're dealing with, yes."

James sighed. "I'll see what we can do."

Jed knew he would. James might embellish the truth to the media, but he tended to be straight with his friends. "Get some sleep, buddy. This is gonna be a long week for all of us."

"Stay safe. I say that as a friend."

"I'll do my best."

Morning brought another death—the woman Jed saw yesterday holding the dead child. Now she'd joined her daughter.

"What are you doing with the bodies?" Jed asked Flavia.

A tear rolled down her cheek inside her face visor. With the hospital desperately short of help and each person only able to wear their PPE for an hour at a time before the heat got the better of them, Jed found himself assisting on the ward.

"That's another problem we've had. The first were buried according to sharia, and the families performed a bathing ritual first. We're not sure yet how the disease is transmitted, but I suspect that contact spread it further."

"And now? What are you doing?"

"We've set aside a new area of land for the burials, and Dr. Abadi is trying to talk the relatives out of touching the bodies. Some agree; others are insistent on doing things their way. We can't force them to do otherwise."

"No, we can't." Jed knew all too well that working successfully in the Middle East meant force was a last resort. Engagement and coercion always came first. Next up on his list of things to do that day was meeting the local leaders to discuss their plans for Al Bidaya. "We'll need to turn them to our way of thinking."

"I'm hoping you can help there. My Arabic isn't fluent, and I can't treat the patients and spend time negotiating." Flavia's voice shook, and Jed understood the toll this must be taking on her.

He tried to sound positive. "Hey, that's why I'm here."

There was little other comfort he could offer while they were both wearing hazmat suits.

"I know, and for the first time in weeks I've got a little hope."

Hope. Flavia said she had hope, but Jed wasn't sure he shared the sentiment. After a series of difficult conversations with the locals, he now had a videoconference with the committee to look forward to before dinner. Not that he was particularly hungry after what he'd seen today.

Despite a momentary blip with the power mid-afternoon, the electricity had been restored in time for him to set up the satellite link on time. Bert and Clint took their places either side of him—the rest of the team was still at the hospital.

Right on time, the screen flickered into life. James sat in the top seat as always, with Emmy on one side, Frank on the other. Lined up along the table were six more men, all guys Jed recognised. But they weren't the only people in the room. Another figure sat in the shadows over Emmy's right shoulder. Who was that?

James started proceedings. "Good evening, gentlemen."

"Mr. President." Jed stuck with formality in light of the audience while Bert and Clint mumbled the same from his side.

"I'll cut to the chase. We've been through the report, and you're right. Any pathogen spreading with that ferocity is a concern not just to us, but to all of Iraq and those beyond its borders. I spoke to the Iraqi president half an hour ago. He's offered assistance and is grateful for any additional expertise we can provide."

"So, what's the plan?"

"The CDC is pulling a team together, including their leading expert on haemorrhagic fever, which they believe is the most likely culprit. I believe you've met Dr. Fielding?"

Jed thought back to a scare they'd had in Pakistan four or five years ago, to the chaos he'd encountered in a small mountain village that had ultimately turned out to be a particularly virulent flu. Dr. Fielding had joined the team for a week, assisting with sampling and diagnostics. A kindly looking man in his fifties, he'd spoken with a quiet confidence that made a difficult job go smoothly. If he was on his way to Iraq, it could only be a good thing.

"I know him. He's coming?"

"We've got a briefing tomorrow morning and a plane ready to go once we get the equipment loaded. It's being gathered together as we speak, and the Iraqis have agreed to transport it from Wadi Al Khirr to Al Bidaya."

"Did you get everything on the list?"

"We're still tracking down the new-generation hazmat suits, but the manufacturers have stepped up to the plate and provided everything else."

"Over-billed too," the man to Emmy's left muttered.

Corbin took care of the project budgets on black ops as well as their more legit cousins. He was forever shuffling money around so nobody knew how much the government spent on things they shouldn't. Welcome to the land of three hundred dollar pencils and "consultants" costing several thousand dollars an hour.

Emmy glared at him. "Look on the bright side. If this outbreak spreads, we're only looking at, like, twenty cents per death."

James narrowed his eyes at both of them. "We're not concerned about money at this point. We're more worried about where this disease originated."

"Your report indicated patient zero operated a café," Frank said. "But we need to know how he got infected."

Jed shook his head. "We don't even know what we're dealing with. The samples only left for the US this afternoon."

Emmy spoke up again. "Option one is that patient zero caught—let's assume it's a virus—from a natural vector. Mammals—sheep, goats, cows, that sort of thing —act as reservoirs for CCHF, and the CDC think it's possible the common strain's mutated to make it more deadly."

"So, what? We're looking for a herd of sick goats?"

"Not quite. The goats carry the virus, but it doesn't make them visibly ill."

A groan escaped Jed's lips. "Let me guess, you want me to chase after the goats and collect blood samples?"

He had a vision of himself running after a herd dressed in hazmat gear, then collapsing from heatstroke.

"The virus can also be carried by rats, hares..." She checked the sheaf of papers in front of her and tried to keep a straight face. Sometimes he hated her. "And, uh, hedgehogs."

"You want me to go out into the desert and shoot hedgehogs?"

James looked from Bert to Clint. "Would you mind leaving us for a few minutes?"

They shrugged and walked out of the room. Probably glad their lack of security clearance allowed them to remove themselves from the situation, Jed figured.

Once the door closed behind them, he raised an eyebrow at Emmy. "Hedgehogs?"

"I only said that was the first option."

Jed almost didn't want to ask his next question. "So, what's option two?"

"That this wasn't an accident."

Deep down, Emmy's words didn't surprise him. For years, tales had abounded of biological experiments being conducted by all sides. Indeed, he recalled the discussions during the last Ebola outbreak, where his superiors voiced concerns about the epidemic being caused by a biological weapon. Or if not, they'd wanted to know, what were the chances of it being made into one?

A harsh whisper floated from the figure in the corner, and Jed's stomach sank. Cronus. Larynx damage left him unable to speak normally, or so Emmy said, and she knew everything she wasn't supposed to. Jed only knew the man was bad news.

"There have been rumours of a test."

"Tell me more."

"A Middle Eastern terrorist group recently made a large purchase from a Russian middle man, and not so long ago, that same middle man offered genetically modified Yersinia pestis on the black market."

"In English."

"Plague. Genetically modified plague."

Jed leaned back on the rickety wooden chair and closed his eyes. "Modified? They're messing around with this shit?"

Emmy nodded and scrunched her lips to one side. "It gets worse."

How? How could it possibly be worse? "I'm not sure I want to know."

Cronus whispered again. "Plague is classified as Biosafety Level 3. Intelligence suggests supplies of modified Level 4 agents are also available."

"You're fucking kidding me? And you only thought to mention this now?"

"Our source has been inactive for several years, is considered unreliable, and this is the first indication we've had that she told the truth on this particular issue."

"She? Who's your source?"

"Lilith."

Lilith? Emmy was right—this was much worse if Lilith was involved. Word said she was made in Russia, a terrifying combination of genetics and training that left a trail of bodies in her wake. And hot, if James was to be believed.

"You used Lilith as a source? I thought she was on the other side?"

"Hades II ran her as a double agent for a year or so." Cronus referred to one of his underlings, a man who had come to a nasty end when his car fell off a bridge one night. Accidental or deliberate? Nobody was quite sure. "But three years ago, she stepped firmly back into the Russian camp."

"So it's the Russians? They're making this shit?"

"It's possible."

"And if this really was a test? Now what happens?"

"I'd say it's been successful so far, wouldn't you?"

If a terrorist group was looking for a way to kill indiscriminately, then they'd certainly done that. But Jed would describe it as horrific, not successful. "You think there's more of this stuff, don't you?"

"That's the theory we're working on."

A ripple of worry crossed James's face, although Emmy remained impassive at his side. Fuck. This was as bad as it got.

"I need that equipment, and I need Fielding."

James nodded. "Everything's on its way. Look after yourself."

After the video conference ended, Jed had one more

call to make. He retired to his bed with the satellite phone beside him, then dialled Quinn.

"Did you sort the papers out?"

"Oliver delivered them this morning, and my flight to Galveston leaves at eight a.m. tomorrow." Oliver was Emmy's lawyer who Jed borrowed on occasion.

"Thanks, buddy. I've got enough shit on my plate without worrying about that too."

"Things aren't going well over there?"

"Half the town has gone down with this virus. Just being in the same room as another person could be lethal."

"Still think this is better than chasing pussy in Richmond?"

No, it definitely was not. And the thought of Quinn flying out to see Chess tomorrow made him want to punch something.

"Drop it, buddy." Quinn might not like talking about his time in Russia, but he was connected and Jed needed to ask a question. "Say, you ever hear of Lilith?"

"The first rule of Lilith is that you don't talk about Lilith."

"This line's secure."

"And Lilith's a ghost. She could be anywhere. Actually, she's not a ghost. She's the grim fucking reaper. Anyone who crosses her path ends up dead, and she makes Emmy look humane."

Fantastic. Apart from his jaunt to Syria last year, where he'd been chained to a wall while a group of sadists took it in turns to beat him, this went down as the worst week of his life. First his accidental marriage followed by Chess knocking him back. Then a trip to a toxic town in hundred-degree heat while a group of terrorists ran around with the biological equivalent of a nuclear weapon, overseen by a Russian she-demon. A couple of months in the little cabin on the shores of Lake Superior he'd inherited from his grandfather suddenly looked like an attractive option. He could fish for supper, repaint the railings on the back deck, and sleep with a gun. Alone.

What would Chess think of the place? He knew so little about her and for a moment, he wished he'd asked more questions about her life. But what would have been the point? That was over.

He lay back on the bed and put the phone on the floor beside him. Why had he let Chess creep back into his thoughts again? Her sweet face, full lips, and those breasts—each one a perfect handful. Fuck it. The blanket rose an inch, and he slid his hand into his boxers. He wouldn't be able to sleep until he gave in to the urge. A few minutes later, he wiped up the mess with yesterday's T-shirt and rolled over, hoping for darkness but still only seeing her.

Chapter 14

WOOHOO! I WANTED to dance around the lab, but that would have been tricky in a hazmat suit. Instead, I settled for grinning behind my visor and high-fiving Chet, my Canadian lab assistant.

The six marmosets I'd vaccinated on Wednesday showed a slight fever yesterday, but today their temperatures were back to normal, and the polymerase chain reaction test I'd just run showed the vaccine replicating in the non-human primates—NHPs in lab-speak, monkeys in English.

I'd never managed to get a reaction that fast before. The other vaccines I'd trialled either took weeks to show an immune reaction, or they never did at all.

But this?

This gave me hope.

"All these years of work are finally starting to pay off, eh?" Chet's voice came through my earpiece. Our hazmat gear came with integrated communication systems as well as built-in breathing apparatus and an air supply that maintained positive pressure inside the suit.

"I sure hope so."

"When do we give the live viruses?"

"Day twenty-two, after the maximum incubation periods for Ebola and Marburg. That way we can be sure that any symptoms are from the viruses we introduce rather than a delayed reaction to the vaccine itself. You're happy with the monitoring instructions?"

He gave me a mock salute. "Yes, boss. You're doing the checks tomorrow morning, and I'll do Sunday?"

"Brian's meeting me here early." We never worked in the lab alone. Firstly, because of the danger aspect—anyone dealing with a needle-stick injury, accidental spillage, or hitch with the air supply needed immediate assistance. Then there were the practical considerations—getting in and out of the bulky Level A hazmat suits was a heck of a lot easier in pairs. "You won't forget to fill in the spreadsheet?"

"You put a notation in my calendar every day, with an alarm fifteen minutes before."

"Okay, okay. Sorry. I'm just kind of excited."

He gave me a toothy grin. "Me too. You ready for lunch?"

I looked at the clock on the lab computer. Two p.m. It would be a late lunch, but I'd been too nervous to eat breakfast and my stomach had that weird, empty feeling. "Let me just give the monkeys some treats."

Until the final experiment, the monkeys were living in individual cages in a shared room. Only one filovirus was suspected to be airborne—the Reston variant of Ebola. Reston infected humans but didn't produce the same deadly symptoms that it did in primates so wasn't part of my trial. That meant the monkeys could keep each other company throughout. I never named them. I couldn't bear to in case I lost them at the end, but I did spoil them with treats while they were in my care. As well as the balanced diet prepared by the "monkey kitchen" at the facility, they loved baby rusks, malt loaf, and mini marshmallows.

"You're gonna end up with twelve fat monkeys."

"They're always active." Their nine-foot-high cages were filled with ropes and ladders, and I swore they never sat still. "And you can't talk. Didn't I see you eat a donut for breakfast?"

"And I've got two more for lunch. Come on, let's celebrate. And in three weeks, we can celebrate again."

I lost my appetite somewhat at his words. Because in two weeks I'd be married, and even if my vaccine was a success, I sure wouldn't feel like celebrating.

No, I'd leave that to my mother. She'd been grinning as far as her botox allowed when she took me to my dress fitting on Monday evening. I'd prayed it wouldn't fit, but the seamstress declared it perfect after a few last-minute stitches.

In my eyes, it was far from that. One of those poofy, meringue-like creations, when I put it on I felt as if I'd stepped right out of the eighties, and after glancing at myself in the mirror, I'd barely held back the tears.

But today, I pushed all thoughts of the wedding to the back of my mind, determined to focus on the positive, and forced myself to smile as I followed Chet into the chemical shower. I once read a study that found even pretending to smile released endorphins and made you happy, so I held that darn grin until I'd changed back into my own clothes and made it to the break room in the next building.

"You got notes to write up?" Chet asked.

"Always."

"I'll go grab lunch, you do the boring bit." He wiggled his hips and waved his arms. "Then we can par-tay."

I couldn't help but laugh. Chet was such a dork but an adorable one. "Deal."

I'd emailed myself the information I needed from the lab, so I headed back to my office, where my creaking laptop filled half the desk. And when I said office, I meant cupboard. By the time I'd filled the single shelf with books and put my purse on the visitor's chair, there was barely room for me to fit.

Before I began typing, I picked up the phone. My supervisor worked at the CDC, and I needed to update him on the latest developments. He'd been waiting for this trial as long as me.

"Dr. Fielding's office," the receptionist greeted me in that cool, professional tone of hers.

"Is Dr. Fielding there? It's Chess Lane."

"I'll put you right through."

Dr. Fielding's warm voice came through almost immediately. "Chess? How did it go?"

"I detected recVSV viremia in all the NHPs."

That was to say, I'd seen the modified virus I was using as a vector for the filoviruses entering the monkey's bloodstream. I quickly ran Dr. Fielding through a more detailed summary of my results, together with my plans for the next few weeks.

"My dear, that's wonderful news." Dr. Fielding always sounded so British, even though he'd lived in America for years. "I told you all your efforts would pay off."

Just like Chet. At least they believed in me. "I still have the hard parts left."

"But there's every chance of those working. Have a little faith in yourself."

At the mention of "faith," I blinked back tears.

Wasn't she why I was doing all this?

"I'll try to stay positive. Really, I will."

By the time I reached the break room, the party was in full swing. Unknown to me, while I wrote up my results Dr. Fielding had called a local bakery to deliver a huge box of cakes, and the other staff chipped in for drinks and more snacks. One of the professors plugged speakers into his laptop, and when the Motown blared out, I surprised myself with a genuine smile.

"Come on, let's dance," Chet said.

He grabbed me and waltzed me around the room, our lab coats flying out behind us. He'd dredged up a party hat from somewhere, and it sat lopsided on his thatch of ginger hair with a piece of elastic under his chin.

"I feel dizzy."

He'd spun me six times in a row, and I had to grab onto his biceps to keep from falling over.

"But you're having fun, eh?"

"I guess. But if you don't let me sit down, I'll be sick."

On his next circuit, he deposited me in a chair. "You get five minutes' rest, then you need to enjoy yourself again. Here, have another cake."

First, I tried to fix my hair back into its ponytail. The band had slipped halfway out, and tendrils were escaping all over the place. I shoved my bangs out of my face, then stared at the doorway. Who was that guy?

Tall and tanned with messy light brown hair and a leather jacket, he sure didn't belong in the science faculty. As I took a bite of my cupcake, Chet stopped to speak to the stranger, and after a bit of gesturing, my assistant pointed at me. Why me? I didn't know the man.

He picked his way towards me, skirting around the other dancers and catching a balloon somebody batted in his direction. What did he want? Did he have me confused with someone else?

"Whose birthday?"

I stared at him. Up close, he was even more darn handsome, and I was even more confused. "It's nobody's birthday."

He raised an eyebrow and pointed at the balloon he was holding, blue, with *Happy Birthday* emblazoned on the front.

"Oh. I think someone must have gotten those by accident."

"You mean lunchtimes are always like this?"

"Of course not! Usually, we're really boring." Oh heck, that made me sound like an idiot. "I mean, not boring, but busy working. And that's not boring, not at all."

He broke out a smile, and if I'd thought he was good looking before, that made him devastating. Not quite as sexy as Jared, nobody ever would be, but still...wow.

"So, what's the occasion?"

"I made a breakthrough on my project."

"Congratulations, Chess. You are Chess, aren't you?"

"How do you know?"

He pointed at Chet, now attempting the moonwalk in rubber-soled shoes. "Michael Jackson told me."

"I mean, why were you looking for me in the first place?"

"Jed sent me. I'm Quinn."

"Jed? Who's Jed?"

"The dude you married in Vegas last week?"

"You mean Jared?"

He burst out laughing. "Nobody calls him Jared but his mother, and that's only when he's fucked up really badly."

"Oh. Jed. He never told me that. I've been thinking of him as Jared all week."

Quinn's lips settled into a wide grin. "You've been thinking of him?"

I clapped a hand over my big mouth. "No! Not at all. In fact, I'd almost forgotten about the whole incident."

"You sure about that?"

"No. I mean, yes. I mean, thank you for coming. It'll be good to put all this behind me."

He held up an envelope. "In that case, I have papers for you to sign."

Wonderful—the annulment. I should feel happy that Jared—Jed—had kept his word and removed the complication from my life, but far from smiling, my heart dropped like a rock. Signing those papers would mean cutting my link to the man who'd taken up residence inside it.

But what choice did I have? "I'll just find a pen."

Quinn produced a shiny, silver one from his pocket. "Would you prefer to go somewhere private so you can read them first?"

"Yes, of course. That would be more appropriate."

In my office, I shoved a pile of papers and my purse

off the chair next to the door and waved him into it. He dwarfed the small room, and the air inside felt suddenly thicker. For the first time, I wished I'd had a quick tidy at some point in, oh, the last year. It may have looked a mess, but I worked best in organised chaos.

Quinn pulled a sheaf of papers out of the envelope and handed them over. "Have a read through these. It should be straightforward, but if you have any questions, I can get Jed's lawyer on the phone to answer them."

"I trust him. Where do I sign?"

He pointed at the space for my signature. If I'd been thinking straight, I'd have spotted the green sticky tab with the arrow pointing right at it. I scribbled my name and handed it back.

"Perfect. Thanks."

"Do you want me to show you out?"

"I can find my own way." He stood but hesitated at the door. "You know the offer Jed made you?"

How could I ever forget? "Yes."

"For what it's worth, it was genuine."

After he left, I stared blankly into space for at least half an hour. That chapter of my life was closed now, but I couldn't deny Quinn's final words stung. And he was wrong, anyway. If Jed really did mean what he said, why hadn't he come to Galveston himself?

I couldn't deny I'd harboured a secret hope that he would.

Stupid, stupid me.

It hadn't happened, and now I was officially single again.

Back in the break room, my colleagues were still

dancing as I crept out of the exit. I didn't feel like celebrating anymore. What I needed was a hug, and there was only one person in Texas I could count on for that.

CHAPTER 15

BY THE TIME I'd walked to my car, fought my way through traffic, and stopped at the thrift store, it took me an hour and a half to get to the Bayview Centre. Lottie had just finished dinner when I walked into her room. Well, not finished it, but finished with it. She'd eaten half and begun pushing the rest around on her plate while a nurse looked on.

"Will you sit with her?" the nurse asked. What she meant was, would I make Lottie eat the rest?

"Yes."

Although if Lottie didn't want to eat, there wasn't much I could do to make her. Over the years, I'd tried bribery, cajoling, getting upset, even angry, but nothing helped.

Today, Lottie looked up at me, her expression almost pleading.

"Could you try and eat a little more?"

"It's cold."

"Shall I get them to reheat it for you?"

"No point. Even when it wasn't cold, it tasted horrible."

I kind of saw her point. It looked like it had once been mashed potato and stew, but now that she'd shovelled it around the plate, I wouldn't want to eat it either. "You need to eat."

"I know, okay. I'm trying, really. I've eaten three meals today."

Three meals was a big thing for Lottie, considering she never used to eat more than one. I tried to look happier than I felt. Fake it until you make it, right? "That's good."

My bad acting didn't wash with Lottie—she'd known me too long. "Please don't be upset. I promise I'm eating."

I sighed. Everything had gotten to me today, not just Lottie's dietary habits. "It's not you; it's me."

"That sounds like a bad break-up."

I managed a tiny laugh. "Sorry."

"What's up? Did your monkey tests go badly?"

"No, they actually went really well. I couldn't have hoped for better."

"Then why do you look like someone just rejected one of your papers?" Her eyes widened. "Oh hell, someone didn't reject one of your papers, did they?"

"Nobody rejected a paper." A tear leaked down my cheek, swiftly followed by another, then another. Darn it—this wasn't supposed to happen.

"What, then?"

"Me. Somebody rejected me."

She wrapped her arms around me and squeezed so hard I worried she'd break. "You broke up with Wade?"

I choked out a laugh, and before I could stop myself, I was bent double at the absurdity of it. "If only."

"Chess? What are you talking about?"

"I got an annulment today." It just slipped out.

"An annulment?" She glanced at her pile of books, and I knew she'd seen it mentioned in at least one of them. "Isn't that what you get when you married and you shouldn't have?"

"Yes, exactly that."

"But I thought the wedding wasn't until next week? Did it get moved and nobody told me?"

She let me go, and the hurt on her face told me how disappointed she was at the thought of missing the upcoming debacle.

At least I wouldn't have to let her down. And it felt surprisingly good to get the secret off my chest. "I didn't marry Wade. It was another guy. In Vegas."

Her jaw dropped. "No way! But... But you never do anything impulsive. You make lists about making lists."

"I didn't do it on purpose. I was drunk."

She let out a low whistle. "I didn't think you had it in you."

Neither did I. But I did have Jared in me, for one night I'd give anything to remember. "Believe me, I had quite a shock when I woke up and saw the ring." And the large, naked guy in bed with me.

"But it's sorted, right? If you got an annulment, Wade never needs to know, and you can live happily ever after."

"Life isn't a romance novel."

I stared past her, out of the window where two men were fitting tyres on a Ford Focus. Both were topless, and the one on the left really needed to put a shirt on. He had bigger breasts than I did.

"But you've found your Prince Charming."

"I did, and he lives in Richmond."

"Wade's moved to Virginia?"

"Not Wade."

"This other guy? Are you crazy?"

Yes. Yes, I was. Crazy for dreaming of a man I'd never have. "Yeah, I am. Forget I said anything."

"What's wrong? Don't you want to marry Wade or something? Everybody says he's a real catch."

"He scares me," I whispered.

I wanted to claw the words back in as she stared at me, her excitement replaced with dawning horror as she gripped my arms.

"You're really serious, aren't you?"

I nodded, not trusting myself to speak.

"Then why are you marrying him?"

"Because Clayton wants me to." I'd said too much. "Forget it. I can't do anything about it now."

"How can I forget about it? Just tell Clayton you don't want to. You're an adult—he can't force you."

"Please, can you drop it?"

Mercifully, she did. Or at least, I thought so. She tucked her head in the crook of my neck and rubbed my back, but I'd forgotten just how smart my little sister could be.

"It's because of me, isn't it? The only good thing about Clayton is that he pays my bills for this place."

"Look, I said drop it. For once in your life, can't you do something I ask?" I practically snarled at her, then watched in horror as her face crumpled. I'd never spoken to her like that before. "I'm sorry! I didn't mean that. Lottie, don't cry."

For the second time, I wished I could take the words away and stuff them inside me. Smart or not, she was incredibly fragile, and I'd forgotten that too.

She looked up at me, blurry eyed. "But is it true?"

"Yes," I whispered.

"What did Clayton say?"

"That he'll stop paying for your medical care and you'll be on your own if I don't marry Wade. Clayton thinks he's the son he never had."

Lottie leapt up and started pacing. "We'll think of a plan. We will. You can't marry Wade, not if you don't want to. It's...it's...it's not right."

"I have a plan already."

"What? Tell me."

"I marry Wade now, but in a year I'll have finished my PhD. I need you to get better by then so we can run away together. That's it. Just get better. I can stick out a year with Wade as long as I know you're getting better." I tried to muster up a smile. "I've got big plans for us, missy, so don't you forget it."

She shook her head, not just a little shake but violent enough that I clasped my palms to her cheeks to keep her still.

"You can't marry him. No way. I can leave Bayview now. I'm eating again, see?" She grabbed the remains of her dinner and began stuffing it into her mouth, making herself gag.

I grabbed at her wrist, and she tried to struggle away. "Lottie, stop. Even if you were well enough, which you're not, we don't have anywhere to go. I don't have any money or a job at the moment, and neither do you."

She dropped the spoon back onto the plate and sobbed again.

"Please, don't cry. It won't get us anywhere."

"Then what can I do to help?"

"Only get better. That's all I need you to do. I'll fix up everything else." I forced myself to smile, something I was getting better at these days.

She did her best to return it. "I will. I'll do that. I'll get better and get a job and then it'll be just the two of us."

We hugged each other, and like that, a pact was formed. Us against the world, or at least that's how it felt. One year and we'd be through this, and we could both live again.

My shoulder was damp from Lottie's tears when my phone interrupted us. *Please, tell me it's not Wade complaining I'm late for dinner again.* I wiggled it out of my pocket and looked at the screen. Dr. Fielding? Why was he calling so late? In the three years I'd known him, he'd never once phoned outside his office hours.

"Dr. Fielding?"

"Chess, thank goodness you picked up."

"What's wrong?" He sounded a little breathless. Was there a problem at the lab? Something with the monkeys? I'd listed Dr. Fielding as an emergency contact for the project, but surely they'd have called me first?

"It's Marjorie."

Marjorie was his wife of thirty-two years, his high school sweetheart, and a prime example of how marriage should work if done properly. Because of them, I knew love really did exist. "What's happened to her?"

"I... I f-f-found her in the living room when I got back. The doctors say she needs a heart bypass."

"Oh my gosh! Will she be okay?"

"She's in intensive care. The doctors won't tell me much, but they want to operate right away."

"I'm so sorry. If there's anything I can do..." Not

that I could help much from Texas when they lived in Atlanta, but I felt compelled to offer.

"That's why I'm calling. It's a terrible imposition, but I don't have anyone else I can ask."

"What is it?" After all he'd done for me over the years, I'd be glad to return a favour.

"I'm due at a meeting in Washington, DC tomorrow. There's been an outbreak of haemorrhagic fever in the Middle East, and they want some advice on what they're dealing with. I know it's last minute, but could you step in?"

Washington, DC? "But I'm in Texas."

"They'll arrange a flight for you. It's three hours each way, and the meeting's at eleven. They only ever last an hour or so. I-I-I just can't leave Marjorie."

I did some rapid thinking. Because I often spent Saturdays at university, me being out for the day wouldn't seem unusual. And in the afternoons I sometimes went to the book group Lottie got us involved in—Wade sure was dumb enough to believe Lassa Fever was a literary heroine, anyway. "Are you sure I'm the right person?"

"Biggs is away on a research trip, and you know more than anyone else."

Could I afford to pass up the opportunity? In a year, I'd be looking for a job, and if I wanted to follow my dream career, being able to add "government adviser" to my résumé sure wouldn't hurt. "They'd have me back by evening? Mom wants me to go over the final arrangements for the wedding."

He let out a long breath. "I'll emphasise the importance of that, and I really am incredibly grateful."

"Don't even think about work tomorrow—just make

sure you look after Marjorie. Where do I need to go? And when?"

"They'll send a car. Would you like to be picked up from home?"

And have my family ask awkward questions? "The lab would be best. I need to go there first thing to record the monkeys' vitals."

"Perfect. I'll email you with the time later."

"Can you wish Marjorie all the best from me?"

"I will." His breath hitched. "I will."

Oh, what had I gotten myself into?

"Are you going somewhere?" Lottie asked.

"Washington, DC, tomorrow. To advise some government people on haemorrhagic fever."

Lottie squealed with excitement. "On an airplane?"

"Yes." Another trip, but at least I wouldn't have to experience it with Wade. He'd booked our honeymoon in the Cayman Islands, and I was dreading that too.

"That's so cool! Like one of those businesswomen who jet off at a moment's notice. Will you get to go in first class?"

"I doubt that."

She waved a hand. "Doesn't matter. It's still awesome. You're going on an adventure."

Her mood was infectious, and I couldn't help smiling. "Washington's still in the same country."

"Barely. Will you take pictures?"

"Sure I will. I'll have to miss our visit tomorrow, but I'll tell you all about it next week."

"Don't worry about me; just enjoy yourself. I've got plenty of books."

I hugged her goodbye and walked outside with a spring in my step. I'd been gifted one last adventure before I married Wade, and even if it was only to meet with a couple of stuffy men in suits, I intended to make the best of it.

CHAPTER 16

"DARN IT!" I kept my voice to a whisper as I stubbed my toe on the kitchen table—one of the many hazards of sneaking out of the house while it was still dark. According to Dr. Fielding's message, a cab would pick me up outside the lab at seven, and I had to deal with the monkeys first.

One bonus of getting up so early was the lack of traffic, and I cracked the door to the lab before the sun came over the horizon. The faint sound of classical music drifted from the office two doors along from mine.

"Morning, Heidi."

She raised a glass of orange juice, looking far too cheerful for five o'clock. Morning people scared me.

"Are you ready to check the NHPs?" she asked.

"Give me a minute. I need to wake up first."

Heidi hailed from Austria and had developed her love of early mornings milking cows on her family's farm. In the six months she'd been at the Galveston National Laboratory, I'd never once beaten her into work. When I realised I needed a buddy for the lab this morning because Brian didn't like dawn any more than I did, I knew she'd oblige. With any luck, I'd be done and on my way to Washington before Mom and Clayton even woke up. They rarely got out of bed before eight.

I hung my only suit on the back of my office door and shoved thirty cents into the vending machine in the break room. Yuck. The instant coffee was every bit as bad as I remembered, but I didn't have time to start up the coffee machine.

Once the caffeine began circulating, I fetched Heidi, who fanned herself on the short walk to the lab building.

"You think the summer will get much hotter?" she asked.

"We're only in June."

"They need to build us a tunnel with air conditioning so we don't melt just getting to work."

"You'll get used to it."

"Every day my brain cooks more."

Despite the coffee, I had to lever my eyelids open as I stared into the iris scanner, then I switched to auto-pilot as I changed my clothes. No personal items were allowed in the lab, not even underwear. We got glamorous paper panties to wear under our scrubs instead.

Then it was into BSL-4. Biosafety Level 4 housed the most dangerous agents in the world—those that caused life-threatening diseases with no cure or those with unknown risks. Not for the first time, I glanced at a biosafety cabinet containing Lassa virus and fantasised about mixing it into Wade's evening meal.

I pushed that thought out of my mind and kept an eye on the clock as I ran through my tasks with help from Heidi, and forty minutes later we reversed the procedure—first a chemical shower, then we took our airtight suits off, scrubbed ourselves under a water shower, and finally changed back into street clothes.

That left me a quarter of an hour to grab my laptop and notes, then change into my suit before my ride arrived. Oh, and sort out my hair. It always looked terrible after those showers.

"Good luck," Heidi called out as I hurried towards the exit.

"Thanks, I'll need it."

I'd been expecting a cab, but when I got outside the only vehicle in sight was a sleek black limousine. Surely that couldn't be meant for me? How would I know? I needed the driver to hold up one of those little name boards like in the movies.

As I got closer, the window rolled down, and a man in a peaked cap stuck his head out. "Miss Lane?"

"That's me."

He climbed out and held the door open. "Would you like me to put your bags in the trunk?"

I'd only brought my laptop case and purse. "I'll keep them with me."

"As you wish. If you're thirsty, there's a drinks cooler built into the armrest." He said it like it was a perfectly normal occurrence.

Lottie was never going to believe this.

I managed to get a few sneaky photos of the interior as the car glided through the still-quiet streets. The limo had leather seats, plush carpet, and individual climate control, and I almost wished Clayton could see me because it put his two-year-old Lexus to shame. All too soon, we pulled into Scholes International Airport, and my luxury ride was over.

Or so I thought.

"Uh, you missed the turning for the terminal," I told the driver.

He'd sailed right past the sign, and I didn't want to miss my flight.

"We're not going to the terminal."

"Then where...?"

I trailed off as he took a left and parked beside a small hangar, just yards away from three private jets lined up on the tarmac.

"Do you need help with your bags, Miss Lane?"

"I'm not going on one of those, am I?"

"Yours is the one at the far end. Can I help with your bags?"

"B-b-but those are private jets."

He rolled his eyes halfway before he remembered his manners. "Yes?"

"I don't understand. Why am I flying on one?"

"It's the fastest way to Washington, although if you don't get on board you'll still be late." He climbed out and pulled my door open, waiting.

"Do I just walk over there?"

"I can call a golf buggy if you'd prefer?"

Was he kidding? I wasn't sure, but I didn't want to get labelled a diva for trying to find out. "I'll walk."

The plane's steps were down, and I hesitated at the bottom until a uniformed hostess beckoned me up them. This was insane. I half expected her to kick me back to the terminal when she realised I wasn't an actress or a pop star.

"Miss Lane?"

"That's me."

"The pilot's ready to take off as soon as you've buckled up."

I must be dreaming. That was the only explanation. I subtly pinched myself as I sat back in the nearest seat, but nothing happened. The walnut-accented cabin didn't suddenly disappear nor did the fear of messing things up in Washington. How many thousands had been spent on my trip today? What would they say when I couldn't deliver the goods?

A gentle hand on my shoulder shook me out of a dream I shouldn't have been having. Jed, the plane, and the comfortable leather seat all featured. I blushed as the hostess looked down at me.

"We'll be landing soon."

Wonderful. My first, most likely only, trip on a private jet and I'd slept through most of it. "Do you know if somebody's coming to meet me?"

"There'll be a car waiting."

The pilot landed smoothly, and a few minutes of taxiing later the hum of the engines wound down. Waiting for me at the bottom of the steps was a twin of the car that picked me up in Galveston. Even the driver looked like a clone.

"Where are we?" I asked.

Not at any of the main airports, that was for sure. One runway, a single terminal, and more private jets than I could count didn't look like Dulles or JFK.

"Hyde Field, ma'am. It's the most convenient airport for the White House."

"I'm sorry, the what?"

He looked at me like I was an imbecile. "The White House, ma'am. It's where the president lives."

"I know that." I took a deep breath. "Sorry, I didn't mean to snap. Mornings don't agree with me. The bit I don't understand is what the White House has to do with me."

"It's where I've been told to take you, ma'am."

"Are you serious?"

I'd been asking that a lot lately. Had I fallen into some weird, parallel dimension in Vegas? Because nothing had been normal since.

"I'm always serious, ma'am."

Yes, I could believe that. Freaking heck, Lottie was going to flip when she heard where I'd been. Photos. I needed to get more photos.

"I don't suppose you know who I'm meeting?"

"Sorry, ma'am. It's a big place. There might be twenty meetings on at any one time. Someone will be able to tell you more once we get there."

This time, I didn't care if the driver thought I was a total tourist. Who wouldn't take pictures on a trip to Washington? The drive took thirty minutes, and as we drove up Pennsylvania Avenue, the home of our president looked every bit as impressive as it did on television.

And I still couldn't believe I'd be going inside.

"Knock knock," a female voice said from outside the car, making me jump.

The driver opened my door to reveal a young brunette with an identity badge hanging around her neck.

"Hi, I'm Molly. I'm here to show you to your meeting."

What was it with these people? It was still only ten and she exuded this freakishly energetic aura.

"Chess Lane."

"First time at the White House?"

"I still can't believe I'm here at all."

She giggled. "I know the feeling. I've been interning here for three months, and I still remember the first time I walked inside. Here, turn right. We need to go through security."

Two security guards patted me down, then X-rayed my purse, pulling half of the contents out as they did so. I tried not to cringe as they held up a box of tampons.

"Can you turn this computer on?"

I did so, only for their eyes to widen at my desktop wallpaper.

"What's that?" one of them asked.

"Ebola." Ebola Zaire, as photographed under a scanning electron microscope, to be precise.

They glanced at each other and took a step back.

"Look, I'm a scientist, okay? I'm not here to cause an incident."

An impeccably dressed platinum blonde swanned past and paused to murmur in the taller man's ear. He visibly shrank an inch and waved me past.

"Who was that?" I whispered to Molly.

She shook her head. "We don't talk about her."

Molly led me along one plushly carpeted hallway after another, each with portraits of people I vaguely recognised staring down at me.

"Am I allowed to take pictures in here?"

"Only in the public areas, and please don't use a flash."

She slowed down so I could snap everything with my cellphone, and when we reached a small waiting area, she waved me into a seat and then took the one opposite. "I've got some paperwork for you to sign."

"What kind of paperwork?"

"A non-disclosure agreement." She giggled again. "It's really wordy, but basically you can't tell anyone about anything you see or hear today. If you do, it's considered treason and you could go to jail."

"So, I can't even tell anyone I visited the White House?" I'd been so looking forward to telling Lottie.

"No, you can say you were here, just not who you spoke to or what you talked about."

That sounded fair. "Where do I sign?"

She pointed out two places, and I scribbled on both of them.

"The briefing started at eleven, but according to the agenda you're not needed until eleven thirty. Somebody will come out to get you."

"Do you know what time it'll finish?"

"The schedule says two, and they usually run on time."

So much for Dr. Fielding's promise the meeting would only last an hour. I'd be cutting it fine to get back home for dinner.

"Is there a restroom I can use first?"

"Of course." She pointed along a corridor. "Through there, second on the left. I'll stay with your bags."

What were the president's bathrooms like? I'd imagined gilt and marble, but they were disappointingly normal, the kind of stalls found in office buildings the world over. Although, the paper towels did have the presidential seal on them. That was pretty neat. I stuffed a couple in my purse as a souvenir.

"I got you water." Molly waved at the cooler in the corner as I sat back down.

"Thanks." My throat had gone a little dry by then. "I don't suppose you know what's expected of me at this meeting?"

Her eyes went big. "Nobody's briefed you?"

"A colleague asked me to stand in late last night. He didn't even tell me I was coming to the White House."

"Oh, my goodness," she whispered. "Uh, I'm not quite sure what they'll want. It's the bi-weekly Middle Eastern briefing, and I've never sat in on one of those. It's reserved for senior staff only. I guess they'll ask you questions if they want to know something."

"Do you know who'll be in there?"

She snatched a breath. "Um..."

The double doors at the far end of the waiting area opened and a man in a suit stepped out. From his earpiece and oh-so-serious expression, I guessed he was a secret service agent.

"Miss Lane?"

I leapt to my feet.

"They're ready for you now. Please come through."

"Good luck," Molly called after me.

I'd sure be needing that.

Chapter 17

THE MEETING ROOM was half the size of Clayton's car showroom, dominated by a long table with thirteen seats around it, one at the head, six on each side. A video screen faced the open end, but it was turned off.

A single man sat on one of the long sides, dressed in a military uniform, and he rose to his feet as I walked in.

"Are you in the wrong room, Miss?"

"Maybe. I'm not sure. I'm looking for the bi-weekly Middle Eastern briefing."

"That's us, but if you don't mind my asking, who are you?"

"Dr. Fielding asked me to come. His wife had a heart attack yesterday, and I agreed to stand in."

"I heard about Marjorie. Such a shame—she and my wife get along very well. But old Wilfred didn't say he'd be sending such a pretty little thing in his place."

I wasn't sure whether to be pleased or offended by his words, so I did the sensible thing and kept my mouth shut as the man held out his hand.

"General Wise, chairman of the Joint Chiefs. But call me Frank."

I shook his offered hand and mustered up a smile. "Francesca Lane. But call me Chess."

"Here, you can take the seat next to me." He

motioned at the only place that didn't have papers on the table. "So, you're our haemorrhagic fever expert?"

"I'm not sure I'd call myself an expert, but I study them."

"Tip number one. Don't run yourself down. Wilfred wouldn't have sent you if he didn't think you were capable, so in here you need to speak with confidence."

"That could be a little difficult—I'm still not sure what I'm here to speak about."

Frank guffawed, although I didn't find the situation funny. "Trust old Wilfred to leave you in the dark. We've had an outbreak of some kind of fever in Iraq, and nobody's quite sure what to make of it. We'll go through the reports we've received, and then the president will most likely ask for your thoughts on the matter."

"The president?" It came out as a squeak.

Frank laughed louder. "Wilfred really didn't tell you anything, did he? Yes, the president will be here, plus representatives from various agencies and a couple of specialist advisors."

"How am I supposed to speak to the president? He's, like...the president."

Frank patted me on the arm. "Don't worry. James Harrison is human, just like the rest of us. Well, most of us. There's one viper."

Before I could ask what he meant, a door on the far side of the room opened and a group of men walked in. I didn't know their names, but I was sure I'd seen one or two on television. Nobody spoke to me as they settled into their chairs, and Frank motioned at me to sit down.

Then the door swung wide again, and the president

himself walked through. My heart began hammering, both from fear and...something else. President Harrison wasn't nicknamed the pin-up president for nothing. At least with all this drama, I hadn't been thinking about Jed and *his* sexy body; that was something positive. Except I just did, didn't I? Darn it.

With the president seated, there was one space empty, directly to his left. The fancy pen in front of it suggested we were missing somebody. Who kept the president waiting?

"So it's just our illustrious leader we're waiting for," a bespectacled man remarked. "What happened? Did her broomstick break down?"

The president narrowed his eyes. "For your information, Donald, she stopped to make a phone call."

She?

Donald sank an inch in his seat and turned to me. "We were hoping to link up with the team in Iraq, but they've had a technical issue."

The door pushed open once more, and the blonde woman I'd seen during my security check walked in. Impeccably dressed in a skirt suit, she glided across the floor in four-inch heels so gracefully she could have been born wearing them. I'd have landed on my face. And while our hair might have been the same colour, if I'd attempted to imitate her perfect chignon, I'd have looked like someone stuck an albino hedgehog to my neck.

She gave Donald a sharp look as she sat down, almost as if she'd heard his words. He stared at his pad, and his knuckles whitened as he gripped his pen.

"Shall we start?" the president asked. "I see we have

a newcomer—would you care to introduce yourself?"

Words stuck in my throat as everyone stared at me. Public speaking had never been my forte, and in front of this audience? Impossible.

Frank stepped in to save me. "This is Francesca Lane. I know you were all expecting Wilfred Fielding, but Miss Lane comes highly recommended."

I shot him a grateful look before he continued.

"For Miss Lane's benefit, I'll give a brief recap of our previous meeting. Approximately one month ago, an outbreak of fever began in the Iraqi town of Al Bidaya. Doctors initially diagnosed food poisoning, but then people began dying at an unexpected rate. Our own team arrived on Thursday and believe the culprit is some sort of haemorrhagic fever, possibly the Crimean-Congo variant."

Talk of a familiar subject helped my tongue recover. "Crimean-Congo is certainly endemic to Iraq. In fact, it pops up all over Africa, the Balkans, and the Middle East. Basically, wherever the ticks that spread it live. The last major outbreak originated at an ostrich abattoir in South Africa."

"Ostriches?"

"Yes, most birds are resistant, but ostriches are susceptible. They don't show symptoms, but the virus stays in their bloodstream for about a week after infection. Then at the abattoir, workers get contaminated with blood and voila, haemorrhagic fever. If people eat the meat, they can get sick too."

I'd turned vegetarian during my first year at university, and the case study my class undertook on the cause and effects of CCHF was a big reason behind that. No ostrich steaks for me.

"We don't see many ostriches in Iraq, but we're working on the theory it could have originated at a restaurant."

"That's certainly possible."

"But we can't afford to rule out other possibilities, so we'd like you to consider what else could cause these symptoms."

One of the other men chipped in. "We've got video footage and another report from the on-site team."

President Harrison picked up a remote control and aimed it at the screen. "Let's take a look at those now."

The lights dimmed, and a disturbingly clear picture appeared, showing the inside of a hospital. Patients lay on beds, on gurneys, even on the floor. And the noise? The sound of a woman's distress as she held a small child made my heart stutter.

I'd worked with viruses for years, but in all that time I'd avoided seeing the human side. To me, Ebola was a stain in a petri dish or an image under an electron microscope, at worst the death of my NHPs. But this? I didn't want to know what Faith went through at the end.

Even if I'd been prepared for the scene, I'd still have been horrified. I closed my eyes, but it was too late to stop the bile rising in my throat. The restroom. I needed to get to the restroom. My legs wobbled as I struggled to my feet and stumbled towards the door, trying to remember whether to go left or right. My stomach protested. Oh hell, oh hell, oh hell. I wasn't going to make it in time. Halfway across the room, a secret service agent thrust a trash can at me, and I hugged it tight as I hurled into it.

Please, somebody shoot me now.

CHAPTER 18

IF I'D HAD a vial of Ebola, I'd have injected myself right there and prayed for a hasty end. Oh, sweet Mary Jane, I'd just thrown up in front of President Harrison, of all people. I risked a glance back at the table. The scene of the hospital was frozen on-screen, and twelve shocked faces stared over at me. Actually, make that eleven. The woman next to the president didn't show any expression at all. Right at that moment, I knew she was the viper Frank told me about.

She remained impassive as Frank leapt to his feet and strode over to me.

"Come on, let's get you sorted out."

He handed the trash can to a disgusted-looking secret service agent, then put an arm around my shoulders and led me out of the room. Molly was sitting where I'd left her, and her jaw dropped.

"What happened?"

"A little accident," Frank told her. "Could you help Miss Lane to clean up?"

She grabbed my hand and tugged me to the restroom, sneaking glances as we went. I kept my mouth shut. I wasn't allowed to talk about it, even if I wanted to.

"You were sick?"

By then I was by the mirror, and I groaned as I

looked at my reflection. My aim hadn't been so good. The sludgy remains of this morning's coffee decorated one of my lapels.

"Yes, I was sick."

She dampened a handful of paper towels and handed them to me, nose crinkled. "Oh my gosh! You're pregnant?"

"No, I'm not pregnant."

"Are you sure? You might be and you just don't know it."

I thought back to the discarded condom on the floor of my Vegas hotel room. "I'm definitely not pregnant. It's just...some of the things in that room aren't very nice."

I cupped my hands under the faucet and rinsed my mouth with lukewarm water, wishing I didn't have to go back out there. But with the president waiting, I could hardly just go home, could I?

"Mint?" Molly held out a package to me, and I took one gratefully.

"Thanks. My mouth doesn't taste so good."

"I bet. Are you okay now? Do you need a doctor?"

"I'm fine, really."

Frank was waiting for me in the hallway, and he gave me a sympathetic smile.

"Feeling better?"

"Not really. But I think that's mostly to do with the fact I threw up in front of the president."

"Don't worry about that. You weren't the only one feeling green in there. I almost grabbed the trash can myself."

It was sweet of him to try and make me feel better, but it didn't work. "The other lady in there didn't throw up." My voice shook, and I hated myself for that.

"She's barely human. You can't judge yourself against her."

"Who is she? What does she do?"

He shook his head. "Can't tell you any of that, I'm afraid. Just know that she's not like you or even me. Now, do you feel up to going back in?"

"What I'd really like to do is start running and not stop until I get to Alaska."

"Ah, Alaska. Spent a couple of years there myself, stationed at Fort Wainwright. It's a lovely place to visit, but I wouldn't recommend going on foot."

I managed a small smile. *Grow a backbone, Chess.* "Okay, let's do this."

I straightened up and marched ahead of Frank, past the secret service robot and across the conference room. As I took my seat, I was sure I'd turned the colour of a tomato, but I held my head high.

"Are you happy for us to proceed with the video, Miss Lane?" the president asked.

I nodded. "Sorry about before."

"Not a problem. I think we all understand where you were coming from."

Not quite all. The ice queen beside him had found time to get an espresso, and she stared at me from over the top of the rim as she sipped.

Frank picked up the remote and started the video again. This time, I tried to detach myself from it and concentrate on the clinical symptoms rather than the people suffering half a world away but at the same time, *right there.* The camera operator moved through the ward, pausing to focus on a face to the left, or a body to the right. Medical staff in hazmat suits tended to the sick, but their lack of success in treating the illness was evident in their posture—slumped shoulders and heads down. A man in a yellow suit and apron passed the lens, and for a second Jed popped into my head. I pinched my eyes closed for a second to gather my composure. Was I really that obsessed with the man that random strangers reminded me of him?

I took a deep breath and began to assess the scene. As far as I could see, the agent presented as a typical haemorrhagic fever. They all shared similar symptoms, and the only sure way to differentiate was by lab tests. Looking at the geographic area usually helped narrow a diagnosis down as did tracing the movements of the first victims.

The screen finally faded out to the presidential seal, and as the lights came back on, Frank handed out copies of a report. We each took the time to read through them. Al Bidaya. The village had a name, and that made things all the more real. I skimmed through the pages, glossing over the names, ages, and descriptions of the victims, and concentrating instead on the scientific data. My eyes widened when I got to the death rate. Out of 139 people who caught the virus, 132 had died. A death rate of ninety-five percent? That was almost unheard of. Crimean-Congo ran at thirty percent, forty percent at a push.

"Your thoughts, Miss Lane?" President Harrison asked.

"My first guess would have been the same as yours, given the area—CCHF, but not with this mortality rate. It's far too high. It would need to have mutated..."

Donald spoke up. "What are the chances of that?"

"Mutations happen, but CCHF doesn't usually

transmit easily among humans either."

"So what else could it be?"

"With a mortality rate that high and that fast? Ebola's the only virus that comes close, specifically the Zaire variant, but ninety-five is at the top end of the scale. And in Iraq? It's never been found in Iraq."

"Usually in West Africa, isn't it?"

"That's right. Every case we've seen can be traced back to Africa. Outside of the continent, it only exists in labs."

"How secure are these labs?"

"You think Ebola escaped from a lab? It's almost impossible."

Any biological specimens leaving BSL-4 were placed in a tube containing chemicals to inactivate infectivity and extract any nucleic acids. Then the tubes got sealed and passed outside through a dunk tank containing disinfectant.

"But not completely impossible?"

"Let's go with extremely unlikely. I don't think Iraq even has a BSL-4 facility."

"It did once."

"Oh." They obviously knew more than I did. "But surely this is all speculative? Some of the symptoms aren't consistent with Ebola. Those lesions on four of the victims' arms, for example. Do you have a diagnosis yet?"

"Samples are on their way to the CDC right now."

"Could an animal have carried Ebola to Iraq?"

That was another of the suits. I hadn't been introduced to anyone except Frank, so apart from Donald, the men in grey were all interchangeable to me.

"Historically, hemorrhagic fevers have always been confined to small geographic areas. In a way, they're too successful for their own good. They kill so many, and so quickly, that they tend not to spread far. It's only now, with car and air travel, that they've begun to cause more widespread problems."

"Can you remind us how Ebola spreads? I seem to remember the last epidemic in Africa was traced back to a monkey?"

"Monkeys can catch the virus and spread it, sure. But it also kills them. Each virus of this type has a natural reservoir—for CCHF it's ticks. For Ebola, we believe it's a type of fruit bat."

"Natural reservoir?" the president asked.

"A host. A creature the virus can live in without killing it. But I don't know how a bat carrying Ebola could get across an entire continent to Iraq, especially without infecting anything else on the way."

The ice queen locked her gaze on me, and I shuffled down my seat a few inches.

"How about if the virus was introduced deliberately?"

"Who on earth would want to do that? It could cause an epidemic. Thousands of people could die."

"If someone did introduce it deliberately, that would kind of be the point."

"Oh."

Like the other scientists I worked with, I'd spent all of my academic life trying to prevent the spread of the world's most deadly viruses. The thought of somebody doing the exact opposite wasn't something I wanted to contemplate.

"It would explain how the virus jumped a continent,

wouldn't it?"

How could she talk so calmly about this?

"I guess. But why Al Bidaya? If somebody had a filovirus, why not infect somebody in New York or Los Angeles?"

"That's the question I've been asking myself."

"And how would they have got the virus in the first place? The last outbreak's over, and at this moment, there are no patients being treated for Ebola anywhere in the world."

"How about if they found the natural reservoir?"

"It's not that easy. Scientists have been looking for years without any luck. Two of my colleagues made a trip to the Kitum Cave in Kenya two years ago to look for the Marburg host, and even though we know people have been infected in the cave, they came away with nothing."

We knew people had been infected because Faith was one of them.

"Okay, so what else would you suggest, Miss Lane?" She didn't take her eyes off me. Did she get a kick out of making people feel uncomfortable?

"We should ask more questions about the origins of the food served at the café and look for the animal hosts. I'd also propose putting a testing regime in place for the patients at the hospital, to ensure you're not quarantining people who don't have the fever in with the people who do."

"Precisely what we had in mind. The CDC is preparing equipment for the field lab as we speak. You know how to test for haemorrhagic fever?"

"Of course. I do it all the time. In the early stages, the most common way is through an enzyme-linked immunosorbent assay—ELISA for short. You can also use a polymerase chain reaction test or isolate the virus through cell culture."

"Excellent." She turned to the suit at her side. "How soon can we get Miss Lane on a flight?"

They were dismissing me already? At least I'd be home on time.

The man looked at his notes. "The plane's due to leave Atlanta at ten p.m. EST."

"Atlanta?" I asked.

"Yes, it's easier to fly you to Atlanta than have everyone in Atlanta fly here."

"But I'm going to Texas."

"No, you're going to Iraq." The ice queen gave me a chilling smile. "You are, after all, our expert in the field."

What? "B-b-but I can't go to Iraq. I'm supposed to be getting married next week."

"Well, that's a good incentive to get things done quickly, isn't it?"

That...that witch! It was all very well for her to sit on her throne and throw out orders. It wasn't her life getting turned upside down.

"I also have an ongoing research project on a possible Ebola vaccine."

"I know. Wilfred told me all about it. I understand you're monitoring the monkeys at the moment, and the next stage doesn't start for two more weeks?"

I gritted my teeth, plotting murder. Why didn't she go herself? If anybody deserved to get Ebola, it was her.

"That's right."

"I'm sure you'll get the lab up and running by then. Think of it as an adventure."

"I've had enough adventures already this week."

The ice queen jotted something on her pad and angled it towards the president. He glanced down and then smiled at me.

"Miss Lane, we really do need you in Iraq. It's a matter of national security, and with Dr. Fielding unavailable, there isn't anyone better we can send. We'll do our utmost to get you back in time for your wedding. There are a lot of people dying over there, and I'm sure you understand when I say we have to do everything we can to help them."

What was I supposed to say to that? He was the president, for heaven's sake. And even if he wasn't, all he'd need to do was smile and any red-blooded woman would parachute straight into the nearest war zone for him. Besides, he was right. People were sick, and if I could do anything to help, I owed it to them and to Faith.

So I blew out a thin breath and said the only thing I could. "Yes, Mr. President."

CHAPTER 19

"CAREFUL THERE."

FRANK grabbed my arm before I walked into a chair in the waiting area. What just happened in that conference room? One minute I was puking in front of everyone, the next I was on my way to one of the most dangerous places on earth. An hour, Dr. Fielding said. An hour. I didn't even bring clean underwear.

"Sorry. I guess... I can't believe they're sending me to Iraq."

"They wouldn't be if they weren't desperate for your help. I don't think it helped that Fielding's recommendation was glowing."

I forced a half smile. "I should be worse at my job, huh?"

He chuckled. "It wouldn't hurt. Ah—these gentlemen are here to look after you."

I looked up to see two men in suits, black polyester this time, bearing down on us. At a glance, they were almost identical, the only difference being the one on the left had a moustache.

"Miss Lane?" he asked.

"That's me." How many other lost-looking blondes were meandering around the White House today?

"If you'll follow us, we'll help you get organised for your trip."

Oh, thank goodness. I needed every bit of help I could get.

Somewhere en route to the small meeting room we picked up Molly, complete with coffee and the expensive kind of cookies. When she set the tray down on the table, the two men descended like gannets and picked out all the double chocolate ones.

"Don't worry; I can get more," she said, picking out a shortbread.

"I'm not all that hungry at the moment."

Moustache swallowed his mouthful and looked down at me. "The boss told us to get whatever you need to take with you."

"The president said that?"

"Not that boss. Apparently, the CDC is supplying the field lab and lab assistants, but if you want anything specific, you'll need to talk to them. Molly can pick up any personal items."

I'd never had free rein to request equipment like that before. Under any other circumstances, it would have been exciting. "Who should I contact at the CDC?"

"We'll get the contact on the phone for you."

Twenty minutes later, I'd been promised everything I needed to test for all five families of the RNA viruses that could cause haemorrhagic fever—Ebola, Marburg, Lassa, Hanta, and Crimean-Congo were the worst of them. They'd also send me sampling kits, hazmat suits, undergarments in my size, and a communications system.

That just left the personal items. I snagged a pad and pen from a side table and sat down to make a list.

Shampoo.

Conditioner.

Shower gel.
Toothpaste and brush.
Tampons.

Just in case I had to go through security again. It was always good to embarrass myself.

Underwear.
Shorts (size four).
T-shirts (size small).
Flip-flops.

How cold did it get in the desert at night? In Texas it could drop sharply, depending on the time of year.

Jeans.
Sneakers (size four).
Hiking boots.
Towel.
Hairbrush.
Hair bands.

I was forever losing those. Each time I tidied my room I found a hundred or so in strange places. What else did I need?

Sunblock.
Sunglasses.

What would the ice queen do if I added something utterly frivolous to the list? Would she veto it? Well, it was worth a try. I added a notation.

Sunglasses (Gucci).

"If I'm going to an Arab country, do you think I'll need one of those long dresses the women wear?"

The two men looked at each other and shrugged.

Molly crinkled her forehead. "I guess you could buy one out there if you do."

"Uh, I don't have much cash." My research grant ran to ramen noodles for lunch, gas for my car, and

Lottie's books.

"I'll see if I can get that too."

Molly grabbed the list and bounded out the door, leaving me with my two sentries. I felt like a spare part. I'd never had anyone shop for me before.

"You don't have to wait with me," I said. "I'm not planning to go anywhere."

Heck, I wouldn't be able to find my way out with SatNav and a map. Besides, I needed to make a phone call, and I didn't particularly want to talk with an audience.

No-moustache shrugged again. "We've got our orders."

"Are you sure you don't want food?" Moustache asked. "You might not get another chance to eat for a while."

"I suppose I should try something." Because if the disease in Al Bidaya came from a café, I sure wouldn't want to eat much in Iraq.

"What do you like?"

"I'm vegetarian."

Moustache rolled his eyes. "I'll see if I can find a salad or something."

Yum. "Can I use the restroom?"

"Yeah, no problem."

In a move vaguely reminiscent of my trip to Vegas, I locked myself into the furthest stall and sat on the closed lid. Why did so many of my important conversations take place in the bathroom? A euphemism for my life, maybe?

I got the easy call out of the way first. Chet agreed to take my samples without hesitation, even though I couldn't tell him much about my trip.

"It's a research project for the CDC, very short notice."

"That's a great opportunity."

"I guess."

"Come on, Chess. Enjoy the experience and think of all the contacts you'll make."

"But..."

"And don't worry about the project. I'll even give the monkeys marshmallows."

Great. As long as the monkeys had marshmallows, everything would be fine. Right, who to call next? Lottie or Mom? I plumped for Lottie—I was a coward, okay?

Except her phone rang six times, then went to voicemail. Odd. She always answered—it wasn't like she went out anywhere. Maybe it was fate because now I needed to make the call I was dreading. I prayed for it to ring out, but my mother answered almost immediately.

"Hi, Mom."

"What do you want? I'm late for my spinning class."

"I'm going to be away for a few days. Someone dropped out of a study trip at the last minute, so I've gotten her place for free. We're going to tour literary landmarks in northern Texas." Were there any literary landmarks in northern Texas? I didn't know, and it was a good thing Mom wouldn't have a clue either.

"Did Clayton give you permission for that?"

"I tried calling but he didn't answer." I hated to lie, but I figured that was the least of my problems. "And the bus is leaving right now."

"You shouldn't go without checking first. And what about the wedding?"

"I'll be back in plenty of time for that; don't worry."

"We haven't finalised the flowers."

"Why don't you pick, Mom?" Because she would anyway, no matter what I said.

"Clayton and Wade won't be happy about this."

"Gotta go—the girls are waiting."

I hung up and stared at the phone, keeping my fingers crossed Mom's spinning class would take precedence over calling me back. It stayed silent— thank goodness for small blessings and stationary bicycles.

When I arrived back in the conference room, I found that Moustache had laid half a deli out on the table. Sandwiches, a pizza, chips, cookies, a selection of olives, a fruit platter. He'd also piled his own plate high —just to help me out, I was sure.

No-moustache picked at the food too. "I've got your itinerary. As soon as Molly gets back, you'll be flying from Hyde Field to Dobbins. From there, you'll hitch a ride on a C-130 to Iraq."

He might as well have been talking a foreign language. I only heard "soon" and "Iraq."

Moustache put down his sandwich. "If you're going on a C-130, you probably don't want to drink much. The toilet on that plane isn't something you'd want to use."

No-moustache glared at him. "Don't scare Miss Lane."

"Just trying to be helpful. I usually take a bottle."

He was right. I'd rather know. "How long is the flight?"

"Thirteen hours, give or take."

Wonderful. Half a day on a plane without a proper

bathroom. For a second, I wished I really had embarked on an English literature degree. I bet Jane Austen never had to worry about peeing in a bottle.

I was sipping a glass of water when Molly came back, laden with bags. A guard trailed behind her, wheeling a suitcase.

"I got everything on the list, plus some extra essentials."

Moisturiser, hairspray, three kinds of lip gloss. Ooh, an MP3 player. I didn't have one of those. A sarong, a bikini, and not one but three pairs of Gucci sunglasses. Yes, Iraq had sand, but did Molly realise I was going to a war zone and not a beach?

"This is a lot of stuff."

She shuddered. "I'm not sure they'll have malls wherever you're going."

"I'm not sure they'll have *any* stores at all."

On the way back to the jet I was going to fly out on, I tried calling Lottie again, and once more it went to voicemail. Fear began to gnaw at me. Where was she? Even if she was in the shower the first time I called, she should have been out by now. I left a quick message before I boarded the plane.

"Lottie, it's me. I have to take a trip for a few days, but I'll call as soon as I can to explain. Just look after yourself, okay?"

CHAPTER 20

WELL, THAT WAS no luxury jet. I stood on the tarmac at Dobbins Air Reserve Base staring up at a huge, drab grey monstrosity. Soldiers bustled around a ramp at the back, loading crates and boxes into the gaping belly of the aircraft.

A tap on my shoulder made me leap out of my skin.

"Sorry, ma'am," a man in fatigues said. "I didn't mean to scare you."

I tried to slow my rapid breathing into something resembling normal. "It's okay—I'm a bit jumpy today. Do I need to get on the airplane?"

"Please, ma'am. We're almost ready to take off."

Without me asking, he wheeled my suitcase as we walked to the back of the plane, and I followed him up the ramp. The entire centre aisle was taken up by equipment, box after box of it. DuPont for the hazmat suits. NuAire for the biosafety cabinet. Husky for the decontamination shower. I was relieved to see everything was tied down in case we hit turbulence. But there seemed to be one tiny thing missing.

The man next to me followed my gaze but misinterpreted. "Don't worry; it's all there. We're just securing the last few items."

"Uh, where are the seats?"

He led me in farther and folded a webbing

contraption down from the side of the airframe. "Right here."

"That's it? I have to spend thirteen hours sitting in that?"

"Afraid so, ma'am. You might want to put your jacket on. There's no heating, so it'll chill off quickly once you're airborne."

"I didn't bring a jacket." Neither Molly nor I figured I'd need one in the desert.

He looked me up and down, taking in my skirt suit with a condescending smile. "I'll see what I can find. You'll be mighty chilly otherwise."

He left me perching on what he laughingly called a seat and disappeared. Well, just when it seemed my life couldn't get any worse, it did. I'd almost have preferred to be walking up the aisle with Wade than stuck in this oversized cigar tube.

Almost.

A minute before takeoff, the soldier returned with a camouflage jacket and matching pants.

"Here you go." He fished around in his pockets and came up with earplugs, a bottle of water and a couple of energy bars too. "Best of luck, ma'am."

"Thanks."

Three times I'd been wished luck today, but it didn't seem to be working. I levered myself out of my seat and wriggled into the clothes over my suit, no longer concerned about minor things like my dignity. More people boarded, the men in uniform securing their bags and settling into their seats with practised ease. My hot pink suitcase stuck out like a princess among vampires. A gaggle of men at the far end of the plane threw curious glances in my direction, and I peeked back.

Were they the team from the CDC? I considered going to introduce myself, but then the engines started and I found out what the earplugs were for.

With nothing else to do, I sank back into my seat, cursing the day I'd abandoned my literary career and then thinking of all the names I'd be calling Dr. Fielding when I arrived back. Finally, I made plans to purchase a voodoo doll, draw the ice queen's face on it, and use it as a pincushion.

I must have been more tired than I thought, because I woke up hours later to a mechanical woman's voice, helpfully informing us we were exceeding various flight parameters. When I opened my eyes, I saw the flashing lights that accompanied the warnings and realised from the angle of the plane we were descending almost vertically.

Was this it? Was I about to die?

I let out a scream, and the men sitting nearby turned to stare at me.

"We're gonna crash! Why are y'all just sitting there?"

A few snickered. Well, I was glad somebody was amused.

"Don't worry, ma'am. This is perfectly normal," the nearest one shouted over the noise. "We always make a steep descent when we fly into an airfield with the potential for surface-to-air missiles."

Oh, perfect, that was totally reassuring.

Surface-to-air missiles?

Freaking hell.

Somehow, we landed without exploding in a ball of flame, and after we'd rumbled along for a couple of minutes the plane ground to a halt. The ramp slowly lowered, and I got my first look at Iraq. The acres and acres of rolling sand coupled with an oppressive heat that seeped into the airplane. Just like Texas—hurrah, I felt right at home.

A man in desert fatigues marched onto the plane, studying a clipboard. I read the name embroidered on his pocket: Samms. "Dr. Fielding?"

Was anybody not looking for the man? I sure would be when I got home. *If* I got home. "He's not coming. They sent me instead."

He looked down at me, and I swear he rolled his eyes.

"Look, I didn't ask to come, okay? The president made me."

Great start, Chess. Name-dropping and sounding like a whiny child all in the same breath.

"Doesn't matter to me. My job's just to deliver you to the major."

He didn't call me ma'am like all the others. Clearly, they didn't stand on ceremony in Iraq.

He started to walk off the plane, and I tried to follow, only to go headfirst down the ramp as I tripped over the ends of my pants. Luckily, one of the other men caught me and stood me back on my feet with a friendly smile.

"Let's get you out of these trousers, shall we?"

He picked me up while a colleague of his pulled on the bottom of the legs. My skirt had bunched around my waist, which gave them both a nice view of my unflattering panties before I managed to pull the skirt down again. For the first time in my life, I regretted choosing comfort over style. He took the jacket as well, leaving me wearing a skirt suit in the middle of the desert while everyone around me wore a military uniform, jeans, or a man-dress. No wonder everybody kept staring at me.

Samms smirked as I walked down the ramp, then pointed to an open-top jeep parked nearby. I tried to climb in without giving everybody another eyeful, but judging by their expressions, I wasn't too successful.

Now what?

Samms joined in with the unloading, leaving me alone in the vehicle. Did they think I was incapable of helping? Fine. Let them be like that. I watched for a minute and then remembered my sister. Was a phone signal too much to hope for in this sandpit?

Miracle of miracles, I had two bars, although I needed to find a power outlet soon. I also had a missed call from Wade, but I ignored that. My fingers trembled as I dialled. Please, Lottie, answer the phone.

"Chess?"

Oh, thank goodness. The boa constrictor coiled around my chest eased its grip a little as her voice crackled through.

"Did you get my message?"

"Yes, I got it. Where have you gone? Is it something to do with Wade?"

Darn the US government and their secrecy paperwork. "Nowhere exciting. Just a quick research trip with some colleagues. What about you? I was worried when you didn't pick up earlier."

"Oh, you don't need to worry. Not now, not ever. I sorted everything out."

Why did I get a bad feeling about this? "Sorted what out? What are you talking about?"

"I've fixed it so you don't need to marry Wade."

"How?"

"By leaving Bayview. You were only getting married so Clayton would pay my fees, and now he doesn't have to."

Stay calm, Chess. Getting hysterical won't help matters. I unclenched my teeth to reply. "You discharged yourself?"

"Not exactly. I figured they'd try to stop me, so I just walked out."

Freaking heck, why did she choose to do this when I was on the other side of the world? "Lottie, listen to me. You need to get right back to Bayview before they notice you're missing. They'll worry if they can't find you."

"No, they won't. I left a note on my bed."

"Please, just go back to your room."

"No way. Uh-uh. You'll thank me for this in the long run. Now, stop getting your panties in a twist, and I'll speak to you when you've come to your senses."

"When I've come to *my* senses?" Heads turned in my direction, and I lowered my voice. "I'm not the one who escaped from a hospital."

"Now you're being all snippy. Enjoy your trip."

She hung up on me. Hung up! And not only that, when I tried to call her back, she'd turned her phone off.

What the heck was I supposed to do?

Short of hijacking the plane, I couldn't go back home and talk sense into my sister, and I could practically feel my blood pressure rising. Dammit, why did I spill my secrets to Lottie? I took a deep breath and blew it out slowly, willing myself to stay calm. I needed to do what the president wanted, then get back to Texas, find my sister, and marry Wade. Simple. I thunked my head back onto the seat and closed my eyes. How had my life turned into such a mess?

Half an hour ticked slowly past before Samms came back, and we set off in a convoy with three trucks and four other jeeps. The tarmac road soon turned into a sandy track, and we kept slowing up to drive around rocks and the occasional camel.

And then we arrived. Al Bidaya. I recognised the main street from the pictures in the report. I should have been eager to unpack my equipment and get on with the project, but all I could think about was finding a bathroom.

Samms drew to a halt in front of a shabby white building and climbed out. He hadn't spoken a word during the entire trip.

"What time is it?" I asked.

"Just turned midday. Follow me."

I trailed him into the building where the morning heat had settled into an oppressive blanket.

"Welcome to our hotel. Five star, of course."

We were staying here? I thought back to my last trip away. This was about as far from Vegas as I could get. Samms led me through a dingy hallway and paused outside a doorway, listening. The soft sound of sobbing came from the inside, and his eyebrows pinched together.

"What's that?" I whispered.

He shrugged, then pushed the door open. Inside, a man dressed in army fatigues with a blond ponytail faced a bank of electronic equipment—screens, keyboards, buttons, and wires everywhere. A woman sobbed in his arms, a curtain of dark brown hair falling over his shoulder.

Samms cleared his throat. "Major Harker, your CDC expert has arrived."

Harker? But that was Jed's...

He turned around, still with an arm around the woman's waist, and his eyes widened about the same time my knees gave way. I stumbled backwards into Samms who shoved me upright again.

"J-J-J..."

Jed recovered faster, cutting me off. "That'll be all, Samms." He leaned closer to the brunette. "Flavia, could you give us a minute?"

She wiped her eyes and nodded, smiling up at him. Of course. Who wouldn't smile at Jed?

He strode over and closed the door behind her, then turned back to face me, eyes flashing. "What the fuck are you doing here?"

I blinked back tears. "I don't want to be here, okay? I've just spent thirteen hours on a plane and three in a truck, and all I want to do is go right back to Texas."

He reached his hands up to his face, sighing as he cradled his head in them. "Sorry. It's been a rough few days, and you're the last person I expected to see here."

"I'm not stalking you if that's what you're worried about."

He laughed, and I relaxed a little. "If you were, that would take stalking to a whole new level of crazy. So was Samms right? You're with the CDC?"

"Not exactly. My thesis supervisor works there, and he was supposed to come, but his wife got sick and he asked me to stand in at the last minute. I thought it was supposed to be an hour's meeting in Washington, but when I arrived at the White House, the president sent me here to help." My voice grew higher as words tumbled out, and I tried to slow myself down. "I've only ever worked in a lab before, never in the field. I threw up in the briefing for goodness' sake!"

"Fuck." Jed pulled the elastic band out of his hair and tugged his fingers through it. "So this was all James Harrison's idea?"

"The ice queen sitting next to him thought of it first, but he went along with it."

"I'll kill her. I swear I'll kill her, the meddling bitch."

I took a step backwards as his hands balled into fists, but the wall was behind me. When he saw me move, his expression softened.

"Sorry, Chess. I'm not mad at you, just her."

That I could understand. "It's like she's got no feelings at all."

"She's out of her mind." His smile looked forced, but he reached out and squeezed my arm. "Excuse me for a minute. I need to make a phone call."

CHAPTER 21

REMEMBERING AT THE last second that Iraqi builders didn't use drywall, Jed refrained from punching the brickwork as he stormed out of the room. The hospital in Al Bidaya wasn't somewhere he wanted to pay an unscheduled visit to for a broken hand. He slammed the door to the store room at the end of the hallway behind him instead and pulled his phone out of his pocket.

"Bitch, bitch, bitch." He jabbed at the buttons until a connection was made.

"Yeah?" Emmy asked.

"Did you know?"

"Give me a clue here. Know what?"

"Don't play dumb. You just sent my wife into a fucking war zone. Did you know who she was?"

"Ex. Ex-wife. And I'm guessing from your tone you'd like my answer to be no?"

"You damn well did, didn't you? She's terrified, you evil bitch. She should be in her lab doing shit with test tubes, not in the middle of this fucked up mess. Did you know she puked in the briefing? That's how upset she was."

"I could hardly miss it. She tossed her cookies into a rubbish bin, then ran out of the room."

And even after that, Emmy still made Chess come

to Iraq. "Haven't you got any compassion? And don't give me bullshit about it being James's decision. Everybody knows he doesn't fart without asking you or Black if it's okay first."

"Are you done yet?"

He kicked the wall and cursed under his breath. "Sweetheart, I'm just getting started."

"Maybe, in amongst all your ranting, you might want to ask why I made the decision I did? By the way, it's cute how you're so defensive over her."

He ignored that last part. "Go on then, enlighten me."

"Reason number one. Fielding's wife had a heart attack the night before last, so even if I'd insisted he go, his mind wouldn't have been on the job. And like it or not, when it comes to haemorrhagic fever, Fielding said Francesca was the next best person for the job."

"And you didn't consider sending the third best person?"

"He's on a research trip in Liberia along with numbers four, five, and six on the list. Then there's reason number two. Chess is due to get married in a little over a week, to a man you insist is a complete arsehole."

"Great, thanks for reminding me."

Emmy ignored his sarcasm. "Except as you quite rightly pointed out, I'm a bitch, so instead of cosying up to her future hubby in Galveston, she's there with you for the next week. All you need to do is change her mind. Oh, and keep the pair of you alive in the process."

Jed sank back against the dirty wall. He still hated Chess being there, but he had to concede that Emmy had a point.

"I don't know whether to kiss you or kill you."

"I'd advise against kissing me, at least in front of Chess. Her opinion of me went down faster than a bargain basement hooker in that briefing. Probably best not to kill me either, because in the unlikely event you managed to succeed, my darling husband would take you out before my body was cold."

"Well, you're definitely off my Christmas card list."

"You've never sent me a Christmas card. Although that time you dressed up as Santa a few years back and gave me a really big present was better than a card any day."

Oh yeah, he remembered. Emmy, comedy underwear and a red hat, two chocolate reindeer and a carton of eggnog. Dammit, he shouldn't be thinking about that. "That's in the past."

"Yes, it is, so stop talking and go charm Chess. And if you wouldn't mind tracking down the source of the outbreak while you're at it, we'd all be very grateful."

"Is there any news on what it is yet?"

"Kind of."

"What's that supposed to mean?"

"The CDC has run a bunch of tests, but that's where the picture gets confusing. Quite literally. They've emailed a load of data through for Chess."

"I'll get her to take a look."

"Just remember she knows more than you do, and you'll be fine."

"Thanks for that gem of advice."

As usual, she blew off the snark. "You're welcome." She puffed out a long breath. "And be careful. My gut's telling me this isn't a natural occurrence. I think

Cronus was right."

"That terrorism's involved?"

"This is a test. A small, isolated town, a sudden epidemic. They wanted to do enough damage to check if this stuff worked and let their target know their capabilities."

"And who's the target?"

"That, hot stuff, is the fifty-million-dollar question. Or maybe a hundred million. If I was holding that stuff for ransom, I'd go high."

"You're sick, you know that?"

"It's been mentioned a time or two."

Find the source of the outbreak, Emmy said. Oh, sure. He'd just go question a bunch of dead people and ask them where they'd been. And on top of that, he had to deal with his feelings for Chess.

Why did she affect him so much? Fuck and forget, that was his motto. Only his actions had eaten away at him ever since he'd done that with Chess. Even Flavia, who would normally have been his type, hadn't warranted a second glance.

Shit—Flavia. She'd broken down after another child died this morning, and he'd sent her packing. Where had she gone? A quick search revealed nothing.

"Have you seen Flavia?" he asked Samms, one of the privates from the original team.

"She said she was going back to the hospital."

Dammit. He'd have to apologise later, but first he needed to deal with Chess.

But what was he supposed to say to her? His

impulsive offer in Vegas had been completely out of character, and he should have felt relief when she turned it down, but instead he'd received his first dose of heartache.

Fucking her out of his system wasn't an option either. Not Chess. Chess wasn't the kind of girl you didn't call the next day, and she'd been hurt enough in her life already, including by him. She needed a gentleman.

So that was what he'd give her. He blew out the breath he'd been holding and forced himself to think with his big head rather than his little one. For however long they were in Iraq, he'd behave like a man of honour rather than the walking cock Emmy constantly accused him of being. Even if he didn't have a future with Chess, he needed to stop her from marrying Wade. That fucker would take all her sweetness and turn it sour.

Okay, he had his plan—be friendly, but not too friendly. Take things slow.

Right?

Except the instant he walked back into the command centre, all he wanted to do was hold her. Sitting in his chair, she looked more worried than ever. And that thing she was doing with her lip? The way she nibbled the corner? Shit—he felt that straight in his cock. It took every bit of his self-control not to carry her up to his room and lock them both in there for the rest of the day.

Which was just as well because a group of his newly arrived colleagues picked that moment to walk in. Great timing, assholes.

Of course, Trent marched straight over to Chess.

Jed had spent enough time with the guy to know he wouldn't play nicely with her.

"How are you feeling after the flight?"

She looked up at Trent and shifted in her seat. Nervous. "Relieved to be on the ground."

"Me too. No matter how many trips I've taken, I'd rather stay at home."

"Have you been to Iraq before?"

"A couple of times. If you like, I can—"

Jed resisted the urge to tear Trent's head off—a court martial wouldn't help matters—but he did shoulder the man out of the way. "Your job is to secure the perimeter, Sergeant Harding, not to entertain our medical team." He'd have to watch the man with Flavia too.

"Just being friendly."

"We don't have time for that. Now Miss Lane's arrived, I need to brief her." Jed motioned Chess to head for the door, and she got up and walked in front of him.

"Debrief her, more like," Trent muttered behind them.

He gritted his teeth and ignored the man. Resorting to violence would hardly endear him to Chess, would it? Instead, he guided her through to the dining room and pulled out a chair, motioning her to sit.

"Hungry?"

"Starving. There wasn't any proper food on the plane. Or a bathroom, or even proper seats."

They sent her on a military transport? Emmy was off his birthday list too. "What did you fly on? A C-130?"

"I don't know. It was grey."

Jed bet it *was* a C-130, and he knew how much of an ordeal that flight would have been for her. "I'll sort out some food. Is there anything you don't eat?"

"Meat."

A cheeky grin popped onto his face before he could stop it. "I'm disappointed to hear that."

Dammit—what happened to acting like a gentleman? Luckily his innuendo flew right over Chess's head, reminding him once more how far from his type she was.

"Don't worry; I'm not one of those militant vegetarians who chain themselves up outside fast food restaurants. It's just that seeing how easily animals transmit deadly diseases put me off eating them."

"You know what? Maybe I'll have vegetables too."

Chess yawned and clapped a hand over her mouth. Damn, she looked cute when she did that. Jed bet she hadn't slept well on the flight either. Which led them to another problem.

"I'll need to find a bed for you. I'd planned to have Fielding bunk in with Trent."

"If you're short of space, I could share with him anyway."

The hell she would. Trent screwed around on his wife every chance he got—another reason Jed wasn't keen on the man. Jed fully admitted he rarely kept it in his pants, but he never, ever cheated. "I'll sort something out."

"I don't want to cause any trouble."

"It's no trouble."

Jed found Maram in the kitchen, kneading bread. "Could you make lunch for two? No meat."

"*Na'am*, right away."

"And we've got a female guest who needs a separate room. I don't suppose you have any more space?"

Maram pounded the bread dough on a wooden board, thinking. "No more guest rooms, but there is a small bedroom on the second floor that my son sleeps in when he comes to visit. You can use that."

Maram's son was in the army, stationed in Baghdad. She'd shown them all photos over dinner the night before.

"Perfect."

"It is the third door on the right. I don't lock it."

Upstairs, the hinges creaked as Jed pushed his way inside. One thing was for sure—Chess wouldn't be sleeping in there. While the guest rooms were basic, they looked luxurious compared to the mattress on the floor and the rickety chair by the window in Maram's son's room. But it would be fine for him.

His smartphone pinged with an incoming email, and he glanced at the screen, thanking Emmy's business partner, Nate, for building him a device that worked anywhere in the world. Ah, the report from the CDC had arrived. He opened it up, but five paragraphs in he was already baffled. He skimmed the rest, looking at the pictures. Nope, didn't help. Jed spoke seven languages, but science wasn't one of them. Marburgvirions, polymer of nucleoproteins, *Variola major*, enzyme-linked immunosorbent assay. What did that mean?

It meant he needed Chess.

CHAPTER 22

LAUGH OR CRY? I had to do one or the other, stuck in hell with the one man who made my breath hitch and my heart beat faster. He'd have made my palms sweat too, if my entire body wasn't dripping already from the oppressive heat. I tried to collect my thoughts, which had scattered the second I saw Jed with that girl in his arms. Who was she, anyway?

A lady came into the room, dressed in a traditional black abaya with a scarf covering her head. She carried a tray and began transferring the dishes from it onto the table. Bread, houmous, some kind of stew served with rice, a plate of dried fruits and nuts. She didn't say a word, but when I caught her eye, she gave me a toothless smile.

After she bustled out, I slid an empty plate over and helped myself to bread and stew, happy to find it tasted as good as it smelled. I'd gotten halfway through my first helping when Jed came back, carrying a laptop and a pile of papers.

"Food okay?"

I quickly swallowed my mouthful. "Really good."

"When you're ready, I have the report from the CDC."

"The sooner I look, the sooner I can go home, right?"

He blew out a breath. "Right."

"Then pass it over."

He set up his laptop next to me, and I popped another piece of bread into my mouth as I started to read. By the time I'd read five paragraphs, I wasn't hungry anymore.

"This is crazy," I whispered.

Jed leaned over my shoulder. "With you there. I can't even pronounce half of those words."

"That's not what I meant." I flicked through the documents until I got to the photos taken under the electron microscope. "Freaking fu...dge."

"If you want to swear, go right ahead."

"I try not to."

He shrugged. "Sometimes, only a good fuck will do."

I glared at him, but even as I did so heat pooled between my legs. "I think fucking has gotten us into quite enough trouble already, don't you?"

And I couldn't even remember whether it had been good or not. Probably it was amazing.

"Sorry."

Jed dropped into a chair beside me, and I blocked him out as I carried on reading. These tests couldn't be right, could they? Because if they were... I glanced out the grimy window to the town beyond. Two children, a brother and sister, maybe, raced up and down with a single bicycle between them, blissfully unaware of the nightmare unfolding in their midst.

"Do we know what it is yet?" Jed asked.

"None of it makes sense."

"In what way?"

I turned the screen so he could see it too, then

scrolled to one of the photographs of the virus. "See this thin part?" I covered up half the picture. "This is Ebola, the Zaire variant." I moved my hand to the other side of the screen. "But this capsule is *Variola major*, or smallpox."

"Smallpox? I thought that was extinct?"

"Eradicated. Yes, it is."

"Then how—?"

"I don't know. But it's not only smallpox—they're joined together. I've never seen anything like it."

"So, the people in the hospital, they're infected with...that?" He pointed at the screen. "Both diseases?"

"It would explain the symptoms. Ebola has the shorter incubation period—two to twenty-one days. Smallpox is seven to fourteen. So the Ebola kicks in first, then if the subject survives that, they get hit with the smallpox. Which would explain the rash in some of the patients."

"Where did it come from? Could it have occurred naturally?"

"I don't see how. Ebola isn't endemic to this region and smallpox only exists in labs."

"It's not completely extinct?"

"The CDC has a supply, as do the Russians, in their State Research Center in Koltsovo. But..."

"What?"

"There could be more out there. In 2014, the CDC found six vials of freeze-dried virus that weren't supposed to exist hidden away in a store room. Who knows if there's more?"

Jed groaned and tipped his head back. "This week gets worse and worse. You think man created this virus?"

I peered again at the picture. "Creating a super-virus wouldn't be straightforward. It's easy to stitch together the DNA letters, but it's less predictable what they'll do. We still don't know that much about the effects of individual genes. And with viruses, there isn't room for extras—they need to be small to do their jobs efficiently. So a scientist would need to work out which of the genes needed to stay and which could go, and then knit them together. It would take years of research."

"When was smallpox prevalent?"

"It's been around forever. The last known case was in...uh, 1978, I think. I've never even seen it in the lab."

"And Ebola?"

"First seen in 1976."

"So, there was a crossover. And if somebody began experimenting back then..."

"They'd have had decades to get it right." I buried my head in my hands and imagined the scene in the hospital multiplied ten times, a hundred times. "I can't believe this."

"And I don't want to believe it, but it's here and we have to stop it."

"How?" I thought for a few seconds. "There was a vaccine for smallpox. We could try that to stop the second stage at least. The vaccination program ended years ago, but there's enough stockpiled to vaccinate everyone in the United States."

"Then we'll get it."

"It still might not work on the engineered virus. And the Ebola... Nothing's proven, even on the strains we know about. Nobody's ever done a proper trial because you can't just go around giving people a deadly virus on the off-chance a cure will work."

"The wider team needs to work on that. For now, your job is to get the field lab up and running so we don't end up with uninfected people in that hospital. My job is to hunt for the source of the outbreak."

I scrolled through the data on the screen again. "The CDC says the Ebola ELISA test is still effective for detecting the virus. I brought all the equipment we need for that."

"Good."

"And we need to stop it spreading. If nothing else, we have to keep it contained here."

"I spent yesterday negotiating with local leaders to set up a perimeter. They agreed, but people are scared."

"I'm one of them."

Jed's expression softened, and he opened his arms. Without thinking, I leaned over and he hugged me against him. Taking the opportunity to steal a little of his strength, I relaxed against his chest, wishing we were anywhere but Al Bidaya. I'd dreamed of being close to him again but not like this.

Anything but this.

"How did you end up here?" I asked him. "Did they practically kidnap you too?"

"Would you believe I volunteered?"

I tilted my head back to look up at him, but I couldn't bring myself to pull away from his warmth. "Why on earth did you volunteer?"

"Felt like getting away for a bit."

"Why? What could possibly be that bad?" Unless... "Was it because of what happened in Vegas?"

"It doesn't matter."

But it did. Had my stupidity upset Jed enough to

make him run to Iraq? Was him being in danger here my fault? A tear leaked down my cheek as I thought of all the ways I'd messed up this week.

I jinxed everything.

"Do you have to go out?" I asked Jed.

He'd finished a call to his boss and announced he was off to speak to the locals.

"Don't have much choice if we want to find out where this virus came from."

"You should be wearing protective clothing."

"People won't speak to me in that. It scares them."

"Then promise you won't touch anything, or shake hands, or let anyone breathe on you."

He chuckled. "And if they cough, run. I know."

"Please, I'm being serious."

His smile dropped. "I know, darlin'. I promise."

That left me to work with the CDC team and a whole group of medical personnel I hadn't met before, and I'd never found it easy to slot in with a group of strangers. Since my school days, I'd been left on the outside, and it had taken me years to find my place at the National Laboratory. As people filed into the dining room armed with notepads and laptops, I shuffled to the back and tried to blend into the furnishings.

A man stood up at the front and knocked on the table. "All right everyone, my name's Clint, and together with Bert here, I've been tasked with putting procedures in place at the hospital to deal with this epidemic. We also have representatives from Washington on speaker. Now our equipment's arrived, we need to work together to stop the spread of this disease."

A bespectacled man in his fifties took his place next to Clint. "We've commandeered the school building next to the hospital to act as a lab, and we also need to set up tents to act as additional wards. It's important patients don't enter the main ward until they've been diagnosed with...well...it doesn't have a name yet. Any ideas?"

"Ebola-pox?" someone suggested.

"I'm not sure that does it justice."

"Euphrates? Like the river? Ebola was named after a river."

Clint wrinkled his nose. "The locals won't like that association."

A voice crackled through the speakerphone, and I recognised the ice queen's clipped English accent. "Azrael."

"Azrael?"

"Archangel of death. A many-headed beast legend says will be the last to die."

"Won't that scare people?"

"They should be scared. If people don't treat this virus with the respect it deserves, it'll kill them."

Much as I disliked the woman, she had a point.

"Okay, we'll go with Azrael. Now, where were we? Ah, yes, we need to put a triage system in place."

Several men taped sheets of paper to the wall, and the woman who had been with Jed when I first arrived drew a diagram of the hospital and the surrounding area. I understood as the afternoon wore on that she was working as a doctor, and I developed a new respect for her, tempered by a touch of jealousy at her closeness to Jed.

Over the next three hours, we drew up plans for two additional wards, plus a holding tent for patients who hadn't yet been diagnosed. The hospital, lab, and morgue were all designated as part of the red zone. We could take equipment inside, but nothing would leave apart from people, and they'd do so via the chemical showers in the grey zone.

Weirdly, now things were getting organised, I began to feel more at home. I'd be even more settled when I unpacked my microscope and testing kits and pulled on my snazzy yellow hazmat suit.

Oh, and when I worked out how the heck I'd cope with being around Jed for the rest of the week.

CHAPTER 23

HOT. SO HOT. The visor on my hazmat suit needed wipers on the inside to deal with the sweat dripping down the inside of it. My home lab may have been in Texas but the air conditioning there was really good. In Iraq? I blew a strand of hair out of my eye. That was it.

A herculean effort by the team got my lab up and running by midday on... What day was it? Oh, yes. Monday. Figured. Diagnosing seven people with a disease that would most likely kill them made a great start to anybody's week.

But still, it was an improvement on previous efforts —over breakfast this morning Jed said confusion had reigned so far, with infected people being sent home, and most likely uninfected people being admitted, both of which undoubtedly led to the virus getting its genetic claws into extra victims.

Jed always looked heart-stoppingly gorgeous, but this morning when he'd drunk two cups of coffee in a row, he'd had a tiredness about him I hadn't seen before. A day's worth of stubble, shadows under his eyes—this situation was taking its toll on him as well as everyone else, and I didn't suppose him giving up his bed for me helped. Actually, it didn't help either of us, because every time I inhaled, I breathed in eau-de-Jed from the sheets, and that kept me awake half the night.

"Is that all the samples?" Clint asked.

Tasked with assisting me in the lab, he was suited up too. We were still learning how each other worked, but so far, he seemed competent.

"For now, yes."

"Is there anything else to do?"

I looked around the lab. The benches were tidy, and the sun burned through the window, glinting off the rows of sample tubes and their deadly contents. Despite the searing temperature, I shuddered.

"Let's go. It's time we stripped out of these suits before we get heatstroke."

I didn't see Jed again until the afternoon, after we'd tested samples taken from the morning's batch of bodies while they waited to be wrapped for burial. More importantly, we collected blood from the handful of people who'd survived Azrael and prepared it for transport to the CDC. According to Clint, their research teams would be working through the night for the foreseeable future.

"Did everything go okay in the lab?" Jed asked from behind me.

Darn it! I'd hoped to sneak in for a shower without anybody seeing, especially Jed. Two shifts wearing a hazmat suit had left my hair plastered to my face, and I'd sweated half of my bodyweight into my boots.

"Yes, fine."

"You don't look fine."

"Because I'm a mess, and all I want to do is sleep."

Jed tilted my chin up so I met his eyes. "You

couldn't look a mess if you tried, darlin'."

I jerked out of his grasp. "I'm all sweaty."

"Then you need to rehydrate before you do anything."

He grabbed my hand and pulled me through the building until we reached the kitchen. Maram stood on the far side, preparing food, and she glanced up at us before returning her attention to the chopping board in front of her.

Jed took a bottle of water out of the fridge, then opened the cupboard next to it and rifled through the contents.

"Every glass is fuckin' chipped."

"It doesn't matter. I'll drink from the bottle."

"No, I'll get you a glass." He reached into the back and came back with his prize. "This one's okay."

Like a sommelier showcasing a fine wine, he uncapped the bottle and poured me a drink. Then he opened a bottle of his own and swigged from it.

"So, it's all right for you to drink from the bottle?"

"Well, yeah."

"Why?"

He shrugged. "Because."

"Because I'm female, is that it?"

"No."

"Then what?"

He advanced, forcing me backwards until I hit the wall, then stopped with just an inch between us. "Because I want you to have the best of everything, okay? If we were in the US, I'd take you out to a fancy restaurant and buy you wine and lobster, but seeing as we're stuck in this hellhole, I'll have to settle for finding you a glass that doesn't have a damn chip in it."

Way to go, Chess. Jed tried to do something nice, and I gave him attitude. Wait—was he serious about taking me out for dinner?

Maram saved me from further embarrassment by bringing over a plate of pastries. She shoved them at me while rattling off a string of rapid-fire Arabic, none of which I understood.

"She hopes you like dates," Jed whispered.

"Dates as in the fruit?"

Duh, why did I say that?

At least it got a smile out of Jed. "Yeah, the fruit. The pastries have dates in them." He took a step back, giving me space to breathe. "It's me that hopes you like the other kind of dates."

Did he just...? No. I couldn't even think about it, not with Wade waiting for me in Norsville. And the wedding. And my stepdaddy. Jed watched me, those blue eyes driving me to distraction as I tried to think of the sorry state of my love life. Blocking him out, I picked up a pastry, forced a smiled for Maram, and took the only sensible option: escape.

The lukewarm shower turned cold before I'd finished rinsing the shampoo out of my hair, but at least I was clean. Well, clean-ish. The water had a worrying brown tint to it. Molly had gone all out and bought me a towel the size of a bedsheet, and I wrapped myself up in it, then scurried back to my room.

While I waited for my hair to dry, I checked my phone. Still no signal—not even one bar since we left the airbase. Just in case the electronic gremlins were playing a trick on me, I turned it off and turned it on again. Nothing. Darn it. Where was Lottie? Please, tell me she'd gone back to Bayview. I couldn't bear to think of her out on her own. Even at home, I'd had to watch what she ate like a hawk with binoculars.

By the time I'd tossed my phone onto the bed in disgust, I'd already begun sweating again. At least I didn't have to put on a hazmat suit again until morning. A quick rummage through Molly's selection revealed a pair of shorts and a camisole top like the ones I used to wear in Texas before Wade started dictating that I showed more skin.

Well, he wasn't here now, was he?

The dining room was almost full when I got downstairs, the low hum of voices drifting over as people ate. Were there any seats left? I spotted two—one next to Jed, and... Why was he looking at me like that? I quickly glanced behind. No, that was definitely me he was scowling at. Had I done something wrong? The men either side of him were smiling, so what was his problem?

His mouth set in a thin line, so I changed direction and sat next to Trent instead. I didn't want to make things worse if I'd managed to upset Jed.

Trent seemed friendly enough, although if I was honest, a tiny bit dull. Like Wade, he seemed rather fond of talking about himself. Milton, a doctor who'd worked all over the world with the Red Cross, had far more interesting stories to tell, especially about the time he'd spent travelling around Africa in his early twenties. Each time I glanced over at Jed, he either glowered at me or was so engrossed in talking to Flavia he didn't notice. If nothing else, his behaviour acted like a bucket of iced water over my libido. I should have thanked him.

As soon as the first people left the table, I made my excuses to Milton and headed for the stairs, stifling a yawn. I needed sleep, not another half hour trying to puzzle out Jed and his mood swings.

Only as I climbed the stairs, footsteps thundered along behind me. I'd barely set foot on the landing when Jed caught up and boxed me in against the wall.

"Have I done something to upset you, or do you just enjoy playing games?" he asked.

Huh? "Do *I* enjoy playing games? You were the one who looked like you wanted to rip my head off all evening."

"Not your *head*, darlin'."

"What are you talking about?"

"You showed up for dinner half naked, then ignored the seat I'd saved for you and spent the evening talking to two other men."

"I am not half naked!" Sure, the shorts were a little...short, but he was being absurd.

"Trent was drooling."

"I hardly spoke to Trent. If you must know, I find him boring. I preferred Milton's stories."

"Milton was telling his damn stories to your breasts."

He was? "Don't you dare lecture me. You spent the evening sitting with Flavia."

"There weren't any other seats left for her to take."

Okay, he had a point there, but...but... "Why does it matter to you who I talk to, anyway?"

The kiss caught me by surprise, and I gasped as I slammed back against the wall. The instant I opened my mouth, Jed's tongue plunged inside, rough yet delicious. There was nothing gentle about his actions, but I couldn't help pressing against him, desperate for more. Then his lips were gone.

"That's why."

Before I could gather my thoughts, he walked off cursing.

I leaned against the wall for support and gingerly lifted a finger, tracing it over my lips. He'd left them swollen and tender. Blood pounded through my veins as I tried to make sense of what just happened. The little spark I'd felt between us in a Vegas restroom had just exploded in a hail of fireworks, and before Jed walked off, he'd primed my belly with a few sticks of dynamite. I knew, just knew, that if he touched me again they'd go off.

When my legs stopped shaking, I took a tentative step towards my room, or rather, Jed's room. Sure, I was sleeping in it, but he'd left most of his stuff behind and the bed still smelled of him. I lay down and hugged the pillow to me, wishing it was the man himself. Why did he walk off after he kissed me? How could he do... that and then leave?

Dammit, I really, really needed Lottie. She'd read so many darn romance books she could get a job as a relationship counsellor, but right now, she'd abandoned me too.

Chapter 24

DAY TWO STARTED much like day one, except I had fourteen samples to test and only eleven of them turned blue to indicate the presence of Azrael. Being able to send three people home with mild stomach flu made me extraordinarily happy—I had to take the small wins under the circumstances.

In the hospital next door, the new tented wards were filling up, as was the morgue, with another seven deaths overnight.

Flavia walked in carrying another vial of blood as I was washing my work table down with bleach solution.

"Are you able to test this one too?"

So much for getting out of my suit. "Of course." She didn't leave, and the silence grew uncomfortable. "How are things in there?"

Her shoulders slumped. "Worse. Three more are developing the blisters."

"Is there any word on the smallpox vaccine?"

"When I ate breakfast with Jed, he said enough doses for the whole town were on their way."

"You saw him this morning?"

All I'd gotten was a note saying he'd gone out to talk to people.

"He came over to the place where I'm staying."

Oh. I unconsciously raised a finger towards my lips,

then stopped when I realised I couldn't touch them anyway. He'd chosen to spend time with Flavia rather than me? That stung more than it should have.

And she was still there, watching me.

I held the vial of blood up. "I'll test this and let you know the results right away."

Her eyes crinkled as she smiled. Even with most of her face hidden she still managed to be really, really pretty. "*Grazie.*"

One extra sample turned into three, then five. The lab was within walking distance of the boarding house, but I was grateful when Trent offered me a ride back because I could barely put one foot in front of the other. Remembering Jed's instruction yesterday, I headed for the kitchen and took a long drink of water before I stumbled up to the shower. Boy, the water sure felt good.

Then I faced the problem of what to wear again. I took one outfit after another out of the suitcase, but everything Molly had picked out was either short or skimpy, apart from jeans and a sweater that I couldn't bear to put on in the heat. I picked out a cute but tiny T-shirt with the slogan *small ones are more juicy* written across it and looked at my chest. I'd be lying if I wore that one, if it even fit.

I blew out a breath and stared around the room, looking for inspiration, and I found it in the form of Jed's bag. He wanted me to cover myself up? Maybe he'd have something I could borrow?

An hour later, my phone alarm woke me from my

nap, and I went in search of food only to find the dining room full of people. Jed was standing on the far side but looked up as I stood in the doorway. I didn't move a muscle as his gaze moved from my head to my feet, then back up again.

The verdict?

He whispered in Flavia's ear, she nodded, and he walked over to me.

"Well?" I asked. "Does this meet with your satisfaction?"

He stretched out the fabric over my left breast, where "HARKER" was sewn onto a badge stitched to the camouflage pattern, and groaned.

I put my hands on my hips. "Look, you said I was 'half naked.'" I used my fingers to make little quotes. "And now I'm practically wearing a dress. So what's your problem?"

He walked forwards, pushing me into an alcove in the hallway. "My problem is that I promised myself I'd act like a gentleman towards you, and you're not making it easy."

Tension crackled between us, and I rested my hands against his chest to stop him getting any closer. "How?"

"Because I want to rip that fuckin' shirt off you." His hand on my thigh made me suck in a breath. "At least you're wearing shorts underneath it."

My skin burned where he touched it, and the heat pulsed through my blood, raising my temperature to boiling point within the space of a few seconds. Suddenly, all those heroines in Lottie's books who swooned at men setting their skin aflame made sense. At least I had the wall behind me for support. *Breathe,*

Chess.

Bert's voice from the dining room snapped me back to reality. "As some of you know already, the smallpox vaccine has arrived, so we need to vaccinate our team before starting a wider program for the town tomorrow."

I sidled back into the room with Jed beside me. Thankfully, everyone's attention was directed towards the front.

"Are we doing that now?" somebody asked.

"Absolutely. We need to be aware of possible side effects. Most people get a mild fever, but encephalitis and severe eczema are also possible. Does anybody have an existing skin or heart condition? Or is anybody pregnant?"

He looked towards Flavia and me when he asked that, as did Jed and everybody else. We both quickly shook our heads.

"Good. Then we'll get started. Who's good with a needle?"

There weren't enough seats for everyone, so Maram set out a buffet, only to find we didn't have enough plates or cutlery either. People milled around, and call me paranoid, but I didn't want to share food or be in such a crowded place. When I managed to get near the door, I slunk out into the living room and slouched onto one of the cushions on the floor.

"Good idea." Jed followed me in and placed a plate piled high with food between us.

"My hero." I sat cross-legged, and Jed's T-shirt

pooled around my hips. "It's like a carpet picnic, except without the carpet."

He waggled an eyebrow. "You've brought the... No, I'm not going to say it."

"The whole gentleman thing?"

"I'm trying."

"Very trying."

He sighed. "Sorry." He pushed the plate towards me and passed a fork. "Here, have something to eat."

Before he could take a mouthful himself, Meredith Brooks' song "Bitch" played from his pocket. He pulled out a phone and glanced at the screen. "Sorry, gotta take this."

How come he had a signal and I didn't? I slid my own phone from my shorts and checked again. Nothing. Dammit, I needed to call Lottie.

Jed came back five minutes later and took a seat opposite me, legs straight out in front of him. "You haven't eaten much."

"I don't have much of an appetite at the moment."

"Lot on your mind?"

I gave a hollow laugh. "Oh, just a few things. Do you think I could borrow your phone? Mine doesn't work here."

"Sure." He slid it towards me but held on when I reached out to take it. "Wade?"

I shuddered in an automatic response to the mention of his name. "No. Lottie. My sister."

"How is she? I remember you said she wasn't well."

Before I could stop it, a tear escaped, then another. "I don't know. We had...well, not exactly an argument before I left, but I let slip that I was only marrying Wade to help her. She quit the hospital just before I was sent here, and I haven't been able to speak to her since."

"Shit, darlin'." A calloused thumb came up and wiped my cheek. "Why didn't you say something?"

"I don't know... I guess because there's nothing I can do from here, anyway."

"But I can." He pressed the phone into my hand. "Call her. See if you can find out where she is."

I punched in the number from memory, noting the five bars of signal Jed had on his magic phone. One ring, two, three... "She's not answering."

Her voicemail picked up, the falsely cheery message she'd recorded a year ago on one of her visits home. "Hi! This is Lottie. I'm not here right now, but leave your number and I'll call you straight back."

"It's Chess. Please call me. I..." I covered the receiver. "What's the number?"

Jed read it out, and I dictated it into the phone, then hung up and handed it back. "She didn't pick up again."

He already had the phone to his ear. "I need a favour... Yeah, I know. I need you to track down a missing girl... Texas...uh..."

He raised an eyebrow at me.

"Galveston."

"Galveston... Lottie Lane." Back to me again. "Is that short for Charlotte?"

"Yes. Charlotte Emily Lane."

"Here, talk to Dan." He passed the phone to me.

Oh, I hated speaking to strangers. "Hello?"

I expected a man, but I got a woman. "Are you Chess?"

"How did you know?"

"I'm an investigator—it's my job to know. I can't believe you and Jed got married."

"It was a total accident."

"Yes, it must have been. Jed's idea of commitment is a season ticket for the Giants. Anyway, I need details of Lottie. She's your sister?"

"Yes, six years younger."

"Is there anywhere we can get a picture? Facebook? Twitter?"

"She doesn't have any of those accounts."

Three years ago, she nearly died after getting involved with an online pro-ana group, and the doctors recommended curbing her internet use. Clayton threw away her smartphone and ensured the hospital didn't let her have access to Wi-Fi. Even back in those days, she'd only posted pictures of her body, never her face.

"But I have an old photo of her in my wallet," I said.

"Get Jed to send it. I'll need her cellphone number as well."

"She won't answer it."

"No, but if it's turned on, we can track her."

Dan asked more questions about Lottie's friends and habits. There wasn't much to go on since she didn't get out much, but when I hung up, I felt a little lighter inside knowing that at least somebody was trying to help.

"Thank you," I whispered to Jed.

"Promise you won't keep things like that from me again? I can't help if you don't share."

"I promise."

"Good. Now, eat some of this food before it gets cold."

CHAPTER 25

THAT EVENING WAS the first chance I got to talk to Jed properly, and under his crude exterior I found more of the sweetness he tried to keep hidden. Not only that, he seemed genuinely interested in what I did, and the questions he asked revealed an intelligence I hadn't been expecting.

"You're smarter than you look," I told him.

"I'm not sure whether to be insulted or flattered by that comment."

Oops. That did come out a bit wrong. "I meant that when I first met you, I thought you were just one of those sexy guys who relied on his looks rather than his brain."

He gave me a smile that melted everything—my heart, my panties, possibly a glacier on the next continent. "You think I'm sexy?"

Darn it, that came out wrong too. Well, not wrong, but it wasn't something I'd wanted him to know. "I..."

"Admit it."

"No."

"Come on, say it. It's not difficult. Three little words. Jed Harker's sexy. Or hot, if you prefer—I'm not fussy."

"Jed Harker's impossible."

He laughed and shuffled a foot closer. "Listen, I'll

go first. Chess Lane's sexy. See how easy that was?"

"Now you're being ridiculous."

"Nope, just honest." He clutched both hands over his heart. "I only ever speak the truth."

"Fine, okay. You win. I think you're sexy. Happy now?"

Oh heck, he needed a licence for that grin. If he did that near traffic, he'd cause a pileup.

"Happy as I can be, under the circumstances."

Thanks—a reminder I didn't need. I stopped giggling and thought about what lay in store for us the next day. "We should get some sleep."

He glanced at his watch. "You're right. Fuck knows what's gonna happen tomorrow. Every day out here is full of surprises, and none of them are good."

"Tell me about it."

"How did you get into this, anyway? The whole virus thing? If we're judging on looks, you should be prancing around on a runway with some asshole taking photos of you."

Jed's innocent question led to the pain I kept firmly locked away spilling over, and I blinked my tears away. I'd never spoken about Faith to anybody but Lottie, Dr. Fielding, and Mom. Mom only tried to take my mind off it with a shopping trip, and when that didn't work, she convinced her doctor to prescribe me a handful of pills. Usually when people asked me why I chose to study virology, I glossed over the answer and muttered something about relishing a challenge. But with Jed? I didn't want to lie to him.

"Because of an old friend. She died from haemorrhagic fever."

"Shit, darlin'. I'm sorry. You want to talk about it?"

"I-I-I don't know. I never have, not properly."

He opened his arms to me, and I was unable to resist their lure. Being wrapped up in Harker—sexy Harker—made everything better.

"Her name was Faith, and back then, I really was going to major in English lit. We both were. Only she'd always dreamed of travelling, so she went to Kenya for six months first. I wanted to go too, but Mom and Clayton forbade it. Faith went with one of those overseas volunteering projects to help build a school, only while she was out there they went on a field trip to Mount Elgon and six of the group caught Marburg."

"That's like Ebola, right?"

"Same symptoms, similar virus. Only one of the six survived, and it wasn't her." I gulped back tears as I recalled first the confusion, the mixed reports from the doctors in Africa, then the horror when I found out she wasn't coming home. "She kept a blog of her trip, and I read it every morning, but one day the postings stopped. She wrote she was off to look for elephants in the national park, then nothing. Not until we heard she was in the hospital."

Jed rubbed my back and held me close, like he had in the restroom in Vegas. Movement at the door caught my eye, and Milton looked in. "Doesn't matter. I'll come back."

"I should..."

Jed didn't let me go. "Ignore him. If it helps to cry, then cry."

"Why are you so damn understanding?"

"Got two sisters. Coped with my fair share of upsets over the years."

"Two sisters?"

All these little snippets of information about him fascinated me.

"One older, one younger. No fun being in the middle, let me tell you."

"Do you see them often?"

"Nah, they both stayed in Florida near my parents."

"Faith's parents moved to Florida. Her dad had a heart attack after she died, and I'm sure it was because of the stress. I hardly hear from them now, just a birthday card each year. I don't think they like to be reminded of the past." The tears fell harder. "I spent so much time with them growing up, and then…and then…"

"It feels like they abandoned you."

I nodded. "I miss them so much, and Faith. When she died, I wanted to stop anyone else going through what they did, so I switched my major to virology, and I've been trying to find a cure for the filoviruses ever since."

"Have you had any success?"

"I'm running a trial at the moment. Dr. Fielding thinks it could be the breakthrough we're looking for, but until I get back, I can't progress it to the next phase."

Jed leaned into me and pressed a kiss into my hair. "Then we have to get you back as soon as we can, darlin'. I need a few more days, and you've got to get the lab into a state where it can be handed over to the rest of the team. You're too valuable to waste out here."

"What if the ice queen doesn't agree?"

"I'll deal with her. Trust me."

He gave me another smile—not the full-beam one, but something softer. And what did I do? Yawned. I clapped a hand over my mouth as he chuckled.

"Looks like somebody needs to go to bed."

Oh, if only. A memory of waking up beside Jed in Vegas popped up unbidden, and I swallowed down a sigh. Being alone around him was hard.

He helped me up and kept an arm around my waist as he guided me to the stairs. Would I get a repeat of last night? Secretly I was hoping for it, and I'd avoided eating anything with garlic just in case.

"Goodnight, Chess."

His fingers left my hip with a gentle caress, and he exited stage right towards his room.

A groan escaped my lips, and he paused mid-step.

"What was that for?"

"Nothing."

"Now, why don't I believe you?"

"I don't know, because it's... Okay, fine. I was just wondering whether you were going to kiss me again."

He reversed his steps, stopping so we were toe-to-toe. "Do you want me to kiss you again?"

What was it with him and his difficult questions? I shrugged, unwilling to admit to anything.

"Say it, Chess."

I couldn't, not in words. I closed my eyes and gave a brief nod instead. Had I lost my mind? The man was most likely a cad, and technically I was engaged. But still I didn't stop him.

At first, I thought he wasn't going to oblige, but after one breath, two, his lips brushed mine so softly I thought I'd imagined it. Then he trailed a line of tiny kisses up my jaw, as faint as the flutter of a butterfly's wings. This was nothing like the vicious duel from last night, that clash of lips, teeth, and tongues. This was heaven, with faint undertones of the spicy tea Maram had brought us after dinner.

One arm slipped around me as he deepened the kiss, and I pressed into him, resisting the urge to wrap both my legs around his waist and remove items of clothing. Was this what that night in Vegas felt like? Oh, how I wished I could remember.

When he pulled back, his breath ragged and blue eyes fixed on mine, I had to remind myself to inhale.

"You're so...so..." What word did I want?

"This is where you say sexy again."

"Unexpected."

"Good unexpected or bad unexpected?"

"I'll let you know."

He chuckled and dropped a kiss on the end of my nose. "Good night, darlin'."

One thing was for sure, I thought as I staggered back to my room. I wouldn't be getting much sleep.

CHAPTER 26

A TOUCH ON my shoulder woke me, and I jerked upright. Who was there? I screamed, but a hand over my mouth muffled the sound, and I began to struggle before I recognised Jed and relaxed. Well, not relaxed, exactly. That was impossible with all the testosterone overflowing just a foot away.

"Shhh, it's only me."

I rubbed my eyes, trying to focus in the dim light from the moon. "What time is it?"

"Quarter past four."

"What's wrong?"

"Nothing. We've found your sister."

I came wide awake in an instant. "Thank goodness! Is she okay?"

"Hungry, pissed off, tired. Take your pick."

"Where was she?"

"Sleeping on a bench behind the library. She refused to go back to the clinic, so Dan took her to stay with some friends of ours instead."

"Do Mom and Clayton know?"

"As far as we could ascertain, they hadn't even noticed she was missing."

Figured. As long as Lottie didn't cause problems or necessitate awkward conversations with the care staff, they ignored her.

"Bayview didn't call them?"

"Apparently, they left messages with you, and when you didn't call back, they phoned your stepfather's car showroom and left a message with some prick called Wade."

Who of course wouldn't have wanted Clayton to know that Lottie had disappeared because she was his leverage. I blew out a long breath as one of the loads I'd been carrying for the last few days evaporated. Each night I'd imagined the worst—Lottie lying in a gutter somewhere, or at the very least wasting away to nothing.

"Thank you," I whispered.

He narrowed his eyes. "Is that another one of my T-shirts?"

"Sorry. I didn't bring any sleepwear, what with this being so last minute."

He pushed down the sheet, taking in *PROPERTY of HARKER* written across my chest in big, black letters.

"Keep it. It looks good on you."

I glanced down, willing my nipples to un-harden before he noticed, but judging by his smirk, it was too late.

"Try to get some sleep, darlin'."

I dropped my head back against the pillow, angry at the way he got me hot and bothered with a mere glance. Why did I feel so drawn to him? He sucked me in like a planet orbiting too close to the sun, and if I lost my grip on my sanity, I was afraid I'd get burned. Everything about him screamed "player"—the way he'd slept with me in Vegas, the question mark over Flavia, and who exactly was Dan?

Mind you, my actions in Vegas were hardly rational

either, so was I being too quick to judge?

Or was this bizarre attraction just a natural reaction to the situation we found ourselves in? Emotions ran high in Al Bidaya, with every nuance of hope and despair amplified by the surrounding desert. With all that stress, seeking comfort was only natural, right? A simple reaction of hormones. What was that thing when people got kidnapped? Helsinki syndrome? No, Stockholm syndrome, that was it. Maybe I had that? After all, the ice queen had practically resorted to abduction to get me here.

The rational, scientific part of my mind liked the idea of a rational, scientific explanation for my strange behaviour, and I relaxed a little. These urges couldn't last forever.

It wouldn't be long until things got back to normal.

Not long...

"Chess?"

Jed's voice and a knock at my door made me roll over in bed. It felt like I'd only been asleep for half an hour. Maybe I had.

"What time is it?"

"Almost six."

"In the morning?" I levered an eyelid open and saw the sun peeping over the building opposite.

"Yup."

"Go away."

The door creaked open, and Jed walked in, looking far hotter than should have been legal at that hour.

"I brought you coffee."

"You'll have to do better than that."

"How about a jug of cold water?"

"I don't like you anymore."

His weight on the edge of the bed made me roll towards him, and I put an arm out to stop myself, my eyes level with...

"You're not a morning person?" he asked, forcing me to look up to his face.

"Not unless I've pulled an all-nighter in the lab."

"Well, it's not quite ten p.m. in Washington, and we've got a conference call with the folks at the White House in fifteen minutes. Are you going dressed like that?" He stared at my chest again. "I don't mind. I'll even carry you."

"I thought you were being a gentleman?"

"Carrying you is gentlemanly. Isn't that what knights did in the old days?"

I followed his gaze down to the word *PROPERTY,* then looked back up again.

"Staring at my chest isn't gentlemanly."

"Shit. Okay, I'll leave the coffee. Just be in the command centre by six."

When I got there, the ice queen, of course, was picture perfect in a tailored dress and scarlet lipstick, and despite the late hour in the capital, the president could have stepped from the set of a magazine shoot. The other two men with them, both suits I recognised from the White House, also looked on with interest.

And me? I needed toothpicks to hold my eyes open, and I clutched my coffee like a lifeline. I stood one side of Jed, Trent stood the other, and I tried to imagine I was anywhere but there.

"So gentlemen," the president began. "And lady, of

course. Can we have an update?"

Trent began with a report on the containment situation. "We've turned back a few people at the perimeter, but in general, people don't want to leave their families. We have our own team plus a detachment from the Iraqi army assisting, and generally the ring seems to be tight."

"Good. The Iraqi government understands the severity, and they have more troops on standby in Najaf if the situation deteriorates. Harker? Any progress in tracking down the origin?"

"Four different people have given me the name of a local man rumoured to have been involved with al-Tariq."

The ice queen nodded. "Al-Tariq. Up and coming terrorist group. They split off from Islamic State when they decided those dudes weren't fucked up enough for them."

"That's them. He was in town right before patient zero got sick, but I can't find anybody who admits to seeing him since."

"He ever visit that café?"

"A regular. His presence there wouldn't have raised any eyebrows."

"We need to cast our net wider and find the man. Name?"

She poised her pen, ready to write it down.

"Hani al-Salih. I'm still going through his known associates, but most of them aren't being cooperative."

"Figures. Now, the situation at the hospital?"

Jed gave a rundown of events. The rate of infection increased every day, not helped by the locals being inherently suspicious of everything the Americans said or did. As more people died, we'd been accused of spreading the disease on purpose.

"Is the death rate still as high?" the president asked.

Trent answered. "Ninety-two percent at the moment. The additional fluids we've been giving the patients seem to have helped a little."

"Worse than Ebola on its own or smallpox?"

"Appears so."

I cut in without thinking. "In areas with a history of Ebola, we see some natural resistance." Darn it! I'd just interrupted the president. "Sorry."

"Please carry on, Miss Lane."

"Uh, I was saying that in Gabon, for example, we see resistance in ten to twenty percent of the population. We don't understand quite why or how, because these people haven't all displayed symptoms of the disease, but it's there. In Iraq, there isn't that history."

"How about those people who've recovered?"

"I've taken samples of their blood and shipped them to the CDC. Without exception, they were younger and in good physical health to begin with."

"Can we use—?"

Before the president could finish, a commotion outside the door to the command centre made us turn our heads. Private Samms burst through the door, red-faced.

"Major Harker, we have a problem." He looked up at the screen, and his eyes widened as he realised who was on it. "Sorry, sir, er, Mr. President."

Jed held a hand up. "What's the problem?"

"That guy from yesterday—he's running for it."

"Fadil al-Ghafar?"

Samms nodded.

"As in literally running for it? On foot?"

"On a horse, sir. One of the patrol teams is pursuing in a jeep."

A string of curse words left Jed's mouth, and I glanced at the president. His expression didn't change.

"How far has he got?" Jed asked.

"Through northern wadi and he's heading up the slope behind."

"Fuck."

Jed scrubbed his hands through his hair. I'd noticed he did that a lot when he got stressed. Behind him on screen, the ice queen's lips moved, but there was no sound. She must have muted it. The president pointed at something on the papers in front of him, and she nodded.

Then her voice came through, loud and clear. "Private, is he within firing range?"

"I believe so, ma'am."

"Then shoot to kill. And tell them not to bloody miss."

Samms gulped and turned to Jed. "Sir?"

Before he could reply, the president spoke. "You heard her, private."

Samms practically sprinted from the room, the crackle from his radio growing fainter as he hurried down the hallway. Bile rose up my throat.

On screen, the ice queen glanced at her watch. "Right, shall we continue?"

CHAPTER 27

BREATHE, CHESS. BREATHE. My pulse raced as I tried to reconcile what had just happened. I'd witnessed the ice queen order a man's execution, cold as, well, ice. Who was Fadil al-Ghafar? If he was capable of escaping on a horse, he was unlikely to have been in the throes of Azrael. Why did they need to kill him? Couldn't they have arrested him instead? Or immobilised him somehow?

The woman was evil. A class one, grade A bitch. How did she stay so calm? Was she a cyborg underneath that pristine veneer?

I heard my name being called and realised the president was speaking to me. *Darn it, Chess, pull yourself together.* Forget that a man just got murdered.

"Uh, could you repeat that, please?"

"I asked whether Azrael appears to be as contagious as Ebola. I know smallpox is more difficult to catch, so can we hope that Azrael has taken on that characteristic?"

I'd carried out an analysis of the spread pattern yesterday with Clint while I was between stints in the lab, so I rattled off an answer, disappointing President Harrison in the process. Azrael seemed every bit as virulent as Ebola Zaire. The only saving grace was that it hadn't gone airborne like the Reston variant.

As I finished speaking, Samms came back, head bowed. "It's done."

The poor man looked distraught, and he was only the messenger.

"Thank you, private," the president said quietly.

Jed patted Samms on the back. "Send another patrol team out to replace that one. Tell them to take the rest of the day off."

President Harrison's expression softened a little. "You can sit down, Miss Lane."

I sank onto the nearest chair, feeling nauseous. The others carried on talking, but my attention was elsewhere, visualising the terrible scene of a man fleeing on horseback, only to fall to his death because of a decision made by somebody thousands of miles away. At one point, I saw the ice queen watching me. When I met her eyes, rather than looking away like a normal person would have, she held the contact, refusing to back down. It was me who looked away first.

She scared me.

When the call wrapped up, I couldn't get out of the room fast enough. Jed caught up with me on the upstairs landing, but when he tried to grab my wrist, I shook him off.

"Are you okay?"

"No, I'm not freaking okay. That woman just had a man killed."

"She wouldn't have made that decision lightly."

"You think? It took her ten seconds. She didn't even ask any questions."

"She's trained to act quickly."

"Poor Fadil was probably scared like everybody else out here, and instead of asking the soldiers to talk to him, she…she murdered him. She sits there in her ivory tower, dishing out words. She doesn't see the horror in the world, the people, the reality."

Tears turned into sobs, great racking sobs that shook my body as Jed pushed me into my room and gathered me into his lap. He wrapped me in his arms and stroked my hair until my eyes ran dry.

"I'm so sorry. Everything's so… It's… I hate it here. I hate all the people dying, and I hate the orders, and I hate that woman. I just want to go home. Except I don't because Wade's there."

"You're still planning to go through with the wedding?"

"I guess." Truth was, I'd been so busy with everything here I'd managed to block it out of my mind for a few days.

"But your sister's not in the hospital anymore, so Clayton's got nothing to pay for."

"I don't know what I'm going to do about Lottie. I still haven't spoken to her."

"Why don't you give her a call now?"

Darn it, these sniffles were hideous. I resisted the urge to wipe my nose on my sweater and nodded.

Seconds later, Lottie's voice came from Jed's phone, and I didn't know whether to be happy or shout at her.

"Lottie, where have you been?"

"Sorry," she mumbled.

"You scared me half to death!"

"But you shouldn't have to marry Wade, not if you don't want to."

"I don't, but we both need somewhere to live."

"I've got somewhere, at least for the moment."

"Since when?"

"Since your friend picked me up and flew me to Virginia. In a damned private jet, Chess. Why didn't you tell me you knew someone with their own airplane?"

Because I didn't? "Uh, who picked you up?"

"Tia. You sent her, right? She said you sent her."

"Tia?" I mouthed at Jed.

"Friend of a friend," he whispered.

I went back to Lottie. "Yes, I sent Tia."

"She's awesome. Anyway, she lives in this, like, mansion with a pool and a cinema and a games room, and she says I can stay as long as I want."

"She was probably just being polite."

"Honestly, it's fine. I mean, it's not Tia's house, but it belongs to a friend of hers, more of a sister she says, but she's not there most of the time so she doesn't even use it."

"You can't move into a...someone's house like that." I almost said a stranger. I had to trust Jed wouldn't send my sister to live with someone awful.

"Well, I met the owner earlier, and she said it's no problem. In fact...more than that. We talked for ages, and she got me thinking about a lot of things. I swear one conversation with her was better than a year in therapy."

"What did you talk about?"

Lottie had always hated her sessions with the counsellor at Bayview, and the psychiatrist had frequently reported on her lack of cooperation.

"I didn't mean to talk, but before I knew it, I just did. She made me see that what I do, and whatever decisions I make, they affect others too. And not everybody who pretends to help is helping me."

"I've only ever tried—"

"Not you. Mom. There's a nutritionist here too and a life coach. Did you know that all those diet foods Mom kept feeding me are actually really bad for me?"

"I did tell you."

"You did?"

"Several times, but you... I couldn't convince you."

"I've been a terrible sister." Her voice quavered. "All this mess is my fault."

"Don't say that."

"But it's true. From now on, I'm going to be a different person. And this place... It's so different to Bayview. Like, normal."

Oh, sure, normal. With a cinema and a swimming pool. I wanted to warn her not to get too used to those luxuries, but I couldn't bring myself to say the words. "Just look after yourself until I get back, okay."

"No need to hurry. Relax and enjoy your trip."

Relax? I rolled my eyes, even though she couldn't see me. "Hopefully I'll be back soon. Whereabouts in Virginia are you?"

"Near Richmond, I think. If you don't know when you're coming back, does that mean the wedding's off?"

"I guess. But I have no idea how I'm going to tell Wade." If he punched the wall over me being a few minutes late for breakfast, what kind of damage would he do when I told him I'd be permanently late for our wedding? "There are only two days to go."

"How about you just don't show up?"

I gasped. "I can't leave him waiting at the altar!"

"Why not? If he tried to force you into this, he deserves it."

For once, I wished I was more like the ice queen.

She wouldn't hesitate to stand him up. "Yes, but I have to think of the guests. That would be embarrassing for them too."

She sighed. "What about a text message?"

"That's not much better." I closed my eyes, relishing the feel of Jed surrounding me. "I'll have to call Mom. She can break it to Wade and Clayton."

"Well, good luck. Don't say hi from me."

"Don't worry. I plan to keep it as short as possible."

Jed raised a questioning eyebrow when I hung up. "Judging by that conversation, it sounds like you've made a decision?"

I nodded, and another weight lifted from my mind. Hearing Lottie sound so happy had clarified things. "Now all I need to do is tell them."

"Do you want me to stay?"

"Please."

A little shiver ran through me as his arms tightened, and I leaned against his chest in my new favourite place to be.

"No time like the present."

Mom answered the phone with a typically friendly greeting. "Where the hell are you? Have you any idea how much we still have left to do?"

"Yes, Mom. Absolutely nothing, because I'm not coming back."

"Francesca, stop being ridiculous and come home this instant! Your father and I are both furious with your behaviour."

"It's not my home anymore; Clayton's not and never has been my father, and Wade's not and never will be my fiancé."

There was a pause, and I heard my mother's

breathing getting faster and faster. I wouldn't have been surprised if fire came from her nostrils.

"You'll pay for this! Do you realise how much Clayton's done for us over the years? The way you've thrown his kindness in his face, he'll have your sister out of that hospital so fast she'll be on the streets barefoot, and it'll serve you right."

"No, you won't. Because she's not in the hospital anymore, and she isn't going back, either."

Mom began spluttering. I couldn't make out everything she was saying, but the bits I did get were decidedly uncomplimentary.

"Goodbye, Mom."

As I threw the phone down on the bed, Jed kissed my hair. "Well done, darlin'. I know that wasn't easy, but it's over now."

I laughed nervously. "Not exactly. I still need to find a job and somewhere to live."

"I said I'd help you with that, and I will."

"Thank you." I went to kiss him on the cheek, but he turned his head and I got his lips instead. "That's cheating," I mumbled, still pressed against them.

He rolled me over on the bed and pinned me underneath him. "I'd say you were fair game now."

"I suppose I *am* single."

"We'll have to work on that."

He supported himself on his arms and kissed me so deeply it felt like the air had been sucked from the room. My hands developed a life of their own and wormed their way under his shirt, caressing each bump of his abs under taut skin.

Jed groaned and rolled off me before I could get any higher. "Wish I could stay here with you all day, darlin', but we have work to do."

"Rain check?"

Oh, who was I kidding? Jed wasn't rain. Jed was a freaking tsunami.

"Too damn fucking right."

CHAPTER 28

WITH JED OUT looking for leads to our suspected culprit, I spent the afternoon packing up samples to send back to Atlanta. The field lab was well-equipped, considering it was in the middle of the desert, but there was a lot it didn't have. I couldn't wait to get home myself and see some of these slides under an electron microscope.

I said home like I actually had one. I'd have to go back to Galveston for now because of my research, but once I'd finished my thesis? Now Lottie wasn't at Bayview, I could move if I wanted to. But where to?

Not anywhere hot, that was for certain. Stuck in my hazmat suit, I couldn't even scritch the trickle of sweat running down my back, and I'd had enough of the beating sun to last a lifetime. Did they have any BSL-4 labs in Alaska?

No.

But they did in Richmond, Virginia.

What would be the chances of me getting a job there? Dr. Fielding would give me a reference—heck, he owed me one after landing me in Al Bidaya. Hey, maybe I could get the president to give me a recommendation? I giggled at the thought, and my lab assistant gave me a quizzical look.

"It's nothing," I said. "Just thinking silly thoughts."

He eyed up the syringe in my hand. "Uh, could you not?"

I tried in vain to block Virginia from my mind. I might attempt to convince myself that the attraction to Richmond was the excellent research facilities, or even the fact that Lottie was there now, but I was kidding myself. The reason was six foot two, with dirty blonde hair and a killer smile.

What would Jed say if I wanted to follow him across the country? He'd offered to help me find accommodation, but was living near him what he had in mind?

Too stalker-ish?

At least Virginia wasn't hot. I tried to wipe the sweat off my chest by rubbing on the outside of my suit. It didn't work.

As we started to lose daylight, I stood under the chemical shower and then stripped off my suit. Now I was over the jet lag, my body had fallen into a routine—lab then dinner then bed. Jed wasn't there when I got back, and the mood at the dining table was subdued. Things hadn't improved much at the hospital, and all seventeen samples I'd tested today had turned blue.

"Now we've started with the smallpox vaccine, the death rate's slowed to eighty-five," Bert said, trying to lighten the atmosphere.

It didn't work. *Only* eighty-five? So far, we'd lost six of the original medical staff, and the replacements were scaring the patients with their space-suits.

Clint blew out a breath. "Yeah, let's look on the bright side—at least the town's running out of people to die."

Boy, that was a cheery thought to end the day with.

Still, at least I could go to bed and get a few hours of respite by dreaming of my favourite sexy major. Part of me was tempted to wait up for him, see if I could get another one of those kisses, but my sensible side knew I needed sleep.

And I got it, at least until the early hours, when the sound of gunfire outside my window made me sit up so violently I fell clean out of bed. I ducked my head down in case of stray bullets as I scrambled across the room. I needed to warn Jed!

His eyes flew open as I burst through his door and stopped by his mattress, panting.

"What is it?"

"Someone's shooting outside!" I hissed.

"Is that all?"

Perhaps he didn't understand. "Like, from a gun."

"Darlin', this is the Middle East. People shoot all the time. If it's a war, they shoot. If they're hunting, they shoot. If it's a birthday party, they shoot."

He stretched his arms lazily above his head.

How could he stay so calm? "What if someone's trying to attack us?"

"One of the guards would have radioed through. Besides, I'll save you."

He lifted one corner of his pillow, revealing a pistol underneath, then gave me a cocky wink.

I put my hands on my hips and glared at him. "Well, that doesn't help me if they come to my room first. I could be dead before you made it out of bed."

He grinned and flipped his blanket back. "Room for one more."

"If you think I..."

Moonlight reflected off his bare chest, and I

followed his happy trail down to a pair of black silk boxer shorts. Did I dare? The devil on my left shoulder politely informed the angel on my right that I was single now, and if I passed up this chance, I must be clinically dead. So I did what any female with a pulse would do and slipped under the covers with him.

"If I think you what?"

"Shut up."

"Is that another one of my shirts?"

"It might be."

He laughed and threw an arm over me. "Get some sleep, darlin'."

That was it? An arm? What happened to the Jed who'd done bad things to me in Vegas? I confess to feeling a teeny bit disappointed at his absence, which raised yet more questions. Who was this man?

A few hours later, I still felt the same frustrations. Jed spooned me as I lay on my side, his hand splayed over my stomach. The beach he'd brought me to was beautiful, with white sand stretching out in both directions and surf gently lapping at the shore. In fact, it reminded me of the honeymoon Wade had booked. Despite not wanting to go, I'll admit to drooling over the hotel in the brochure on occasion.

But now I was there with the man of my dreams, relaxing under the fronds of a swaying palm tree. Overhead, a brightly coloured bird flew in lazy circles, and a monkey chattered in the forest behind us.

Paradise. Perfect, except for being a tiny bit hot even in the shade, and the fact that Jed wasn't *doing* anything. Like me, for example.

I wiggled back into him, trying to get comfortable on the blanket underneath us, and his lips tickled my ear as he leaned closer.

"Keep still, would ya?"

Why? I loved feeling him around me, so hard in all the right places. "But I want you."

"Darlin', I mean it." His whisper was louder this time. "If you don't keep still, we'll have one hell of a mess to clean up."

Huh?

His hand tightened on my belly, and consciousness began to seep into me. Oh, heck, this wasn't all a dream, was it? I really was lying there with Jed behind me, and his *thing* really was pressing into my butt.

Please, somebody kill me now.

At least I'd woken, because who knows what I'd have said next. The ache between my thighs told me it wouldn't have been anything appropriate. I tried to get up so I could go and die quietly in a corner, but Jed's arm didn't move.

"So you want me, huh?"

"I was asleep when I said that. You can't hold it against me."

He flexed his hips forwards and I stiffened. "I can hold all sorts of things against you."

"What happened to being a gentleman?"

"It's harder than I thought."

So were other things. I clenched my fists, resisting the urge to reach behind me and explore.

"Can I get up now? Please?"

"I quite like you where you are."

"It's not funny, Jed. I just made a total fool of

myself."

He whispered in my ear again. "Shall I let you into a secret?"

"What?"

"I want you too." He nibbled gently on my earlobe and I gasped. "You can feel what you do to me."

I could, and it brought back glorious memories of him naked in Vegas. I blew out a breath and clenched my thighs together. On occasion, I'd given in to temptation and touched myself down there, and I desperately needed to get back to my room so I could take care of things. Either that or I'd spontaneously combust.

"Hot and bothered, I see."

He swept my hair to the side and fluttered his lips across the back of my neck.

"Please, just stop," I said through gritted teeth.

"Oh, I don't think so. I'm enjoying myself, and so are you, even if you don't want to admit it."

I sucked in air as his hand crept downwards, lower, lower, until it slipped under the edge of my panties. Panic welled up inside me. Should I beg him to stop or plead with him to keep going? A man like Jed must surely know what he was doing, and curiosity kept my mouth shut as his finger reached farther, hitting the magic spot that sent ripples of pleasure through me.

"You're soaked, darlin'. What the fuck were you dreaming about?"

"Nothing."

"I don't believe you." His finger slid away. "Tell me the truth, and I'll make it come true."

Oh, shoot. How did I get into these situations?

"I can't. It's embarrassing."

Grr, that smirk was infuriating.

"So it was a *dirty* dream."

"No! Well, maybe a little." I closed my eyes and sighed. "I wanted you to touch me, and you wouldn't."

"And how did you want me to touch you?"

"I—"

"Like this?" He ran a digit along my centre and I shuddered.

"Uh, I don't..."

"Or this?"

One finger pushed inside me, followed by a second. The intrusion made me gasp, but in a good way, as he stroked parts of me I didn't even know existed. I clenched around him, and he quickly withdrew.

"Not yet, darlin'." He brought his fingers to his mouth and sucked. "You taste delicious."

Oh. My. Goodness. Before I could process what he'd just done, his fingers slid back inside me, stroking, as he moved my shirt to one side and dropped soft kisses across my shoulder. Then his free hand reached underneath to my bare breasts, pausing to roll my nipples between his thumb and forefinger. Every touch and every caress shot heat through me, leaving me a writhing mess of flames until I detonated, volcano-style.

"So, was that what you were thinking about?"

He sounded smug and with good reason.

"I can't even..."

"I love seeing you come apart like that." His tongue running around the edge of my ear made me shiver. "So responsive."

I sagged back against him as the pleasure drained out of me, leaving me awash with unfulfilled need. His hard cock nestling between my butt cheeks reminded me the last few minutes had been all mine.

"What about you?" I asked.

"There's a time and a place, and this isn't it."

"But—"

He flipped me over and silenced me with a kiss. "The first—second—time I'm buried in you, I want you in my apartment, not in this shithole."

I'd blocked out our surroundings while Jed distracted me, but now I took in the grubby mattress, the bare concrete floor, the sun shining through a cracked window. And Jed's words filtered into my brain.

"You want me in your apartment?"

"I want you in my apartment."

I couldn't stop the huge grin that spread over my face.

"You didn't run screaming. I'm taking that as a good sign."

"There's only one kind of screaming I'm going to be doing near you." Oh, good heavens, I couldn't believe those words just passed my lips.

He groaned. "Don't say that, or I'll be tempted to take back everything I said and have you right here."

"I wouldn't say no."

"That's it. I'm getting up now or we'll never get anything done today."

He rolled away and climbed out of bed. As he dropped his boxers, I glimpsed his hard cock before he wrapped a towel around his waist. Holy moly, he was huge! No wonder I'd been sore the morning after in Vegas.

Jed disappeared to the bathroom, and I allowed

myself a few more minutes in his bed. My legs were still weak from orgasm, so even if I'd wanted to get up, I'd have struggled. The smell of him, of my arousal, drifted around me, and when I closed my eyes I could still feel him pressed against my back.

How I longed to wake up like that every morning, except maybe somewhere other than Iraq.

All too soon, Jed finished in the shower. When the door clicked open, I clambered to my knees, and he held out a hand to help me to my feet.

I took a moment to admire the view. Damp hair and a taut, golden chest with a smattering of blonde hair. A drop of water rolled down his pecs, and I couldn't resist chasing it with my tongue. Big mistake. My skin sizzled as he pressed me up against the wall and plundered my mouth in a kiss reminiscent of our first. Fingers dug into my hips, hard enough to bruise, but I didn't care. I'd wear those marks with pride.

Jed pulled back and looked down. "Oh fuck it, not again. I just took care of that."

I followed his gaze to the tented front of his towel. Ohhhh... The thought of him stroking himself in the shower had me instantly wet between my legs again. Honestly, the man needed to come with a flood warning.

For a moment, neither of us moved, and then insanity took over as I untucked his towel, letting it slither to the floor. I wrapped one hand around him, waiting for him to stop me, but apart from a slight widening of his eyes, he didn't move a muscle. It felt...odd. Unexpected, much like everything else about him. Silk over steel, soft yet unyielding.

And smooth, so smooth. I stroked along the shaft

and then, before logic prevailed again, I dropped to my knees and gave it a tentative lick.

Not that I had a clue what I was doing or anything, but like any biology student, I'd studied books. I held it at the root, my fingers barely meeting around it, and took as much of the length as I could into my mouth. It hit the back of my throat, and I fought against gagging. Well, none of Lottie's romance novels talked about that part.

I slid most of it out again, and as Jed's fingers fisted in my hair, I began experimenting like a good scientist. A lick got me a harsh breath. Sucking the tip caused Jed to push harder into me. Adding my hands to the party made him gasp.

Salty pre-cum oozed into my mouth, and I figured I must be doing something right. I swirled my tongue, trying to get more as Jed rocked his hips and groaned. Lottie's stories made this sound so glamorous, but the reality was kind of messy. Saliva dribbled down my hands as Jed began to thrust.

"Not gonna last much longer, darlin'. If you don't want me to shoot in your mouth, you need to get off."

I may have been on my knees, but right then, I had all the power and I wasn't about to relinquish it. I gave one last suck and gripped his butt cheeks as he exploded down my throat. Freaking heck—his legs were trembling.

As he pulled me to my feet, I took a second to analyse the situation. Yes, that seemed to go well.

"Now we're even," I said.

He kissed me, the two tastes of him mingling in my mouth.

"Not even close, darlin'."

CHAPTER 29

I'D ONLY BEEN in the lab for a couple of hours when Jed radioed through. A couple of hours where my legs would barely hold me up, and I had to delegate all the dangerous work to Clint because my hands kept shaking. Jed was a bad, bad man, but in the best way.

"We've got a new plan," he said. Even the sound of his voice did funny things to my stomach.

"We're only halfway through testing this morning's samples."

"How long will they take?"

"Another forty-five minutes. Maybe an hour."

"When you're done, meet me back at the boarding house."

There was no sense in trying to hurry—that would only lead to a mistake, and in BSL-4, that was the one thing we couldn't afford. By the time I escaped and went through decontamination, an hour and a half had passed, and Jed was pacing in the command centre.

"What's the plan?"

He glanced at the empty doorway, then squeezed my ass. Yup, he'd totally given up on the gentleman thing, not that I cared. I rather liked the liberties he took.

"The perimeter team's reported seeing dead rats in one of the wadis."

Great, rats. "What's a wadi?"

"A dried-up riverbed."

"You think they could be infected with Azrael?"

"Possibly. That's why I need you to come with me to take samples."

"And there was I thinking you wanted to take me out for a romantic lunch."

He smiled, sweet but sexy. "Just wait until we get back to Virginia, darlin'. I'll take you for as many romantic lunches as you want."

"Bribery will get you everywhere." Feeling brave, I stood on tiptoes and kissed him on the cheek. "I'll need to get bags for the samples."

"Not so fast, Miss Lane." He kicked the door shut and backed me up against the wall. "Lesson number one—don't expect to tease me and get away with it."

Unlike mine, his kiss involved a lot of tongue, a helping of hands, and a whole lot of heat. Right before I melted totally, he let me go. "Now we can leave."

"Are we going on foot?" I hoped not because my legs didn't feel much like walking.

"A man's waiting outside with our horses."

"Horses? Are you kidding?" I didn't know how to ride a horse. In fact, I'd always considered them to be four-legged spawns of Satan.

"Quickest way up the mountain."

An hour later, Jed slid a backpack over his shoulders and swung into the saddle. As his shirt slid up, I glimpsed the pistol tucked into his waistband.

"Why do you need that?"

"In case we need to shoot anything."

"Like what?"

He shrugged. "Potential hosts."

My legs went wobbly and not in a good way. "I don't want to kill anything."

"You don't have to, darlin'. You don't even need to watch. But if we do find any Azrael-infected animals, shooting's the kindest thing for them."

I thought back to the hospital, and before that, my own experiments in the lab. Unpalatable though it may be, he was right.

Jed must have seen the look on my face because he tried a tentative smile. "Come on, a nice romantic horseback ride through the desert. It'll be like Lawrence of Arabia."

Except Lawrence hadn't had to wear a hazmat suit —we had ours strapped to the back of our saddles—or ride the horsey equivalent of a pogo stick. Shergar, as some joker had called my mount, bounced around like he was on springs, shying at anything that moved. Jed's horse stood like a donkey, and he, of course, looked as if he'd been born in the saddle.

"Just relax," he called.

"That's easy for you to say."

Eventually, when he realised he was going to be left behind alone, Shergar bounded after Jed's mount with me hanging on for dear life, stopping three inches from its ass.

"Stop smirking. This isn't funny."

"It's a little bit funny."

"It's a good thing I'm not the one with the gun right now."

Jed pulled a sad face. "You can't shoot poor

Shergar."

"I wasn't thinking of shooting Shergar."

He clutched at his heart. "I'm hurt."

The bottom of the wadi lay a couple of hundred yards behind the hotel. It was wide at first, but after we passed the perimeter guard stationed part way up, the rocky track narrowed in places, and I understood why we needed the horses. Shergar settled into a steady pace, stumbling every so often as the ground got particularly uneven.

The sun rose higher, and I alternated sipping from one of the water bottles Jed made me bring and wiping sweat out of my eyes. An hour passed before we saw the first carcass, a goat-sized skeleton picked almost clean by scavengers.

Jed peered down from his saddle. "Shit. If other animals have eaten that, we could have a whole bunch of deadly-as-fuck wildlife running around out here. How long do you reckon Azrael lives in a dead body?"

I gazed around at the silent landscape. "The heat is our friend here. Outside a live host, in these temperatures, Ebola could survive a few hours. Less if it dries out. I've never studied smallpox myself, but the data says it's more fragile."

"Some good news, at least."

"I'm not sure there's much left to sample."

Jed fiddled with his phone. "I've marked it with GPS. Let's see what else we can find and take the samples on the way back. That way we don't have to put the hazmat suits on yet."

"As it's me who's gonna be suiting up, I'm all for that plan."

"I can—"

"How much experience do you have with biological sampling?"

"Not a lot. Okay, none."

Behind the next outcropping, we found another goat, fresher, then three rats. Then...nothing.

We rode on for half an hour, searching both sides of the wadi as the horses steadied themselves over the rocks. Shergar proved more sure-footed than Jed's mount, who tripped a couple of times and went down on his knees at one point.

"Maybe we've found everything?"

Jed pointed at a pair of large birds in the air over the next ridge. "See those?"

"The birds?"

"Cinereous vultures. They feed on carrion, and from the way they're circling, I bet there's something down there for them to snack on."

Why did I get a bad feeling about this?

Jed urged his horse faster, and Shergar trotted along behind with me bobbing about in the saddle as we rode along the old riverbank. The drop into the wadi was steep there, and with the land arid as far as I could see, I struggled to imagine a day when water flowed plentifully in the channel next to us. As we got closer to the vultures, they cried out and moved back a distance, settling on a high boulder to eye up the two humans invading their territory. Jed hopped off and handed me the reins.

"Hold him—I'll go up to the edge on foot."

"Can you see anything?" I called out as he peered over.

"Another body."

"Goat? Dog?"

"Human."

Sadness overcame me. Some poor Azrael victim came out to the desert to die?

"Did they pass away recently?"

"Hard to tell. I want to go down and take a look."

"No! What if it's still contagious? I'll suit up and go."

"I don't think this guy died from Azrael."

"What? How do you know?"

"He has a hole in his skull and a gun in his hand."

"Suicide?"

"Either that or someone wanted it to seem that way."

Jed stepped back and walked towards the skeleton of a tree a few yards away, sizing it up.

"What are you doing?"

He broke off a branch. "Like I said, I'm going down to take a look."

Before I could protest further, he hopped over the edge, and I heard the clatter of loose stones as they followed him to the bottom. Darn it, Jed! Please, don't do anything stupid. Okay, stupider.

I couldn't stand there doing nothing, so I wrapped both horses' reins around the tree trunk and inched forwards. The drop looked to be about thirty feet, and at the bottom lay a man's body, the tatters of his traditional dress blowing in the breeze. Little remained of his face, but white bone fragments lay around his skull in a bizarre halo. The vultures had done a good job.

"Why come all the way out here to kill himself?" I called.

"Maybe that was his plan all along?"

"What do you mean by that?"

Jed used his stick to poke at a leather satchel slung across the man's body, and a canister rolled out, clattering across the desert floor until it hit a rock.

He stooped to take a closer look. "Oh, fuck."

CHAPTER 30

I SQUINTED INTO the gully, but to me, the canister just looked like a thermos flask.

"What is it?" I called.

"You don't want to know. I don't want to know. Nobody wants to know."

Jed dropped the stick and began snapping photos, first of the scene and then close-ups of the canister itself.

"Can you throw me down one of those sample bags?"

"Do you want a suit?"

"I'm not planning to touch anything."

I dropped one of the largest bags down for him, and he turned it inside out and used it to pick up the mystery object.

"And another? I want to double-bag this."

Once he'd sealed it in two layers, he gingerly picked it up by the corner and began the climb back up. I held out a hand to help him over the edge, but he passed me the bag instead.

"Thanks."

I peered inside at the cylinder. It didn't weigh as much as I expected, and the bottom had some sort of symbols on it. I held it up to the light and almost dropped it when I spotted the biohazard warning symbol on the side.

Jed took it back from me once he rose to his feet. "Unless I'm very much mistaken, we've found our reservoir."

"Is that writing on the bottom of it?"

"I think it's Cyrillic."

"You know what it says?"

"I don't speak Russian."

"It looks like the number thirteen at the end."

"Yeah, it does."

I slumped onto a rock, its surface hot from the sun, and stared at the cylinder in Jed's hand. "I can't believe someone would deliberately infect the town like that. Why?"

"We're working on the theory it was both a test and a demonstration. To check if Azrael worked and show people what it's capable of."

The information filtered slowly into my brain, too huge to comprehend properly at first. "B-b-but that would be genocide. Biological warfare."

If the canister could decimate a town like Al Bidaya as quickly as it had, what could it do to New York or Los Angeles? People would get on trains and planes and carry it everywhere. The death toll would number in the millions. The world as we knew it would end.

"And at any one time, there are tens, maybe hundreds of groups in the world working towards that ultimate goal."

I shut my eyes and pictured the ward in the hospital. Men, women, and children dying almost every hour, and the people left in town growing more scared with each passing day. When I'd arrived there had been children playing on the streets. Now, those same streets were deserted.

"We have to stop them."

"That's what we intend to do, darlin'. You up to getting back on ol' Shergar here?"

As the horses picked their way through the wadi, Jed tapped away on his phone, no doubt sending pictures and other information on what we'd found. The moment we got back to the boarding house, he gave my shoulder a squeeze, distracted, and disappeared into the command centre.

Upstairs, I tried to wash away both the cloying heat and the feeling of dread that had settled over me. I was marginally successful with the first, but nothing shifted the second. I stared into the cracked mirror over the sink, wondering what would have happened if I'd chosen another path in life. Would I rather have been blissfully unaware of the monster brewing in a twin canister somewhere? And were there more than two of them?

"Oof." I left the bathroom and walked straight into Jed. "Sorry."

"We need to leave. Washington wants us back in the US with the canister. There's a plane on its way."

"What about everything here?"

"I've done what I needed to do, and Major Walsh is on his way to take over the command. The plan never called for me to be here long-term. You have the lab up and running now, haven't you?"

"Clint and my assistant should be able to cope with the day-to-day testing."

"Good. The powers that be have decided you're more valuable back home. Fielding told them more about your research, and they want you to advance that. The more we know about the Ebola side of things, the better."

"But this is all happening now, and research isn't that fast. Getting to the stage I'm at took years. There are processes I need to go through."

"President Harrison has promised anything you need to expedite those processes."

So far, I'd done everything on a shoestring budget. Being given free rein for extra lab space and assistants would have been exciting under normal circumstances, but knowing the reasons behind it made me feel ill.

"Besides," Jed continued. "They're not exactly giving you a choice."

"I take it the ice queen was involved in that decision?"

"She's not that bad once you get to know her."

I rolled my eyes at him. "Oh, please. She sent me to hell without a second thought. Since I've been here, she's ordered a man's execution, and now she's telling me what to do yet again. She's got a serious god complex."

"She's not what you think."

"Stop defending her. She might be pretty on the outside, but she's hideous on the inside."

He turned away, ending the conversation. "We need to pack," he said as he walked off.

Shoot. I shouldn't have snapped at him, but that woman made my blood boil. Now I needed to apologise.

First, I packed in record time—not difficult when I hardly owned anything. I stared down at the suitcase Molly had bought with its inappropriate selection of clothing. That really was it for me. After my conversation with Mom, going back to Norsville to collect any of my belongings was out of the question, and with the state of my bank balance I'd be wearing thrift store chic for the foreseeable future. And if I couldn't find somewhere to live, I'd be taking Lottie's space on the bench outside the library. Jed might have offered me a bed in his apartment, but that was in Virginia, and if the president wanted me to work, I needed to be in Galveston.

Jed was already waiting in the hallway, his bag at his feet.

"I'm sorry about—"

He waved a hand. "Doesn't matter. Are you ready to go?"

"Yes, but I need to pick up the samples from the lab."

"Your assistant's loaded them already."

Guess I didn't pack as fast as I thought. I peered into the back of the jeep, and sure enough, there was a sealed crate waiting in the trunk, still damp and smelling of bleach from the sanitisation procedure.

"Shall I sit in the back?" I asked Jed.

"Take the front. I'm driving."

"Is anyone else coming?"

"No. There's a bunch of guys coming in on the plane, so one of them'll drive the jeep back."

Travelling alone with Jed was an unexpected bonus, and a day ago I'd have felt euphoric on the trip, knowing I was going back home with the man I hoped to share my future with. But today, tension fogged the air, both from the words we'd had about the ice queen earlier and the fear of what waited for us in the United States.

I stared out the window at the passing desert until I could stand the silence no longer.

"Do you think the government will pay for me to stay in a hotel in Galveston?"

"Right now, the government would buy you a house in Galveston if you asked for one."

He was kidding, right? "I don't need a house."

"Yes, they'll pay for a hotel. And a consultancy fee too. Make sure you don't short-change yourself. Go in high. What's your normal rate?"

"I don't have a normal rate. My research grant buys paperclips and ramen noodles for lunch."

"You eat paperclips for lunch? Don't they damage your teeth?"

I elbowed him in the side. "Be serious." But I was laughing from sheer relief at the tension being broken.

"Have you tried staples? I hear they double up as toothpicks."

"Jed!"

"Okay, okay. I'll help you sort the money out when we get back."

"Thanks."

He held out an arm, and I snuggled underneath it with the parking brake digging into my waist. But I didn't care. I was more comfortable there than I had been in a long time.

"And you can stay with me tonight. There are a lot of things I've been waiting a week to do to you."

His smile was back too, the sparkling one that made my insides do somersaults.

"I can't wait."

"Not long now, darlin'."

To my untrained eye, the ugly grey plane looked the same as the one I'd flown in on. I peered up the ramp as Jed pulled to a stop beside it. Yes, there were the awful canvas seats. But at least I had Jed to keep me warm on the trip this time, even if there still wasn't a bathroom.

A group of men milled around, some talking, some unloading cargo. Jed hopped out of the jeep and came to open my door for me.

"Jed, you asshole! How's it going?" one of the men shouted.

"Better now I'm leaving."

The man turned his attention to me. "And who's the lovely lady?"

Jed answered for me. "Chess Lane, lead scientist on the team. She's leaving too."

The man grasped my hand. "Gary Walsh. I was in the Rangers with Jed."

Rangers? Wasn't that some kind of special forces? Jed was in the special forces? I glanced over at him. Special forces or not, he didn't seem happy as he looked at my hand in Gary Walsh's. I politely extricated myself and took a step back.

"Shame you're going home, Miss Lane. We could have gotten to know each other."

Jed's look got blacker, and I attempted to make light of the situation. "We've both been summoned by the ice queen."

"Ice queen?"

"She's talking about Emerson," Jed put in.

Emerson? That was her name?

Gary chuckled. "The ice queen—that's about right. She ever thaw out in bed, Jed? Or is it like fucking one of those fancy ice sculptures?"

My brain froze for a few moments while his words trickled in. Jed and the ice queen? Together? In bed?

I looked to Jed, expecting him to deny it but all I saw was shock, then guilt, and I knew Gary's words were true.

"How could you?"

"It's in the past."

Gary's head turned between us like a spectator at a tennis match. "Shit—shouldn't I have mentioned that? Wait. You're screwing the scientist too? Nice work, buddy, even for you."

Even for him? So Jed *did* make a habit of this. I barely knew this man, did I? Vegas Jed—the player who'd fallen in bed with me and then left in the morning—that was the real him, wasn't it? Not the man who'd tried so hard to be a gentleman all week and failed in the sweetest of ways. I was just a game, wasn't I?

I backed away, determined not to cry while the men were still watching me, but I only made it a handful of steps before Jed followed.

"Get away from me!"

"Chess, listen, please. It's not what you think."

"You're gonna tell me you didn't sleep with her?"

"I did, but it didn't mean anything. One night with you was worth a hundred with her."

"You've spent a hundred nights with her?" Freaking heck, I really didn't know Jed at all.

"Fuck, I don't know. I lost count."

"Oh, this just gets better and better."

"With you, it's different."

"The first night we spent together, you don't even remember it. That's how much I meant."

"But in the time we've spent together since, you've made me feel... I don't know; I can't explain it."

"Don't even bother trying. You knew how I felt about the ice queen, and you didn't even hint at your history with her. That alone shows you weren't thinking of a long-term future with me, despite everything you said."

Because surely he must have known I'd find out eventually? She'd probably have dropped it into a conversation to see me squirm, the manipulative bitch.

"Chess, please..."

"Don't. Just don't. If you ever felt *anything* for me, you'll leave me alone."

I whirled around and strode to the plane, relieved when I managed to walk away without breaking on the outside like I was on the inside. Up the ramp I went, into the furthest, darkest corner I could find, and threw myself into one of the stupid seats.

Then I buried my head in my hands and cried.

CHAPTER 31

JED DIDN'T TRY to talk to me again on the flight, which left me in no doubt where I stood. On my own.

I wasn't entirely stupid—of course I'd realised he was a player, and if he'd been playing with anyone but her, I could have dealt with it. But...ugh! Little things began to make sense, like the way he defended her after that poor man got shot fleeing on his horse.

And Jed didn't seem to care about our split, though granted, what we'd had could barely be called a relationship in the first place. Each time I snuck a glance at him in his seat at the other end of the airplane, he was either asleep or chatting to some of the other men on board. He did get up at one point, and my heart sped up as he walked towards me, but he stopped halfway up the hold to pee in a tube. Guess Moustache hadn't been kidding about the bathroom.

So, what should I do when we landed? I needed to find somewhere to stay, to start with. When a stranger walked past on his way to the cockpit, I grabbed his sleeve.

"Excuse me, do you know where this plane is landing?"

He gave me a look as if to say, "You don't?" but answered anyway. "Andrews Field."

"Where's that?"

"Maryland."

The instant the wheels touched tarmac, I pulled out my phone, thankful I'd kept it fully charged in Iraq, just in case. Gah! Nineteen missed calls from Wade, and I ignored them all. With no money and nobody else left to try, I dialled Lottie, trying to inject some cheer I absolutely didn't feel into my voice.

"How are things in Virginia?"

"Awesome! I went to the mall with Tia yesterday for ice cream."

"You ate ice cream?"

For years, Lottie had refused to touch dairy produce, citing an excess of calories, fat, and cholesterol.

She giggled. "I know. Toby says I can eat anything I want in moderation."

"Toby?"

"The nutritionist who's been helping me. And did you know eggs are actually really good for you?"

"You've been eating eggs too?"

"Scrambled every morning."

I needed to meet this nutritionist and kiss his feet, but first I had a bigger issue to deal with. "Uh, I don't suppose one of your new friends would be able to arrange a ride for me?"

"A ride? From where?"

"I've just landed in Maryland, at Andrews Field, but it was all a bit sudden, and I haven't sorted out transport or anywhere to stay."

She squealed so loudly I had to hold the phone away from my ear or risk hearing damage. At least somebody was happy to see me. "You can stay here. It'll be awesome! And Tia will pick you up; I know she won't mind."

"Shouldn't you check with her first? It's, like…" I did some rapid calculations. "Midnight, isn't it?"

"Yeah, but we were up late watching movies last night so we didn't get out of bed until lunchtime. Trust me; it'll be fine."

Rain hammered down as I walked off the plane, and I shivered in my jeans and thin sweater. But after a week in the dry desert heat, I was almost grateful for the chill, so I stepped into the downpour and followed the rest of the men into a hangar. A member of the ground crew came round with coffee as the men began to unload, and I went out into the storm again to supervise the retrieval of the samples.

"These are going straight to the CDC, ma'am."

I watched almost wistfully as they loaded the crate onto the truck, ready to head for another plane. I wanted to get a better look at Azrael. Removed from the red zone in Al Bidaya, my professional curiosity came to the fore, and I longed to delve into its inner workings.

Jed had been in the hangar earlier, but when I returned, he was nowhere to be seen. Figured. At least I knew how important I was in his life now. He still hadn't reappeared by the time I heard a shriek at the door in the far corner. A Lottie-style shriek. I looked up to see her sprinting towards me, watched by a couple of dozen men wearing camouflage and bemused expressions. She threw herself into my arms and I hugged her tightly, relieved to find she hadn't gotten any thinner. If anything, she'd filled out an inch or two.

"How did you get onto the base? I thought you'd call me when you got close."

"Tia talked to the guy on the gate."

A brunette walked up behind Lottie, wearing brightly patterned leggings and an off-the-shoulder sweater only one in a hundred girls could carry off.

"You're Tia?"

"That's me."

Oh. Her accent was English—not what I'd been expecting. Refined, like the ice queen, but softer in a Bridget Jones sort of way. Suddenly, I felt a little ashamed of my Texas drawl.

"Thank you for coming to pick me up. I don't know many people on this side of the country."

"I'm always ready for an adventure. Do you have luggage?"

"Just a suitcase."

One of the men had wheeled my case into the hangar, where it stood as a beacon in a sea of browns and greens. I retrieved it from its spot next to a toolbox and dragged it behind Tia as she led us to a BMW parked right outside. How old was she? Nineteen? Twenty? When I was her age, I'd still been taking the bus.

"This is a really nice car."

"Thanks! It was a birthday present."

Wow. I couldn't imagine being given a birthday present like that. In fact, I hadn't had any presents at all since my father died.

"You have very generous parents."

"Oh, no, it wasn't them. My dad's gone and my mother bought me a china dinner service for my eighteenth. She said every girl should have one." She wrinkled her nose in disgust, then laughed. "The car was from my brother's ex-girlfriend. He went mental at her for buying it. It was hilarious."

"That's whose house we're staying in," Lottie added.

"Your brother's ex? Isn't that...slightly strange?" I asked.

"Nah, she's awesome. Besides, my brother's engaged now, and when I stay with him and his fiancé, they're all smoochy-smoochy, and it's like...such...." She made a gagging noise.

"And you're sure she won't mind?"

"She's not even there at the moment. Mostly she stays somewhere else. Work and stuff. We're, like, house-sitting."

"It'll only be for a night or two. I need to head back to Galveston."

Lottie clutched my hand. "So soon? I thought you could stay awhile?"

"I have to do some lab work there. The research project on Ebola needs to be finished. I plan to move after that, but it won't be for a few weeks."

"You'll come back to Virginia?"

"I was thinking of Atlanta."

With Wade in Texas and Jed in Richmond, both of those destinations were out. Too many bad memories. If Dr. Fielding could find something for me in Atlanta, even a low-level position, that seemed like my best bet. I didn't need to earn much, just enough for Lottie and me to live on.

"But I want to stay in Virginia."

"Please, Lottie. I've only been back five minutes. Can we talk about this later?"

"Sorry." She cast her eyes downwards. "I just like it there; that's all."

When we got in the car, the mood lightened as Tia

and Lottie began singing to the radio. An old pop song by... What was that boyband called? Red Alert. I hadn't heard them for years. Hadn't the lead singer disappeared or something? I stayed quiet in the back for the two-hour journey, forcing myself to concentrate on the music rather than my disaster of a life. I'd almost drifted off to sleep when Tia slowed up and turned into a driveway.

As we waited for a huge pair of metal gates to open, I took in my surroundings. Woods gave way to vast, rolling lawns as we drove towards the house, and what a house! Lottie said it was big but nothing prepared me for the glass and metal behemoth ahead—a juxtaposition of curves and sharp angles lit up by a row of security lights that put the sun to shame.

"Is this all one house?" I asked.

"Yeah," Lottie replied. "And it's got a sauna and a steam room."

"This place must have cost millions," I muttered to myself.

"Probably," Tia said. "It was custom built."

Inside, the double-height atrium was dominated by a life-size silver sculpture of a rearing horse. Tia led us under the flashing hooves, past a set of glass stairs that made me feel a little queasy because I could see straight through them, then stopped in front of an elevator.

"I'll show you to a guest room. We can sort everything else out in the morning."

We followed her through the maze to a beautiful bedroom done out in pale purple with accents of silver. To match the horse? I couldn't help smiling at its simple elegance, and Lottie bounced on her toes.

"Isn't it pretty? My room's green."

"It's lovely."

Tia pointed to a door on the far side. "There's toiletries in the bathroom—just help yourself to whatever. Clothes too, if there's anything in the wardrobe. People leave things all over the place here. When you get up, head back the way we came and find us downstairs."

I raised an eyebrow. "I'll need a map."

"Don't worry. If you get lost, there are two more sets of stairs. Keep wandering until you get to the kitchen."

Oh, it was easy for her to say. I'd probably still be wandering tomorrow at lunchtime. But tonight, I was too tired to care. I rummaged through my bag for something to wear, choking back a sob when I found Jed's T-shirt. Dammit. I flung it across the room, cursing in a manner I never did in public.

Even after he betrayed me, I couldn't help missing him.

Rather than be reminded of him again, I crawled into bed naked and pulled the covers up to my chin. Even so, he still haunted my dreams. Although when his blonde hair and blue eyes mingled with the cold features of the ice queen, those dreams were more like nightmares.

CHAPTER 32

THE NEXT MORNING, well, almost lunchtime, I only had time for a quick breakfast with Lottie and Tia before my phone rang. My worries about finding the kitchen had proved unfounded because Lottie had come to my room to get me before I'd finished dressing.

"Dr. Fielding? How's Marjorie?"

"I keep asking you to call me Wilfred. And Marjorie's much improved, thank you."

Try as I might, calling him by his first name seemed to imply a lack of respect from me. "Did she have the operation?"

"It went as smoothly as we could have hoped."

"Thank goodness."

Dr. Fielding blew out a breath. "How was Iraq?"

"It was—"

"Honestly, Chess, I didn't realise they wanted me to go straight out there. A trip was mentioned, but I thought we'd have a few days first."

It was done now. And while I never wanted to think about Jed again, we still had the super-virus to deal with.

"Do you know about...?" I thought back to the paperwork I'd signed at the White House. Should I mention its name?

"Azrael?"

"Yes, Azrael. It was...horrific. But as a genetically engineered virus it's..."

I felt guilty voicing my fascination with it. A man-made monster, let loose on earth with the power to destroy the human race. So tiny, yet so deadly.

"Fascinating. It's okay to say it, Chess. Whoever designed Azrael was both a genius and a madman."

"We've got to stop it," I whispered.

"We do. Which is why we need to go to Galveston today."

"Today?"

"You need to continue your trial, and I'd like us to take a look at Azrael together."

Dr. Fielding was bringing Azrael? The thought both terrified and intrigued me, but the chance to study the beast on my own turf was one I couldn't pass up. Not to mention the opportunity to work with Dr. Fielding. Until now, almost all our contact had been by phone or email.

"I think I'd like that too."

"A car will be waiting for you outside in an hour. I'll see you soon, Chess."

"Wait! How do you know where I am?"

He chuckled. "The government keeps an eye on that sort of thing."

Like Azrael, the idea that the ice queen was tracking my every move both scared and fascinated me.

For the next few days, I lost track of time. The hours melded together as I trekked in and out of BSL-4 in a whirl of chemical showers and disposable underwear.

Dr. Fielding and Chet were by my side the entire time, but you know who wasn't? Jed.

I'd secretly hoped he might try to contact me—I mean, he had to know where I was—but I heard nothing. Not a word.

In the lab, with the deadly charms of Azrael to explore, I could block him out, but at night in the hotel room Dr. Fielding arranged for me, Jed's face and other parts of him still paraded through my mind. In the end, I took to sleeping in the break room, and each time Jed bothered me, I got up and worked at my computer until I was too exhausted to dream anymore.

Like the other filoviruses, Ebola contained RNA rather than DNA as its genetic material. When RNA was copied, the natural replication process made many more mistakes than with double-stranded DNA, giving viruses like Ebola a higher mutation rate compared to DNA-based viruses like smallpox. Through analysis of Azrael's RNA, we tracked its lineage to the 1976 Ebola outbreak in what was then called Zaire—now the Democratic Republic of Congo. This backed up the theory that Azrael had been under development for a considerable amount of time.

"If only our governments had put this much effort into finding a cure, eh?" Dr. Fielding said.

"There's only so much funding to go around."

He took a sip of vending machine coffee and grimaced. "Not just the funding situation. I bet the lab that developed this didn't pay so much attention to ethics. Wonder how they tested it?"

"NHPs?"

"Not everything that works on monkeys works on humans."

I dropped the cookie I was holding. "You don't think...?"

"Developing Azrael didn't fall within the clinical trial guidelines."

Human testing? The idea sickened me. Who did they use? Unwitting volunteers? Prisoners?

"Our trial is going to be done properly."

"Speaking of trials, are you ready?"

Today was the day. Day twenty-two. The day we'd inject my twelve healthy monkeys with three Ebola variants taken from freeze-dried samples, plus Azrael. We'd modified the trial protocol, dropping out the Taï Forest strain and replacing it with Azrael, while also using the spare pair of monkeys, and President Harrison ensured the amendments were approved quickly.

"I am, but I'm so darn nervous. What if this doesn't work? So much of my time will have been wasted."

"Not wasted. Everything's a learning curve, and with Ebola, that curve's steeper than most."

"Failing scares me," I whispered.

"The only people who never fail are those who never try."

And I didn't want to be the girl who never tried. Fall down seven times, get up eight, that was what my daddy always used to say whenever I came in with another grazed knee.

"Let's do this."

Two hours later, we had five vaccinated infected monkeys and one vaccinated control in the first BSL-4 room, five unvaccinated infected monkeys and a control in the second, and a whole lot of waiting to do. I stood under the chemical shower, emptying my brain of the looks the monkeys had given me as I injected them. They knew. They understood something bad was about to happen.

Until the trial was over twenty-one days from now, only Dr. Fielding, Chet, and I were allowed to enter the room, and all we could do was watch, wait, and measure.

"Better update the man above," Dr. Fielding said, as we headed out of the lab.

"Sorry?"

"We've got a conference call with the president in half an hour. I didn't mention it earlier because you had enough to worry about."

I hated when people kept things from me, but before I chided Dr. Fielding, I managed to bite my tongue. He'd only been doing what he thought was best for me. And when I saw who was sitting at the president's side on the screen a few minutes later, I was grateful I hadn't had more time to think about it.

There she was. The ice queen on the president's left with perfect lipstick, perfect hair, and perfect bitch glint in her eyes. But more surprising was the man on Harrison's right. Jed—looking like he'd rather be anywhere but there. Well, that made two of us.

The president began. "Miss Lane, I'm glad to see you made it back from Iraq in one piece."

"Good afternoon, sir. I'm glad to be back."

"How's Galveston?" the ice queen asked.

"It's okay." Why was she being nice?

"Good. If you haven't noticed already, we've put some pocket money in your bank account."

I hadn't noticed. Dr. Fielding had taken care of my accommodation and all of our food costs since we arrived in Galveston.

"How did you get my account number?"

"Miss Lane, I know you had a slice of watermelon and a bowl of granola for breakfast this morning. Believe me, getting your bank details wasn't a problem."

How the heck did she know that? Did she have a spy in the hotel dining room? The blond man at the next table reading the paper? The couple opposite discussing local landmarks? What else had she found out about me?

Did she have no respect for personal privacy?

The suit next to Jed asked for an update, but thankfully Dr. Fielding jumped in and ran through today's events.

Then the president spilled the bad news. "We'd better hope your vaccine has some effect, Miss Lane, because intelligence suggests we might need it."

"What intelligence?"

"Firstly, we have reason to believe a second canister of Azrael is on US soil."

I slumped back in my seat and gripped Dr. Fielding's hand under the table. He squeezed mine back.

"And secondly?" he asked.

"We've studied the canister Major Harker brought back and concluded it has a suitable mechanism for dispensing the one-micrometre droplets able to cause infection through inhalation. I don't believe I need to explain what could happen if that canister was set off in a crowd."

It was a good thing I was sitting down because if I hadn't been, my legs would have given way. Yes, a release of Ebola in a city would kill thousands. Hundreds of thousands, even. Life as we knew it would grind to a halt. I nodded slowly.

"In light of the importance of your work, we've assigned bodyguards to both of you around the clock, just to be on the safe side," said the suit. "They'll escort you to and from your hotel and wait outside while you're in the lab."

"Thank you, Mr. President," Dr. Fielding answered for both of us.

Great, more people following me around. I didn't relish the idea, but if they thought there was a real danger, I had to be grateful.

"Is there anything else?"

We both shook our heads.

"In that case, best of luck, Miss Lane. We're all rooting for you."

"Can we make a quick stop at the ATM?" I asked Dr. Fielding on the way back to the hotel.

He was driving our rented Honda. We'd decided to finish early that evening and catch up on sleep. Or, in my case, some tossing and turning.

"Of course. Where's the nearest one?"

"Uh, take a left at the lights. There's a mall real close."

My phone rang as he turned, and I glanced at the screen. Wade. Again. He'd been calling a couple of times a day, but I'd gotten real good at ignoring him. At least being in BSL-4 meant I rarely heard the phone ring. A tiny piece of me wanted to answer and tell him what an asshole he was, but the bigger part never wanted to hear his voice again.

I suppose at least he was persistent. How many times had Jed called? Zero. And worse, my subconscious still missed him because I'd dreamed about him last night. Okay, every night, despite my efforts not to. If he phoned, I very much suspected I'd answer before I could stop myself.

Dr. Fielding went into the pharmacy to pick up more antacids while I fished out my ATM card, fumbling to get it into the slot in the machine outside. How much had the ice queen given me? A hundred dollars? Five hundred?

Ten thousand dollars?

She considered ten thousand dollars pocket money? Was she out of her perfectly ordered mind?

Or had I gone out of mine?

CHAPTER 33

TWENTY-THREE DAYS.

Twenty-three long, agonising days.

But they'd passed, along with all five of the unvaccinated monkeys we'd dosed with Ebola and Azrael.

I'd ridden the whole roller coaster of emotions, from worry at the beginning, to sorrow as I mourned the loss of one monkey after another, relief as I talked to Lottie and she told me she'd put on three more pounds and learned to cook an omelette, and finally, euphoria.

Because by day twenty-two, all the unvaccinated monkeys had died except the control. Of the six vaccinated monkeys, only one had gotten sick—number four, the marmoset we'd protected against Ebola only and then infected with Azrael. Monkey four had shown symptoms of smallpox on day thirteen and was currently sitting miserably in his cage, covered in pustules and refusing marshmallows. Monkey five, another participant in our hastily modified trial, who received both the Ebola and smallpox vaccines, remained healthy but cheesed off about being pricked with a needle every day. The only other symptoms in the infected monkeys were slightly elevated temperatures on days five and six.

In short, the trial had gone as well as any of us could have hoped for.

And now, everything was about to change.

Chet would stay on to monitor monkey number four, Dr. Fielding had returned to Marjorie in Atlanta, and I was packing up my entire operation and moving to Richmond. The president himself had intervened to provide the funding to extend my trial, and only Richmond had enough space to accommodate my newly expanded team.

With the virus still raging in Al Bidaya, we needed to test the vaccine on a bigger sample, and the next stage would be human trials, maybe even on some of the townsfolk in Iraq. Little protocol existed on running a trial in the midst of an epidemic, but with Ebola, and indeed Azrael, it was impossible to test on humans otherwise—that's why proving the basic safety of the vaccine was so important.

Dr. Fielding and I had synthesised further stocks of Apollo, as we were calling the trial vaccine, named after the Greek god of healing. The vials in the refrigerator looked so small and dull to the untrained eye, but I couldn't help feeling a sense of pride each time I looked at them. Six years, from undergraduate to PhD student, and I'd achieved something.

Something but not everything.

As I packed my books and papers into a box, I kept telling myself Richmond was a big place. The chances of running into Jed were slim, especially as he seemed to spend so much of his time abroad or in Washington, DC.

I ambled through to the break room for another cup of bad coffee. Since the ice queen dumped a pile of cash in my bank account, I'd taken to spending it in the vending machine rather than setting up the filter for one person. Black coffee funded by a black heart. It seemed fitting.

"Do you want...?"

I trailed off as I realised my guard had stepped outside again, most probably for a cigarette. The guy who took the afternoon shift had a real nicotine problem. Not that I minded him leaving. As well as smelling bad, he was a lecherous slime ball who insisted on talking constantly so I couldn't concentrate. I understood his job wasn't that exciting, but he needed to remember I had work to do as well.

Footsteps behind signalled his return, and by association, an end to my peace and quiet. Wonderful.

"Would you like—?"

My skull slamming forward into the machine cut off my words, and the stars in my head matched the cracks radiating out through the glass front. Another hit and the room went fuzzy then black as I was dragged backwards by my ponytail. I tried to scream as the person behind shoved me into a store cupboard, but no sound came out.

Where was the damn guard? Why wasn't he here to help me?

Blood dribbled down my face as the man—and it could only have been a man from his size and strength —pressed me against the wall. When the president told me I could be in danger, I'd thought he was overreacting, but now? Was I about to die?

A hand pressed roughly between my legs, and the horrible realisation dawned.

"I'm here for what's mine, bitch."

"Wade?" I gasped the word, barely able to breathe.

My knees buckled, but his weight against my back held me up, suffocating me.

"Thought you could get away from me, did you? You dumped me a day before our wedding, you stupid cunt. You must have known I wouldn't let you get away with that."

He wrenched my arm, twisting me so I cracked the back of my head on the wall, then wrapped one hand around my throat. His face faded in and out as one hand went to his zipper, the noise of it coming down so loud above our panting. I retched, and he whacked my head against the wall again before he forced his mouth onto mine.

"Let...me...go."

He only laughed. The man weighed twice as much as me, and when I pushed against him with all my strength, he didn't move an inch. I tried to knee him where it hurt, but he'd pinned my legs, and when I tried to swing a fist, he wrenched my wrist hard enough to make me see not only stars but the whole universe.

"Struggle all you like, bitch. It'll just make this more fun."

Tears mingled with blood as I braced myself for the rest. Where was that *fucking* guard? At that moment, I wished I'd never sent Jed away, no matter what he'd done. He was the one man I *knew* would have protected me.

"What the—?"

I was on the verge of blacking out when Wade was ripped away from me. As I crumpled to the floor, a flash of blonde hair caught in my peripheral vision.

Jed?

Had he finally come back?

I sucked in air as thumps and crashes came from the break room. Please, please don't let Jed be hurt! I'd never forgive myself if Wade injured him because of me. I tried to crawl outside, but my limbs wouldn't cooperate. Inch by inch, I slithered across to the doorway...

And came face to face with Wade. He lay sprawled on the floor, his face a mass of blood and mangled flesh. He wasn't moving. Was he...was he dead? Blood and snot bubbled from his nose as he struggled to breathe. Shoot. He was alive. But how was Jed?

"Are you okay?" I croaked.

"Fine, thanks. I thought for a moment I might have broken a nail, but it's all good."

What on earth...? That wasn't Jed's voice. I followed a pair of legs that also weren't Jed's upwards, all the way to the ice queen's expressionless face.

"Sorry, it looks like I was a few minutes late. Here, let me help you." She took my arm and half carried me to a chair. "If you feel faint, lean forwards with your head between your knees."

The guard meandered back in and surveyed the damage, wide-eyed. "What happened?"

The ice queen turned on him. "You fucked up. That's what happened. Guard duty doesn't mean stopping for a cigarette, it doesn't mean texting your mates, and it doesn't mean chatting up co-eds. Now get out of my damn sight."

He slunk off, and I was glad she was on my side for once. There was nothing like having a pit bull in your corner.

"I need medics and cops. Now," she barked into her

phone.

Oh, thank goodness. I slumped forward as she crouched next to me, perfectly balanced on four-inch pumps, her hair a honey blonde rather than its usual white. She hadn't even creased her charcoal pantsuit.

"Did you black out?"

"I don't think so."

She gently pulled my fingers away from my neck, then rocked back on her heels as she appraised me critically.

"There's a lot of swelling, and you need X-rays."

"What about Wade?"

"Wade's lucky he doesn't need a body bag. Forget about him."

Sirens sounded outside, and in record time I was being loaded into the back of an ambulance. I turned my head sideways and saw the ice queen personally handcuffing Wade to his own stretcher.

"Don't worry; he's not coming with us," she said.

"You're coming to the hospital?"

"Seeing as your ex-bodyguard is looking for a new job, somebody's got to stand in."

I wasn't up to arguing, especially since I didn't stand a chance of winning, anyway. Besides, I soon found having her there had other advantages. The doctors seemed as scared of her as I was, and I got whizzed from department to department before they deposited me back in reception with a selection of anti-inflammatories and a bag of painkillers.

"Here, I brought you a clean jumper." She held out a bag from Target.

"Thanks." I wriggled out of my bloodstained sweater and stuck my arms and head through the new one.

"Have you eaten?"

"Not since lunch."

"We'll pick something up on the way back to the hotel. You like pizza? Italian?"

Outside the White House, she seemed more human. Now she'd thawed, I didn't want to claw her eyes out quite so much. Especially as I needed to lean on her as we walked—I'd twisted my ankle somewhere along the way and a twinge of pain shot up my calf with every step.

"Uh, either's—oh, shit! I mean, shoot!"

"What?"

She followed my line of vision to the hospital doors where a solid man in a three-piece suit was walking in with a tall, thin woman on his arm.

"It's Wade's parents."

I knew the instant his father saw me because Mr. Bruckman's eyes narrowed, and he steered his wife in my direction. Oh, heck. His father made Clayton look like a saint, and his mother was such a bitch she should have been registered with the American Kennel Club.

The ice queen stepped forward and put her hands on her hips. Wade's father tried to cut around her, but she blocked him.

"You little whore! What have you done?" he spat at me over her shoulder.

Emerson, who was six inches shorter than Mr. Bruckman, put her hands on his chest and gave him a hard shove. "Get out of my fucking face." He stepped back and balled up his fists, but she stood her ground. "What? You want to hit me? The apple didn't fall very far from the tree, did it?"

He let fly with a right hook, face red with anger. In the time it took me to blink, she had him on the floor with his arm twisted up behind his back. Wade's mom ran forward, swinging her designer purse like a club.

"Be careful! She's—"

Mrs. Bruckman sprawled across the floor as Emerson sidestepped and tripped her, and the entire waiting room fell silent.

Emerson raised an eyebrow. "Sorry, you were saying?"

"Uh, it doesn't matter."

Footsteps sounded as cops came running. They must have been nearby. Wade's father clambered to his knees and coughed a tooth onto the floor.

"That woman attacked me." He pointed at the ice queen. "Arrest her."

One of the policemen peered down at Wade's mother. "Say, is that Lorna Bruckman?"

The ice queen shrugged. "She doesn't look too steady on her feet. You should breathalyse her."

The older cop walked over to us. "Care to tell us what happened, Mrs. Black?"

Mrs. Black? The ice queen was married?

"These are the parents of the man I laid out earlier. They decided to try doing the same to me."

The cop smirked, then quickly straightened his face. "Didn't work, did it?"

"Nope." I'd never seen her smile before, but it made her look almost normal. "Pass me your cuffs and I'll do the honours."

I watched from the sidelines as the cops hauled off Wade's parents. Mrs. Bruckman came to her senses after a few minutes and began wailing about lawsuits and court.

The ice queen let out a thin breath. "Good grief. Is she always like that?"

"Unfortunately, yes. Aren't you worried?"

"Do I look worried?"

"I guess not."

"In that case, shall we carry on?"

I followed her outside, marvelling at the way she stayed so calm. She'd fought three people and won without even breaking a sweat. I'd always thought she lived behind a desk in Washington, but it seemed she got her hands dirty after all.

Maybe I'd been wrong about her?

CHAPTER 34

THE ICE QUEEN had a car waiting outside, a limousine no less. I guess I shouldn't have been surprised. I guess I wouldn't have been surprised to see a Lamborghini, a Hummer, or a tank either. The driver opened the door, and I climbed in, sinking into one of the leather seats and sighing in relief that this nightmare of an evening was over.

The ice queen sat next to me, stretching out her legs. "Drink?"

"Is there any water?"

She fished a bottle out of a built-in cooler, passed it over, then pulled a tablet out of her purse. I was left alone with my thoughts as she began tapping away at the screen.

The ice queen. I never thought I'd get so close to her and live to tell the tale, but she'd surprised me. Maybe I should start calling her Emerson instead. After all, wasn't that what Jed said her name was?

Jed. After almost a month in Galveston, the hurt had gradually begun to fade, but tonight in the break room, he'd been the first person in my head when I thought my life was over. I still wanted him. Nothing like a near-death experience to crystallise my thoughts. But what could I do about it? He'd most likely lost interest in me by now thanks to my actions. Even if I called him and apologised, would it be enough? What if he hung up? Or worse, told me he'd already moved onto the next girl like he had so many times in the past.

"Penny for them?"

I looked up to find Emerson watching me. "Huh?"

"What are you thinking? If it's about Wade, he's not worth wasting your brainwaves."

"Jed," I blurted.

"I haven't told him, if that's what you're wondering. He doesn't even know I'm here."

"It's not that."

"Then what's the problem?"

Oh, heck. How did I get myself into these awkward situations? Without knowing what the exact nature of their relationship was, it was difficult to answer. Were they still involved? But hang on, the cop had called her Mrs.

I decided to go with vague. "Jed and I had a little argument at the airport in Iraq, and I said some things I wish I hadn't."

"You mean the bit where you found out we used to fuck and you wouldn't let him explain anything? That little argument?"

So much for subtlety. I nodded, cheeks burning. "He told you about that?"

"No, my spy pixies reported back to me. Of course he told me."

"Oh."

I wouldn't have put it past her to have spy pixies. I'd seen pictures of those tiny cameras mounted on bees.

"Look, we talk, okay? We're friends, have been for a long time. And we used to be friends with benefits, but that's all in the past. My husband would kick both our asses if we slept together again."

I gave a nervous laugh. "I didn't know any of that."

"Because you never gave him the chance to tell you. Nor did it escape my notice that you're not my biggest fan."

"Sorry about that," I mumbled.

"Well, now's a good time to clear the air, isn't it?"

I nodded.

"So, first thing. You didn't like that I sent you out to Iraq, right?"

"No. I thought it was mean." Heck, I sounded like a twelve-year-old.

"I did that for two reasons. Most importantly, because Wilfred recommended you. He knew you'd do a good job, which you did, and he also knew you needed funding, which you've now got."

"I guess I should thank you for that. What was the other reason?"

"Because Jed told me you were about to marry a complete prick, and I thought I'd perform a public service by stopping you."

"And another tonight."

"It's been ages since I had a good punch-up, although the calibre of tonight's opponents was disappointing."

"Where did you learn to fight like that?"

She shrugged. "My stepdad. The streets. But that doesn't matter. We're talking about you tonight, and I'm guessing another big thing for you was when I ordered the death of Fadil al-Ghafar."

"Yes, it was. How you could order the death of an innocent man like that?"

"Because he wasn't so innocent. Again, you don't have the full story. Al-Ghafar was a nasty little shit. We suspect he was involved with setting at least three car bombs in Ramadi last year, one of which killed half a dozen US soldiers."

"Really?"

"I had a report in front of me showing that both his wife and children had been infected with Azrael, so he'd been exposed, even if he wasn't yet showing symptoms. He knew that, and we knew that. The night before, we'd intercepted a phone call where he discussed his plan to get to Najaf and infect as many people as possible. At the time I ordered his death, he was one ridge away from his partner's truck, and if he'd reached it, we wouldn't have found him until his body showed up."

I closed my eyes. Yes, I'd totally misjudged her.

"I'm sorry."

"Apology accepted. I fully admit I am a total bitch, just not in the way you think."

She grinned at me.

"So, what can I do about Jed? Do you think he'll speak to me?"

"Yeah, he will."

"But he hasn't called."

"Only because you told him not to."

Oh. "I thought—"

"Don't worry—he still wants you. He's been a miserable bastard this last month, and he hasn't even looked at another woman. Which for him is a bloody miracle, let me tell you."

"He's had a lot of other women?"

Why did I ask that? Of course he had. They probably threw themselves at his feet wherever he went.

"I'll be honest, he's not been a saint in the past. But since you came along, he's changed. I swear, I've never laughed so hard as I did when my husband called to tell me Jed had accidentally got married. If I'd needed to pick one person I thought would never settle down, it would have been him."

"Your husband was there? In Vegas?"

"Sure. They're friends."

Who had a husband who got on with their ex? Emerson surprised me with every turn. "You know we got an annulment?"

"Yeah, but not because of Jed. He did that for you because you wanted to go for your second marriage in as many weeks."

"Oh, hell." I put my head in my hands, then winced as I touched a bruise. "I need to speak to him."

"I'd suggest leaving it until you get to Virginia because otherwise Jed's gonna be here before you can blink and we'll be bailing him out on a murder charge. Even I might struggle to make that one disappear."

"Okay, tomorrow then."

"Tomorrow works."

CHAPTER 35

EMERSON, OR EMMY, as she told me to call her, met me in the hotel dining room early the next morning. I slid into the seat as she waved the waiter over and ordered three coffees.

"Is someone else joining us?"

"Nah, two are for me."

"You're not a morning person either?"

"Not until I've been drip-fed caffeine."

I went to rub sleep away from my eyes, then thought the better of it. When I'd looked in the mirror ten minutes ago, I'd seen a panda looking back at me.

"Thanks for staying to help me this morning."

"Like I said, you need someone with you."

"It shouldn't take me long to finish up. I just have my books and the live vaccines to take back with me. The BSL-4 stuff has already gone."

"Including the live viruses?"

"Yes. My new lab team said they've arrived already. I'm dying to see the place, but I wanted to travel with the vaccines myself. You said we'd be on a private flight?"

"You can strap them in the seat next to you. They don't even need to leave your sight."

"I really appreciate this."

I buttered a slice of toast and nibbled it as Emmy

downed one cup after the other. I still hadn't quite gotten my appetite back. My stomach wouldn't stop churning about the prospect of seeing Jed later on.

"Ready to go?" she asked.

"As I'll ever be."

Emmy carried the boxes of books out to the limousine and stacked them in the trunk while I packed the vaccines into a cooler, each vial nestled into a protective packing cell. I'd never imagined her to be the type for manual labour either, but she did the job without complaint and then headed for the coffee machine.

"You know how that works?" I asked her.

"I'm pretty good with coffee machines. Had a lot of practice over the years." She slotted the filter into place and nodded at the floor. "They did a good job of cleaning up the blood."

"I don't want to think about it."

"As soon as I've drunk this, you won't have to. You're done?"

I waved an arm at the cooler. "All packed."

"Can I see?"

I felt a little overprotective of the magic within, but I flipped the lid back to reveal the milky liquid. "That's them."

"Looks like aloe vera juice."

I stared at her.

"Sorry. My nutritionist's been making me drink a lot of that stuff lately. Apparently it's better for me than coffee, but I'm not feeling it. So, how many people will one of those vials do?"

"Sixteen monkeys. I'd guess four humans, but we haven't started the second-stage trials yet, so we'll need to work that out more precisely."

"Presumably you could scale up production?"

"Yes, if it works. But I'd need additional funding."

"Trust me, that won't be a problem."

With one last look, I closed the lid again and clipped it shut, feeling like Gollum from *Lord of the Rings*. My precious.

I didn't share quite the same affection for the break room anymore. Although I remembered the good times, the bad ones overshadowed everything—Quinn's visit, then Wade's last act. A fresh start in Richmond was just what I needed, especially if it came with the possibility of seeing Jed again.

I carried the cooler to the car myself, then settled it between my feet for the ride to the airport.

Goodbye, Texas.

When I called Lottie last night, she'd assured me it was fine to stay with her and Tia again. She even promised to arrange a ride from my new lab once I dropped off the vaccine. I hated being so dependent on other people, but I didn't have much choice at the moment. One day, I'd find a way to repay Tia's kindness.

And Emmy's.

The limo pulled up next to a plane that looked the same as the one I'd flown on to Galveston, but once I climbed on board, I took in the subtle differences. Black leather seats instead of grey. Soft woollen throws on the seats. The aroma of fresh coffee.

"This is a different plane?"

"Yeah, it is. You get settled, and I'll put the books in the hold."

I picked a seat near the window and strapped the cooler into the one opposite. My phone pinged with a message as I sat down.

Lottie: We're making carrot cake. I'll save you some.

She knew that was my favourite.

Chess: Make it a big slice.

Lottie's new-found obsession with eating proper food mystified me, but I wasn't complaining. If I didn't need to worry about her health, I could focus all of my attention on tackling the Azrael problem. And my disastrous non-relationship.

Emmy climbed on board, and the pilot scooted out of the cockpit and sealed the door. Five minutes later we were rumbling along the runway.

Getting closer to Virginia.

Closer to Jed.

"You want a drink?" Emmy asked as we levelled off.

There was no hostess on this flight—it was strictly self-service.

"Is that coffee I can smell?"

"It is, but you should get some sleep. How about hot chocolate?"

If I was going to speak to Jed again, she was probably right. Being awake when we arrived would give me an advantage. "Chocolate sounds great."

I noticed the coffee rule didn't apply to her. "You're not gonna rest?"

"I don't sleep well on planes. Besides, I've got

emails to catch up on. You know, orders to dish out, mayhem to create."

I forced a laugh. "Yep, I know."

Closing my eyes avoided further awkwardness, and after Emmy tapped me on the shoulder and handed me a drink, she focused her attention on her laptop. Despite thinking I wouldn't be able to sleep, I soon drifted off.

The next thing I knew, Emmy was shaking me awake. Not even Jed had disturbed my dreams. Maybe I should try sleeping on planes more often if it left me dead to the world like that?

"We've landed, and our ride is here."

"I feel exhausted." My jaw cracked as I yawned. Why did I always feel so sleepy right after I woke up?

"You want me to carry the cooler?"

"No! Sorry, I mean no, thank you."

She laughed. "Don't worry; I get it. You put it in the car, and I'll make a start on the hold."

Once the cooler was secure, I joined Emmy in staring at the mess in the belly of the plane. The boxes of books I'd packed so carefully were scattered all over the place.

"What happened?"

"We hit turbulence on the way back." She lifted up her sweater to reveal a coffee stain splashed across her cream top. "Made a bit of a mess. You slept right through the whole thing."

I did? Those leather seats sure were comfortable. Together, we stacked the loose books back into the boxes and carried them to the trunk of the Galveston limo's twin.

It didn't take long to get to the lab, and once there,

my new team came out to help with the unloading. Two scientists and six lab assistants, with me running things. If somebody had told me three months ago this would happen, I'd have pinched myself, but there I was. I only wished it hadn't taken Al Bidaya to get me there.

"I'll stay out here," Emmy said. "I've got calls to make."

"Won't be long."

Resisting the urge to explore my new lab, I carried the cooler inside and put on my hazmat suit. Now, I just needed to get my vaccines into the refrigerator. All sixteen... Oh, shit.

I knelt in BSL-4 and held up a vial from the top layer to the light. A drop of liquid fell from the crack in the bottom and landed on my shoe.

"You okay?" an assistant asked. He'd come in to help.

"One of these broke in transit. We hit turbulence, and I guess with the pressure changes..."

"Is it dangerous?"

"Not this one. But it took us a month to synthesise these quantities, and that means we'll have more work to do before the next phase of the trial."

He gave me a mock salute. "We're all here to help, ma'am."

"Everything okay?" Emmy asked.

"Almost. We lost one sample in transit, but the rest made it intact."

"What happened?"

"A vial cracked."

Her eyes widened. "Could anything have contaminated the plane? Do we need to ground it?"

"All our work says Apollo is good, not bad."

"Okay. But tell me if you find anything that suggests otherwise."

"Believe me, you'll be the first to know."

I suspected she would be even if I didn't tell her directly. I gave my head a shake to clear it, needing to put the accident behind me because I had bigger things to worry about. Quite literally. Jed.

"I need to call my sister. She promised to arrange a ride."

"She did. Me."

"I don't want to put you to any more trouble. Wait— how do you know my sister?"

"It's no trouble. You're both staying at my house."

I tripped along behind as she led the way to a brutal-looking black sports car. "That place is yours?"

"Being a bitch pays well. Are you coming?"

I groaned as I looked down at the car. She'd played me at every turn, hadn't she? "What is this thing? Where's the limo?"

"A Dodge Viper, and it's far more fun than the limo. You can throw your bag in the trunk."

Daddy always taught me that as long as I learned something new every day, my life would never be wasted. During my time with Wade, I'd existed, not lived, and that curiosity to seek out knowledge went on hold. But now I'd passed that bump in the road, I was determined to get back to the old Chess—the one who sought out new facts at every opportunity.

And that day, I learned something very important.

Never, ever get in a car with Emmy driving.

In one of the few moments I opened my eyes, we nearly sideswiped a truck, and each time we went around a sharp bend I felt the back end of the car slide out. At one point, Emmy patted my white knuckles and laughed.

"Don't worry. I've had plenty of practice at this."

"What, killing yourself?"

"Never myself, sweetheart."

She pulled into the driveway at the glass house with a screech of tyres and parked by pulling the parking brake on and throwing the car into a skid. I was hyperventilating by the time I stumbled out onto solid ground.

"You need to relax," she said.

"You need to slow down."

Running feet sounded, slapping on the paved drive, and I looked up to see Lottie racing towards me. Her wide smile faltered as she took in the mess of my face.

"What happened?" she whispered.

"Wade found me."

She burst into tears and threw her arms around my waist. I winced as she squeezed the bruises on my back, but I didn't have the heart to pry her off. Instead, I bent my head, and as the events of the past couple of days caught up with me, I cried too.

"I hate Wade," she sobbed. "Hate him."

"That's all over now."

With my face pressed into her hair, I barely noticed another car pull up. At least not until I heard Jed's growl.

"What the hell?"

"Oh, fuck," Emmy groaned.

I raised my eyes and took in the man striding towards me, his expression getting blacker with every step.

"Uh, hi?"

"What the hell happened to your face?"

"I, uh, bumped into Wade."

"Son-of-a-bitch." He cracked his knuckles. "Ems, I need your plane."

She poked him in the chest. "You're not going anywhere. I've already taken care of it, and Wade's busy having his spleen removed. You won't help Chess if you're in a prison cell."

He stepped backwards and stared out across the lawns. I heard him take a few deep breaths, slowly, in and out, as he flexed his fists. When he turned back around his eyes were clearer, pleading almost.

"Will you talk to me?"

He held out a hand.

I nodded and took it in both of mine. "I think that's a good idea."

CHAPTER 36

JED LED ME into the house, past the horse that glittered in the sunlight and up the glass stairs. He didn't stop until we reached one of the bedrooms, and once I'd crossed the threshold, he turned to close the door behind us.

I took in the rumpled sheets and the men's clothes draped over the couch by the window. Jed's bag from Iraq sat on the floor by the bed.

"Did you sleep here?"

"Yes. And no, Emmy wasn't with me."

"I know. She was with me last night." I tried to hold it together but my face crumpled. "I'm so sorry. I made some stupid assumptions without knowing all the facts."

"It wasn't all your fault. I should have told you more about my past, but I was afraid you'd leave."

"I was scared and confused. I still am, except about one thing."

I took one tentative step forward, and Jed's eyes flicked down towards the floor.

"And what's that?"

"I want to get to know you better."

He blew out a long breath as my heart fluttered in my chest. *Please, don't crush it.*

Seconds ticked by, then he closed the distance

between us and tilted my chin up. "Promise me you'll talk rather than running away in future. I've barely slept for the past month."

We had a future? I wrapped my arms around him and laid my cheek against his shoulder. We had a future.

"I promise."

He feathered soft kisses across my forehead. "What happened yesterday?"

"Wade must have talked to somebody at the university to find me, and he got into the break room at the lab. He... He forced me into a cupboard and said he was going to take what was his."

"He didn't...?"

"No, Emmy came and dragged him off. I still can't believe she took down a man Wade's size."

"I wouldn't bet on anybody against her. She'd kick my ass any day."

"Weren't you in the Rangers?"

"Yes, but that woman still scares the shit out of me. There are only three people who stand a chance against her. One's her husband, one's her trainer, and the other's one of her exes and he's a vicious bastard. Even then, as I said, I wouldn't bet against her."

"I'm glad she was on my side."

"Me too. So..."

"So what?"

"So where does this leave us?" he asked.

I bit my lip, and he pressed his thumb against it until my teeth let go. Even that tiny contact sent threads of fire through me.

"I don't know what to do," I whispered. "I've never been in this situation. Not sober, anyway."

He answered me with a kiss, soft at first, then so deep it sucked my mind away, leaving only my senses to guide me. Goosebumps popped up on my arms as he ran his fingers along bare flesh, and I pressed into him, wanting more.

My hands crept up inside his T-shirt, over the golden skin I'd been dreaming of and around his rippling back. He took his lips away from mine for a second and tore his shirt over his head, giving me the view I craved before distracting me again.

My fingers explored as his hands did the same, running over my back and my stomach. He made short work of my bra catch, and a ripping sound drowned out our laboured breathing as he tore my top off.

"Not small, but I bet they're juicy," he murmured, pausing to read the slogan splashed across it. "Let me taste."

I'd run out of clean clothes, okay? And when he dipped his head and sucked, I was kind of glad about that.

When my knees felt as if they'd give way, Jed picked me up and laid me on the bed, following me down so he lay on top, trapping me in a place I never wanted to escape from. One hand popped open my jeans while the other caressed every bit of exposed skin, swift and light, making me writhe beneath him.

"This time's gonna be quick, darlin'. I can't wait."

"Just hurry up."

He reached over to the nightstand drawer and rolled on a condom with a practised ease I didn't want to think about. Luckily, I didn't think about anything for very long as he slid my panties to the side and pushed slowly inside, stretching me more than I thought possible.

"Okay?"

He stayed still until I nodded, and then he began to move.

Nothing else mattered aside from Jed, me, and the connection between us. He took me on a wild ride through darkness then light until the world exploded in a burst of heat, sparks, and noise.

"Oh, shit!"

I clapped a hand over my mouth as the last of my screams died away.

He shifted his hips, tiny movements that sent a few last shockwaves through me, and laughed.

"Doesn't matter. You think they don't know what we're doing up here?"

"I hope not. How will I be able to face any of them ever again? Oh gosh, my sister..."

"Is an adult. And much less fragile than you think."

I thought back to the Lottie I'd seen earlier. The way she'd run out of the house with an energy I hadn't seen in years. "She's changed since she came here." I closed my eyes as I realised why. "She said Emmy spoke to her when she first arrived and made her look at things differently."

"Emmy has a habit of doing that, but she can't take all the credit this time."

"The nutritionist?"

Jed chuckled. "And Nigel, the life coach."

There was something about the way he said it. "What? You mean..." I struggled to get up, but Jed held me tight. "Let go! Who is this boy? Lottie's my little sister."

He pressed a kiss to my lips. "That there, that told

me everything I needed to know about the type of woman you are. One day, you're gonna make a great mom."

I stiffened. "What? What are you talking about?"

Another kiss. "One day. Not now. There are other things I want to do right now."

He rolled us so I lay on his chest, and I gave up thinking and just felt again as Jed ran warm hands down my back. Thinking was overrated anyway.

"What a first," I murmured. "At least the first that I remember."

"First for me too, darlin'."

I raised an eyebrow. "What about Emmy? And she said you, uh, that you weren't all that well behaved."

"Done a lot of fucking, but I've never made love before."

The last part of my core melted at his words, not caring about the crudeness. "I'm looking forward to the second."

"So am I." He brushed his lips over one of the purple marks on my arm. "I hope I didn't hurt you."

"I forgot about the bruises. I'm not even sure I was in my own body."

"No, but I was."

I giggled. "Can we stay here for the rest of the day?"

He ran his nose down the side of mine, making me wriggle. "Ticklish?"

"A bit," I admitted.

"I'll remember that." He let out a long sigh. "I wish we could stay here, but I've got a meeting in Washington. I came over to pick Emmy up."

He watched me carefully, waiting for a reaction, but I was over the whole jealousy thing now. "Will I be able to see you later?"

I got rewarded with the beaming smile he kept hidden most of the time. "Nothing could keep me away. Do you want to stay here or go to my apartment?"

"Staying here would be weird."

"Because of Emmy?"

"It's her house."

He squeezed my ass, and I couldn't help smiling. "She doesn't mind if people crash here. She's been staying at her husband's place most of the time lately in any case."

"Hang on—they have separate houses?"

"Yeah. Emmy likes modern and her husband likes traditional, so they compromised and got one of each. They have other houses abroad too."

"That's crazy."

"And that surprises you? Her husband's loaded. So is she, in her own right, but he's in a whole other league."

Jed's phone rang on the nightstand, and he groaned as he leaned over to pick it up. "Talk of the she-devil."

The phone was close enough for me to hear her speak. "Have you finished your fuck-fest or shall I make an excuse for you? I'm sure James will understand if I explain."

"No, I'm coming."

"I hope that's past tense or we're going to be late."

Yep, they totally knew what we'd been doing.

CHAPTER 37

EMMY TAPPED HER watch as Jed jogged down the stairs. "Come on, we're late."

"Stop complaining. It's normally you who cuts it fine."

"At least you're smiling. I take it things are back on track with Chess?"

"Yeah. Yeah, they are."

"Oh, fuck. You've gone all dreamy." She smacked him in the chest. "You'd better get your brain in gear before we get to the White House."

"Are you piloting?"

"Yes, because it's my helicopter."

She flew like she drove, swooping in low over the back lawn of 1600 Pennsylvania Avenue while snipers looked on from the roofline. Only Emmy could perform that manoeuvre and get away with it.

"There, bang on time." She slowed the rotors and hopped out, throwing the key to the nearest secret service agent. "I don't want any dings, dents, or scratches."

The guy just stared at her.

"Fuck me. Another one with a sense of humour bypass?"

She marched past, heading for the back entrance.

The rest of the committee was already seated when

they walked in, maybe because Emmy had delayed things further with a stop at the coffee machine. Still, James smiled when she appeared. Jed figured if you'd once had the president balls deep in you, he probably allowed a little more leeway with timekeeping.

Jed pulled out his seat, and as he did so, movement from the corner of the room caught his eye. Cronus. His presence, together with the short notice given for the meeting, meant Jed really didn't want to hear whatever James had to say.

"Good morning, gentlemen. And lady."

"That's debatable," one of the men muttered, and James glared at him.

"Emmy, can you give us an update on your end?"

"Not much of one, I'm afraid. I spent two weeks in Russia, but Lilith's a ghost. Every lead panned out. Her last suspected kill was a British politician on holiday in Tunisia five months ago, then she disappeared."

"Anything else on Azrael?"

"Not that anybody's admitting to."

"How about Base 13?"

Base 13, the words etched in Cyrillic on the bottom of the canister. They'd been researching the place for the last month, but information on the army base in Southern Siberia proved almost as elusive as Lilith.

Cronus's whisper came from the corner. "Word from the top is that the Russian government has lost control of General Zacharov. His men remain loyal to him, and every day he grows more powerful."

Emmy scrunched her lips sideways the way she often did when she was thinking. "Zacharov's name came up in connection with Lilith too. She took out a commander who tried to rein him in, and I believe she was seen with one of his acquaintances."

"Does Zacharov have the capabilities to work with biological agents?" James asked.

"Back in the Cold War, Base 13 was used to develop experimental weapons. That most likely included biological elements as well as explosives, missiles, and chemicals," Cronus whispered.

"And since the Cold War ended?"

"Officially, the base was decommissioned."

"And unofficially?"

"Zacharov treats it like his own personal playground."

"So it's possible, likely even, that Azrael originated at Base 13. But at the moment, its birthplace is our secondary concern. I'm more worried about how much of it was made and where the rest of it is."

Frank cleared his throat. "The day before yesterday, we intercepted a communication we believe to be from al-Tariq. Unfortunately, processing delays meant we didn't realise its importance until this morning, and that doesn't give us much time to act."

"Act on what?"

"We believe they're planning an attack."

"When?"

"On the first Saturday in September."

"Shit." James pinched the bridge of his nose. "That's less than two weeks away. What else do we have?"

"The message originated in Syria and was sent via an instant messaging app to a contact in New Jersey."

"Do we know who?"

Frank pressed a button on the remote, and a picture of a dark-haired man in jeans and a sweater sitting astride a motorcycle appeared on the screen. Clothes by Nike, bike by Honda, haircut styled on Abercrombie & Fitch—just like thousands of other American men in their early twenties.

"Amin Abdallah, also known as Sal Abbott. We had him pegged as a low-level sympathiser, but it looks like we underestimated him."

"Tell me he's in custody?"

Frank shook his head. "Afraid not. We've lost track of him."

"What was the message?" Emmy asked.

Frank pulled up a paragraph of text written in Arabic and flipped through the papers in his hand. Before he could find the translation, Emmy read aloud.

"Use the pass to go through the door on the right of the stadium, behind the hospitality lounge. Detonate the weapon in the air for maximum effect, then take your trip to paradise."

The room fell silent, save for Cronus's heavy breathing.

James spoke first, his voice reflecting the horror they all felt. "They're going to attack a stadium? Fuck."

A suit spoke up. "We need to call off all sporting events next Saturday. And music concerts. And any other type of gathering."

Emmy rolled her eyes. "And what do you think'll happen if we do that? Either they'll attack a different week or change the target—it's not rocket science."

"We'd buy ourselves time."

"And alert al-Tariq that we're onto them. They'll tighten up their communications and go farther underground."

The suit looked like he was about to argue, but

James cut him off. "Emmy's right. Cancelling events isn't an option. We know who we're looking for, we know the type of target, and we've got a clue which entrance he'll use. Let's use this as an opportunity to catch the asshole."

"You're risking thousands of lives. Millions, even."

A discussion of the benefits and drawbacks of each approach ensued, with Emmy staying calm while a couple of the suits grew more argumentative. As one of them opened their mouth again, no doubt to labour the same points he'd been making for the last fifteen minutes, James held up a hand.

"Let's take a vote. This isn't getting anywhere."

Everyone nodded, some more grudgingly than others.

"Everyone in favour of cancelling everything."

"Postponing," one of the men clarified.

"Sorry. Postponing."

Three men raised their hands.

"And those who'd prefer to use the opportunity to stop this group?"

Nine hands went up, including Jed's and the president's. Jed glanced behind him and noticed Cronus voting with Emmy as well.

James blew out a thin breath. "Looks like we have some fast planning to do."

Over the next two hours, they hammered out some of the finer details. Extra training, extra manpower, all leave cancelled. Intelligence on al-Tariq was thin on the ground, but everything useful would be distributed among local law enforcement.

"And me?" Emmy asked James. "Do you want me here or in Iraq? Presumably we want to take out their leadership as well?"

"I'll speak to you after the meeting ends."

The group made a few calls, liaising with top-level officials and contacts in the FBI and various police forces. The sheer size of this operation was something never attempted before, and the timescale made it all the more difficult. Jed felt drained as he trailed out of the room behind Frank. Before the door closed, he glanced back. Cronus's corner was empty. Only Emmy and James remained at the table—the other man had disappeared like a wisp of smoke.

Molly, the pretty brunette Jed had spent one crazy night with six months back, appeared with a carafe of coffee and a shy smile. He accepted a cup while vowing never to touch an intern again. Nothing they had to offer could compete with Chess's charms. Or her brain. Being able to have a conversation over breakfast was somewhat of a novelty, Emmy excepted.

"Did you pick up my pen, Jed?" Frank asked.

Jed patted his pockets. "Didn't even pick up my own."

The fountain pen he carried was a little old fashioned, but his father had given it to him for his eighteenth birthday. It had been one of the few constants in Jed's life over the last decade. A lucky charm. He gave the guard a salute as he pushed open the door to the conference room to retrieve it.

Then froze.

The only sound was the soft click of the door closing behind him, and he really wished he'd stayed on the other side of it.

James had Emmy pinned against the wall to his right, one elbow either side of her ears, the length of his body pressed into hers. Jed may have always wondered about their relationship, but if they were planning to get down and dirty in a White House conference room, he didn't want to witness it.

They must have noticed him come in, surely? But nobody moved.

Except Emmy.

Her right knee hammered into James's groin, and Jed doubled over in sympathy for his old friend. Her harsh tone was audible even over James's groans.

"Never forget what I am, James."

The president fell to his knees as she strode from the room, ignoring Jed as she passed. He took one look at her face and thought the better of going after her. Best to let her thaw out first.

"You okay, buddy?"

"Do I look okay?"

James waved the secret service agents away as they snuck out the back entrance of the conference room and headed upstairs to the apartment he shared with the First Lady, his arm slung over Jed's shoulders.

Diana raised an eyebrow as he limped inside.

"Do I want to know?"

"I bumped into something."

"Like what?"

"One of the chairs in the conference room. I tripped over the rug and landed on the arm."

She screwed up her face in sympathy. "Can I get you anything? Do you need a doctor?"

"Ice." James collapsed onto the couch. "Ice would be good."

"Do you want me to pull out of tonight's dinner?"

"No, you go. The press would have a field day

speculating if you didn't."

Diana disappeared in the direction of the kitchen, and Jed nodded after her. "Will she ask questions about...you know?"

James shook his head. "No. Black found me the perfect first lady. Loyal, compliant, devoted..."

From his sigh, he left "boring" off the end. Jed got the distinct impression James wished for imperfect and borderline insane.

Speaking of which... Jed's phone buzzed with an incoming message, and he pulled it out of his pocket.

Emmy: Gone home. I've left you the helicopter.

How did she get home? Maybe she really did have a broomstick as Donald was always suggesting.

James raised an eyebrow and adjusted the tea towel full of ice Diana had just brought. "Was that her?"

Jed stuffed the phone back in his pocket. "She's left. What happened between you two, anyway?"

"I told her she wasn't getting involved with this one, and she didn't take it too well."

"Why? I mean, why don't you want her on the team? Her instincts are spooky."

"Just because." He shifted in the seat and winced. "Fuck. Why do I always get things wrong with that woman?"

"Because she's an enigma wrapped up in a puzzle tied in a Gordian knot." He nodded at James's nuts. "If she'd done that to me, I'd send her straight into the lion's den."

"Which is exactly what she wants. Why do you think she did it?"

Jed hadn't thought about the reasons, only about buying a cup so she didn't do the same to him if he accidentally said the wrong thing. "I don't know. I wasn't privy to the rest of the conversation."

"She knows exactly which buttons to push. It's not the first time we've had that argument."

"You mean..." Jed pointed at James's tackle.

He shook his head. "Last time it wouldn't have been in her best interests to do that, and besides, I gave in." He leaned back and closed his eyes. "And somebody close to both of us died. She may act like she's got over it, but I can't." Ten seconds passed before he threw the ice on the floor and stomped over to the drinks cabinet, picked up a bottle of scotch, then put it down again. "Fuck it. I can't even drink because of what's going on. The woman makes me want to rewire my whole damn brain."

Jed knew the feeling, but he also knew it was a waste of time trying to change Emmy's mind. "Why don't you just leave it? She'll do whatever she pleases, anyway."

James's face hardened. Jed had seen that look many times before on soldiers heading into battle, and in a way, James was.

He pulled out his phone and blew a long breath. "Not this time, she won't."

CHAPTER 38

"I FEEL LIKE I should carry you over the threshold or something," Jed said.

I'd expected him to have a small bachelor pad, but when he led me into the elevator in a surprisingly swanky apartment building, he pushed the button for the penthouse. Really? Jed looked like he'd be more at home in a surf shack.

"You don't have to do that. It's not like we're married anymore."

He swept me off my feet anyway, and I shrieked as I grabbed his shoulders. Of course, that put our lips within touching distance, and we got delayed as he kissed me thoroughly.

"Why don't we do this inside? What if the neighbours see?"

"I don't care." But he did stoop and stare into a black lens, and the bolts shot back. "Retina scanner. I kept losing my keys."

He used a knee to shove the door open, revealing a large, open-plan living-slash-dining room done out in black, grey, and white, with a few red accents. Through an archway to the left, I glimpsed a modern kitchen, and floor-to-ceiling windows on the right gave me a view of the roof terrace.

"Wow. Is that a hot tub outside?"

"Yeah. Haven't used it for ages, but with you here I'd better get it cleaned out."

I'd hoped for a tour, but he didn't stop, just kept walking through the great room and out of a door on the far side.

"Aren't you going to show me the kitchen?"

"Later. First, I'm going to show you the bedroom."

Oh. In that case, the food could wait. Everything else could wait.

I didn't see the kitchen until the next morning. Jed left me laid out on the bed unable to move while he ordered a pizza, and we ate that in the bedroom too.

But the next morning we both had to go to work, so I put on the clothes I'd borrowed from the closet in Emmy's house and ventured out into what was to be my new home. It was clearly designed for a man, although it was still beautiful in every way, from the furniture to the view across the city. But there was something missing.

"What do you think?" Jed asked.

There were no books on the coffee table, no letters in the hallway, no plants on the terrace.

"It's got no soul."

"Yet. No soul *yet*. I bought it three years ago, but I've barely stayed here since." He wrapped his arms around me as we waited for the kettle to boil. "But with you here, it's got a soul now."

"You're too darn sweet, Jed Harker."

"And too darn yours, darlin'."

While Jed rooted around in near-empty cupboards

for something to eat, I took the opportunity to explore. The apartment had three bedrooms, each with an en suite, plus a further half-bath for guests. Clayton had always bragged he owned the nicest house in Norsville, but Jed's home put that to shame. I couldn't help the smile that crept across my face at the thought of sharing it with him.

"There's a car coming for you at eight," Jed told me when I went back into the kitchen. "You still need guards, but Emmy's providing them this time rather than the local police."

"I hope hers are a little better trained."

"A wasp would struggle to get past Emmy's team."

I had to admit, I felt better walking into the lab with two armed men at my side, not only because of the incident with Wade but because of the ongoing situation with Azrael. Jed tried to gloss over things, but I saw the tension around his eyes whenever he received a phone call.

I looked at my own eyes in the mirrored elevator as I travelled up to BSL-4. Wade's handiwork had turned an ugly shade of yellow-green, but with any luck, it would fade enough in a few days that I wouldn't draw curious glances from every stranger I passed. At least my muscles didn't ache quite so much now. Wearing a hazmat suit was uncomfortable enough without it pressing on all the bruises.

That day, I pushed myself to do three sessions in the lab. My own discomfort was nothing compared to what would happen if Azrael escaped into the general population. With Dr. Fielding at my side, I synthesised additional vaccine in between writing up the procedures and protocols for a wider trial. If that worked, the next step would be to give Apollo to healthy volunteers and monitor them for a reaction.

I'd just crumpled onto the couch after my fifth straight day in the lab when the front door clicked open. I looked up, expecting to see Jed, but it was Emmy instead, this time with brown hair and vivid violet eyes.

"Are those contacts?"

"No, my real colour. I wear contacts most of the time or people stare."

Exactly like I was doing. Oops. I tore my gaze away.

"Uh, Jed isn't here."

"I know. He's out having fun, and I'm not allowed to join in." She mock-pouted and threw herself down onto the couch beside me. "So, I thought I'd come over and say hi. I brought wine."

"You came all this way to bring me wine?"

"Okay, so I'm sick of my own house. President *fucking* Harrison convinced my husband to wrap me in cotton wool, and I've got not only a nutritionist but a life coach on the rampage, plus your sister, who's just given me a lecture on the dangers of too much alcohol."

"I'm so sorry. Do you want her to leave?"

She gave a dry laugh. "Of course not. It's good for Tia to have some company."

"Jed mentioned she was quite taken with the life coach?"

"Nigel. Yeah, but don't worry; I've already had the talk with him. He understands that if his hands go anywhere they shouldn't, he'll lose body parts."

"I'm not sure whether to thank you or not."

She laughed again. "Shall we open the wine?"

Jed arrived home half an hour later, and Emmy swiftly dispatched him to pick up Chinese takeout and another bottle of white. He pretended to groan, but his eyes lit up at the mention of kung pao chicken.

He'd only just walked back into the kitchen with the food when a knock at the door made us all look up.

"I'll get it," Emmy said.

It was only when her hand moved to the small of her back that I realised she had a gun there.

My eyes went wide, but Jed put a finger to his lips. "She always carries. But don't worry—she only shoots when it's necessary."

Oh, that was comforting.

I watched nervously as she opened the door to a woman who definitely didn't have a weapon unless you counted the nipple piercing clearly visible through her lace bra. Her barely there thong didn't leave much to the imagination either.

"Oh, shit," Jed groaned from behind me.

"Room for one more at the party?" the woman purred.

She took a step forward, but Emmy blocked her way.

"Jed's upgraded. He books his hookers by the night now, not the hour."

Emmy pushed her backwards and slammed the door, but not before I'd caught the look of shock on the girl's face. Heels clicked on the tile followed by the ding of the elevator as she beat a hasty retreat.

Emmy sauntered past and snagged a prawn cracker as I narrowed my eyes at Jed. "Do you get many naked women turning up?"

"It's not entirely unknown, but I swear I've never done anything to encourage them."

I didn't know whether to be angry or upset, but in the end I just laughed. Out of all his women, he'd chosen me to move in with him, and I wasn't about to let petty jealousy mess up the opportunity that came to me out of the blue one crazy night in Vegas.

The next Friday night, Jed came home late, looking exhausted. I'd finished in the lab at six and made us lasagne with a green salad, but he could barely hold the cutlery.

"Are you okay?"

"Long day." The fork clattered to the table. "Look, there's a possibility something might kick off tomorrow. Promise me you'll stay away from City Stadium and The Diamond tomorrow."

I dropped my fork as well. "Is this about Azrael?"

"We've had information something might happen, but we haven't been able to confirm it, and the details were fuzzy."

"At a sporting event?"

"Maybe."

I'd seen a slot on the local news before Jed got back, about a schoolboy who'd won tickets for his entire class to tomorrow's baseball game. They'd interviewed him, his parents, and his teacher, and the kid hadn't been able to sit still from excitement. And Jed was telling me about a suspected attack?

"Why haven't the games been cancelled?"

"The suggestion was made but discounted."

"By that committee?" His refusal to confirm or deny it gave me my answer. "Are they crazy?"

"Please, just keep away. In fact, why don't you stay here all day? A guy came out and fixed up the hot tub."

"You're crazy too, if you think I want to sit in that thing all day when people could be dying."

"I wish I could give you the details, but I can't. I promise this wasn't a decision made lightly."

"You're making a mistake."

That was the first night we didn't make love after dinner. Jed went straight to sleep while I lay awake for hours, wondering if I'd been too harsh but knowing in my heart I hadn't. Risking the exposure of thousands of people to Azrael deserved those words.

When I woke on Saturday, he'd already left. After a tiring week, I'd decided to take a day off from the lab and brought my laptop home with a pile of notes to type up instead. I only hoped I'd be able to read my own scribbles.

By mid-morning, I gave up on the idea of concentrating. Visions of a canister exploding in a crowded place haunted me, and the last thing I wanted to do was remind myself of that by studying more photographs of the virus.

The feed from the security camera on the monitor in the study told me Jed had taken the Porsche to work, leaving his Explorer in its assigned slot in the garage. Thank goodness—the idea of driving the Porsche terrified me, but I could handle the Ford. It took me a while to set up the SatNav, but if I could synthesise a vaccine, I could find my way to Emmy's house. A few hours with Lottie would make me feel better. Maybe we could test out that movie theatre?

Only when I arrived at the glass and steel edifice, I found Lottie wasn't there. Emmy was sitting on a white couch in the hallway while a small man with pink hair paced up and down, a phone clamped to his ear.

"Lottie went hiking out the back with Tia and Nigel."

"Nigel? That boy she's seeing?"

"Yeah. Apparently, they're going foraging for wild food. Nigel's doing a correspondence course on holistic lifestyle, and he's taking the module on organic nutrition a bit too seriously."

"Is she still eating okay?"

"Porridge for breakfast."

The pink-haired man walked between us, and Emmy waved a hand at him. "Have you met my assistant, Bradley?"

I shook my head, and he blew me a kiss as he continued to bark into the phone.

"I most certainly did say eleven and sending someone at twelve-thirty isn't good enough."

"Bradley, leave it. I'll drive us to the airport," Emmy said.

He put his hand over the mouthpiece. "No, you will not. Last time I went on a car journey with you, I needed counselling and a week of acupuncture to recover."

"Well, you're not driving because we won't get there until tomorrow."

He flipped her the bird and resumed pacing.

"What's wrong?" I asked her.

"One of our jets is in England, and the other's undergoing maintenance so we have to fly commercial. And as if that wasn't bad enough, my chauffeur's off sick, and the car service failed to send a replacement." She rolled her eyes. "First world problems."

"Where are you going?"

"Dulles."

"I can drive you if you like? If Lottie's not around, I'm at loose ends."

Bradley threw both hands in the air. "Hallelujah! Perfect. A compromise. Emmy, do you know the meaning of the word compromise?"

"I hate being a passenger."

"Tough. Grab the cases." He paused to kiss me on the cheek. "Thanks, doll."

Emmy hefted one olive-green duffle and four bubblegum-pink suitcases into the trunk, then slouched in the front seat fiddling with her phone. At least I didn't make a complete mess of programming the SatNav with her next to me.

"Are you going somewhere nice?" I asked as we pulled out of the drive.

"Boston," Bradley told me from the backseat. "An old friend of ours is moving there from Japan, and we're flying out to welcome her."

"That's nice of you."

In the rearview mirror, I saw him glare at Emmy. "Yes, it is, isn't it? But Miss Sulkypants here needs to cheer up before we get there."

"I hear Boston's nice. It has a wonderful science museum."

"And a baseball team," Bradley muttered.

Emmy flashed a grin. "What? I thought I'd take in a

ball game tonight, and where better to do that than at Fenway Park, home of the Red Sox?"

"You're gonna be dead if Black or James find out," Bradley muttered.

Black? "Is Black your husband?" I asked.

"He's Black by name and black by nature," Bradley said.

"Are you sure visiting a sporting event is a good idea? Jed said..."

She patted me on the arm. "Don't worry. I'm full of good ideas. And I'm sick of sitting on my arse doing nothing."

CHAPTER 39

"NOW LOOK, WE'RE two and a half hours early." Emmy turned to me. "This is what happens when Bradley's in charge of timings."

My life in Norsville had been sheltered, admittedly, and I'd never met anyone quite like Bradley before. Or even a little bit like Bradley. But I already knew we'd be firm friends, not least because of the way he stood up to Emmy. She rolled her eyes as he bumped two of his suitcases down the kerb. I also had one, and she wheeled the fourth, muttering derogatory things about the colour.

Bradley glared at her. "If you took care of your own schedule, you'd miss every appointment. Besides, now we have time to have coffee with Chess first. And to do a spot of shopping."

"Ah, that's the real reason, isn't it? You haven't been shopping since Wednesday and you're suffering from withdrawal symptoms."

Bradley tossed his head and moved next to me. "Ignore her. She just doesn't understand fashion."

Their bickering was all good-natured, and I had to admit Bradley fascinated me. Maybe stopping off for a drink and a chocolate muffin before I headed back to Jed's empty apartment wouldn't be so bad?

"Check-in isn't even open yet," Emmy grumbled.

"But the stores are." Bradley's eyes lit up. "Coffee first or shopping? We can get you one of those triple chocolate cookies Toby won't let you have."

"I'm not trailing around the shops with five bloody bags. Did you really have to pack so much? We're only going for a few days."

"The weather's unpredictable. Plus I have gifts for Akari and toys for Hisashi."

"He's only a year old, and last time we saw him his favourite toy was a sock."

"Ooh, look. That place over there sells earplugs."

I couldn't help laughing, and Emmy smiled at me. "You see what I have to live with?"

Bradley paused in the departures hall, scanning the refreshment options while I watched the travellers milling around. Despite all my flights in recent weeks, this was only my third time in an airport terminal. A lady walked by carrying a screaming toddler, and I gave her a look of sympathy. Hopefully she'd get him settled before their flight took off.

"Okay, we have a café, fast food, or the sports bar. Any preferences?"

What with being vegetarian, fast food wasn't a great choice for me. Half the time, the only option was fries and a cheeseburger without the meat, and that gave me indigestion. I followed Emmy's gaze to the blinking neon sign above the sports bar. The *t* was faulty, leaving the name as *The S adium*.

"Uh oh," Bradley whispered.

"What?"

"Emmy's thinking. That's not always a good thing."

She glanced up at the ceiling, but when I looked too, there was nothing to see but the air-conditioning vents. Okay, this was strange. And Bradley was right. It wasn't a good thing. I'd seen that look on her face before, right before she ordered me to fly into a war zone.

All the humour had gone from her eyes as she turned back to us. "Leave, both of you. Get out of here. Wait in the car, and I'll phone you in a minute."

"What? Why?" I asked.

But Emmy had already dropped her bag and walked away, heading towards a cleaning cart a few yards away. She palmed something from the top of it and carried on walking to the staff entrance on the right of The Stadium, nestled between it and the business lounge.

She waved her hand over the card reader next to the door and disappeared inside as Bradley backed away.

"We're leaving?" I asked.

He'd turned serious too. "When Emmy says something like that, you don't argue. We'll wait outside with the bags. Hopefully it'll turn out to be nothing."

Ten minutes turned into twenty. I flipped through a magazine Bradley had given me while he drummed his fingers on the dash. The words blurred as edginess gnawed at me, just a nibble at first, but as the second hand on my watch kept ticking, it full on attacked.

"What do you think she's doing in there?" I asked.

He shrugged, but that gesture was at odds with the fear in his eyes.

"Is this normal? I mean, has she done this before?"

"Nothing's normal with Emmy."

I thought about calling Jed, but what could I tell him? That Emmy snuck into a restricted area at the airport rather than going for a burger? Only instinct told me there was a big problem, but my instincts hadn't exactly been reliable lately, had they? I only had to look at the Wade debacle to understand that. And Jed had enough on his plate today without me bothering him with Emmy's antics.

Finally, Bradley's phone rang, and he jabbed the speaker button. Emmy's voice came through clearly, and for the first time ever, it held a hint of worry. And if Emmy was worried, I was extremely nervous.

"Okay, that didn't go so well," she said. "You'll need to fly out of Reagan National now."

"What are you talking about?" Bradley asked.

"There's a small issue here I need to sort out. Chess, could you drive Bradley?"

"Of course."

"Thanks. And I'd leave now because in a few minutes, traffic's gonna start backing up and you won't get out."

"What happened?" I asked, trying to keep the quake out of my voice.

"I'll explain later, but I don't want Bradley to be late meeting Akari."

The line went dead, and I started the engine while dread pooled in my stomach. Emmy might have glossed over the problem, but I knew there was one, and if she was passing up the opportunity to gallivant around Fenway Park, then it must be big.

The first sirens sounded as we pulled out of the airport—four squad cars racing down the other side of the street. Bradley craned his neck as he watched them pass.

"Maybe we should go back. I'm worried about Emmy."

His voice trembled. I didn't want him to get any more upset, and if I'd learned one thing during my time with Emmy, it was that you followed her orders.

"I think we should do as she asked. She said it was only a small issue, and I'm sure she'll get it all sorted out soon."

"I hope you're right."

At Reagan National, my nerves jangled as I shovelled Bradley out of the car and into the terminal. He'd booked himself a ticket online as I drove, and by the time we reached the second airport he was half-heartedly complaining that the new flight didn't allow time for retail opportunities.

I leaned over and squeezed his hand. "Why don't we go out for lunch and shopping when you get back?"

"I'd like that."

The instant he'd checked in his pink luggage, I dropped my smile and jogged back to the car. Emmy's behaviour scared me. I pulled out my phone to call Jed, but before I could dial, he rang. Just seeing his name on the screen made my heart skip, but the feeling of joy only lasted a split second before I realised this call was most likely about business.

"Hey. Everything okay?" I asked.

"Where are you? Tell me you got away from the airport before the shit hit the fan?"

If I'd been a little worried before, Jed's tone ratcheted my fears up the scale, as did his mention of the airport. "I just dropped Bradley off at Reagan National. Emmy asked me to. What shit?"

"Thank goodness." He paused briefly, then blew out a breath. "Can you get back to Dulles? They need anybody who knows how to put on a hazmat suit out here ten minutes ago."

A hazmat suit? That meant a chemical or biological incident, and with Azrael on the loose, I could guess which one.

"What the heck happened? Emmy told us to go outside, then disappeared through a staff entrance."

"Intelligence suggested Azrael was going to be released into the air in a stadium, but it turned out the terrorists meant into the air-conditioning system at Dulles."

My hand froze halfway to the ignition. "They set it off? Holy fu...dge. There were thousands of people there."

I thought back to the mom, her baby, the children running around. What if carriers had boarded flights? Azrael could already be on its way across continents.

"Emmy shut down the air-conditioning system before the guy got the canister inside, but it went off, and the way she tells it, she was covered in the stuff."

"Oh, shit."

"She's sealed inside the mechanical room with the terrorist, and we need to get both of them out. Then we need to swab the terminal just in case anything did escape. The cancelled flights are already causing chaos, and it's only going to get worse."

"I'll be there as fast as I can."

Traffic jams meant I abandoned Jed's car a mile away and set off on foot. I called to let him know, half jogging down the side of the road.

"I'm walking the last bit. Everything's stuck."

"Go to the main entrance. I've given your name to the police. If you have any problems getting through, give me a call."

His voice sounded brisk and business-like, but with the same undercurrent of the fear I'd heard in Emmy's. I quickened my steps as I hurried past the lines of stationary cars, the air punctuated with honking horns as irate tourists tried to find a way through. Little did they know they wouldn't be going anywhere out of Dulles, not for a while at least.

With every step, the fear of Azrael squeezed tighter around my chest. *Azrael, Azrael, Azrael.* My mind superimposed Emmy into the hospital in Al Bidaya, her body twisted as the virus attacked, her face marred by smallpox pustules. *Azrael, Azrael, Azrael.*

I quickened to a run, my breath rasping as I got closer. Just a few more steps. A few more. The entrance loomed in front of me, and I scraped sweaty strands of hair away from my face as I choked out my name to the nearest cop.

"Chess Lane. I'm with the, uh, CDC." That sounded plausible,

The cop radioed through to a colleague, then nodded at his reply. "Follow me, ma'am."

Inside the perimeter, police were trying to herd the evacuated travellers into different areas, but the overall atmosphere was one of chaos. My escort elbowed people out of the way until we reached an enclave of semi-calm right next to the terminal I'd left only hours before. Seconds later, Jed jogged towards me wearing his usual home attire of jeans, a white T-shirt, and his favourite leather jacket. The only difference was he'd aged ten years since yesterday. When we got within touching distance, he pulled me in for a kiss, rough and hard. A couple of men gave us strange looks, but I didn't care.

With all the evil in the world today, I needed to feel love.

"Fuck," he said, tearing his lips away.

"Is she still in there?"

"Yeah, and so is the terrorist."

My heart seized. "What if he hurts her?"

"He's just sprayed her with Azrael. I don't think there's much more he can do." Jed sank down to the kerb. "Besides, she's incapacitated him."

As he put his head in his hands, I knelt on the sidewalk and wrapped an arm around his shoulders. Wrong. All wrong. Jed was supposed to be the strong one.

"We'll get her out and do everything we can." I sat up straight. "We need to get her the smallpox vaccine right away. Even if it's given after exposure it can lessen the symptoms."

"She's had it. She had it at the same time we did."

I sagged back against the wall next to him. Over the last few weeks I'd grown to like the woman I'd once thought had the personality of a glacier, and even this morning her first thought had been to get Bradley and me to safety.

"Do you know where they'll take her?"

"There's a military hospital not too far from here with a quarantine facility. Doctors are on their way with bubble stretchers for her and the terrorist to travel in."

"What can I do to help? Test the terminal? Or do you want me to go with Emmy?"

For a moment, all his self-control melted away, and a tear slipped down his cheek. "It should have been me."

"No..."

"It was my operation. She wasn't even supposed to be involved."

Should I tell him about her plans for Boston? I decided against it. What would it gain? It wasn't like she'd actually made it that far.

"From what I've seen of Emmy, nobody could have stopped her. And her actions saved hundreds of thousands of people. We have one room at the airport infected, not all those people about to catch their flights."

"I know that logically, but it doesn't make it any easier. I wouldn't even be here if it wasn't for Emmy. Did you know she saved my life last year?"

I shook my head.

"I'd be rotting in a hole in Syria if it wasn't for her, and she nearly died that time as well."

More tears fell, and I cuddled him against me, trying to comfort him but not doing a great job. I wasn't used to being the stronger person.

A vibration on Jed's hip made us both look down. His phone carried on ringing as he fumbled in his pocket and then stared at the screen.

"It's her."

CHAPTER 40

SQUASHED UP AGAINST Jed, I could hear every word Emmy said. For someone who'd just been given a likely death sentence, she sounded remarkably calm.

"Why are you sitting on the ground?" she asked.

He jerked his head up. "How do you know?"

"I know everything. You should've realised that by now."

Those darn spy pixies again—it had to be. I waited for her to tell him what he'd eaten for breakfast.

"Quit the bullshit."

She sighed. "Fine, Mack patched me into the airport's CCTV system on my phone. Are you going to put Chess down and do some work? Because maybe, just maybe, I'd like to get out of here. Old Abdallah here isn't great company. Too quiet."

I heard a thump, then a grunt—presumably Abdallah.

"And he doesn't like football."

Jed gave a small smile, focusing on the camera jutting out from under a nearby roof. "Do your worst."

"Do you know what he had in his pocket?"

"What?"

"A one-way ticket to Hawaii. When they talked about taking a trip to paradise, they meant literally."

Jed kicked a heel into the ground. "That fucker."

"Got that right."

"Hold on, babe. We'll get you out of there; I promise."

Getting the pair of them out of there was easier said than done. Jed wasn't keen on me going into the red zone, but at the police commander's request, I donned a hazmat suit with a self-contained air supply and headed inside. Emmy was on the phone when I arrived, kneeling on a man's back, twisting his arms behind him.

"Look, I'm sorry, okay? What did you want me to do? Sit back and call 911?"

A pause and she pursed her lips.

"That's bollocks. Call me when you calm down." She tossed the phone on the floor and the screen cracked. "Oh, fuck it."

I crouched beside her as best as I could in my protective clothing and tried to make her feel better. "You can't take the phone out with you, anyway."

"Yeah, I know. I'll get someone to wipe the data remotely."

"How are you feeling?"

"No different to last time I saw you, except my knuckles are bruised from punching that arsehole. What's the average incubation period been running at?"

"Uh, maybe we should talk about this later?"

"Don't bullshit me."

I took a deep breath, and it echoed around my suit. "We've seen a minimum of two days, maximum of seventeen. The average has been five days."

"So, now we wait."

"We get you out of here, then we wait."

As well as the dangers of Azrael, we had to contend with several thousand irritated passengers, the eyes of the world's media, and Abdallah himself, who didn't help by trying to claw through one doctor's hazmat suit with his fingernails. He struggled so much that Emmy lost patience and knocked him out again, then she lifted him onto his stretcher herself and cuffed his wrists and ankles to the rails at the side.

Once she'd climbed onto her own stretcher, she lay back and stared at the ceiling. "Ready to go?"

Two men covered both bubbles in sheets to keep away prying eyes. We'd made an improvised grey zone in the hallway outside, and before we went outside, we scrubbed each other and the stretchers down with diluted bleach. Once we'd wheeled our two patients into the green zone, two men taped new blankets securely over the top of the bubbles. Thanks to the no-fly zone over the airport, we escaped the beady eyes of the news helicopters, but ghouls with camera phones lurked at every turn. I kept my head down and flipped my hair over my face. Nobody wanted to be a TV star today.

We only uncovered the bubbles when we arrived at the medical facility an hour and a half later.

"What is this place?" I whispered to Jed as we stopped at the gate so soldiers could search the car we were travelling in. Even the police weren't allowed to pass.

"I can't tell you, and trust me, you wouldn't want to know, anyway."

As we descended below ground and rushed along corridors, I glimpsed an operating theatre and silent wards but no other patients. The place had an ominous air about it, not so much death, more like it was waiting for something. Azrael? Or were there other deadly pathogens out there that the government didn't want us to know about?

A cavernous room at the end of the corridor housed the isolation unit. There were six individual pods made from thick glass, each containing a bed, a bathroom, and monitoring equipment, accessed through a chemical shower and then an airlock. A narrow corridor behind allowed staff to observe the occupants without wearing protective suits, but right now we were going inside. Three of us donned hazmat suits and proceeded through the airlock.

"Do you want to be at the opposite end to him?" a doctor asked Emmy, pointing at Abdallah.

Emmy shook her head. "No. Put me next door."

The two men with me escorted Abdallah into the end room, and only once they'd Tasered him did they un-cuff his wrists and ankles. By the time he came around, they'd already secured him to the bed, which came with a set of built-in shackles. The sight of them made me shudder. Who was this place designed for?

Even restrained in that manner, Abdallah still struggled against his bonds, hate in his eyes as he glared at all those present. I hoped I didn't have to get involved with his treatment. I didn't want him to live in any case.

When I looked back at Emmy, she'd put on the mask she wore in public. Face impassive, eyes blank. It would only be a matter of time before she began showing symptoms and by rights, she should have been scared—no, terrified—but she just sat on the edge of the bed, occasionally showing mild interest and nothing more. Frozen, pretty much. Chills ran through me as well.

Outside, an empty ward next door to the quarantine suite was filling with people. Jed stood on the far side, talking to two men I was pretty sure I'd glimpsed in Vegas with him. I took a few tentative steps in their direction until I caught Jed's eye, and he beckoned me over.

"This is Nate." He waved at a gruff-looking man with hair the colour of milk chocolate and skin a little lighter.

Nate gave me a salute. "Forgive me if I don't shake hands. This place gives me the creeps."

I was glad I wasn't the only one.

"And this is Nick," Jed said.

Nick smiled at least, and I gave him a finger wave. "I'm Chess."

"I know. We all know. Congratulations, by the way."

On what? My scientific efforts? "We're still such a long way off from a cure. I mean, the early trials have shown promise..."

He shook his head and tapped his ring finger. "I was talking about Vegas."

"Uh, we're not quite married anymore."

"Way Jed looks at you, it won't be long."

A flicker of fear crossed Jed's face, and I sought to reassure him. The last thing I wanted was for him to get cold feet. After all, this relationship thing was as new to him as it was to me. "This may sound strange after the way we met, but I'd like to take things slowly."

Jed's worry lines didn't ease, but thankfully, Nate stepped in and changed the subject.

"How's Emmy?" he asked.

"Calm." Almost back to the ice queen I'd first met. "She's out of the stretcher and in an isolation room now."

"And if it follows the same pattern as Al Bidaya, we'd expect her to start showing symptoms in, what, a couple of days?"

"It could be as long as three weeks."

"Fuck. How does she get into these situations?"

"By saving everyone's asses," Nick reminded him.

A commotion behind us made my hair stand on end. Honestly, it was like all the air had been sucked out of the room. My head, along with everyone else's, turned to stare at the newcomer.

Taller than Jed and more muscular, he looked to be around forty, one of those men who only grew more beautiful with age. My breath caught just looking at him. As he strode over to us, the crowds parted, and I realised how dark he was. Not just his clothes, but his eyes. They spoke of a thousand horrors witnessed and a thousand more to come.

"Who's that?" I whispered to Jed although I suspected I already knew.

"Emmy's husband."

Yes, I was right. He exuded the same odd magnetism that she did, the certain something that made everyone in the room stop what they were doing to watch him. He halted in front of Jed, and I took half a step back without even thinking.

"Where is she?"

"In a containment room," Jed answered.

"I need to see her."

"Chess, can you take him?"

"Of course. You can talk to her from outside, but if you want to go in, you'll need a hazmat suit."

"If they can find one big enough," Nate muttered.

"We'll start with outside."

Halfway down the corridor, a guard licked his lips nervously and asked to see Black's clearance papers.

Black stayed silent for a few seconds, enough time for the man to swallow three times.

"If you try to stop me from seeing my wife, you'll spend the rest of your military career scrubbing toilets in a place where running water is a luxury. Do you understand?"

The guard stepped to the side. I would have too.

I led Black into the corridor and showed him how to use the intercom. Emmy shuffled up to the glass, dragging her heels.

"Leave us," Black instructed, and I retreated so fast I nearly tripped over my own feet.

Back in the ward, Jed was still with Nick and Nate, only two more men had shown up along with a pair of women—one brunette, one redhead.

"Chess, meet Luke and his fiancé, Mack." Jed motioned at the man on the left plus the flame-haired lady he had his arm around. "The woman who forgot to put her skirt on this morning is Dan." He was joking, but barely. Her outfit only just covered her ass. "And this is Xavier."

Xavier came out of the same mould as Emmy's

husband, but his eyes were a little lighter. A little softer.

"What happens to Emmy now?" he asked.

"We wait."

"That's it?"

"She needs to eat to keep her strength up, and once the symptoms begin, we can give her supportive therapy—fluids and the like. But essentially, yes, we wait. The virus won't hit for two days at least."

It was almost midnight when a ripple went through the room. By then, most people had claimed a spot on one of the spare beds to try and get some sleep. Not one person had gone home, despite the base commander's best efforts to evict them, and Black had taken a pillow and blanket and bedded down in the corridor next to Emmy.

And now we had a new visitor, complete with a team of secret service agents shadowing his every move.

"Jed." I elbowed him awake. "President Harrison's just walked in."

Jed sat up, and President Harrison walked straight over. "How is she?"

"Pragmatic. Black's with her at the moment."

"At least she'll keep her shit together if he's around."

I gawped at the president, surprised by his choice of language. I still hadn't closed my mouth when he turned towards me.

"Miss Lane, I'd hoped when we met again it would be under better circumstances."

"Uh, me too." In truth, I hadn't expected to be in the same building as him again.

"I understand you were with Emmy when this incident started?"

"That's right."

"Would you mind running me through it? I've heard the short version from Emmy, but that was soon after it happened and punctuated by every profanity known to man as well as a few she made up."

I recapped events outside The Stadium, then Jed and the president meandered off, deep in conversation. I couldn't sleep, especially without Jed next to me, so I borrowed his tablet to review some papers on experimental serums used to lessen the symptoms of Ebola. One in particular looked promising, but it had never been used on humans before.

Without windows to the outside, I'd lost track of whether it was day or night when a tightness in my chest followed by a shadow falling over the bed alerted me to the fact I had a visitor. A glance at my watch told me it was six a.m., and I rolled over to find Black staring down.

"Would you mind coming to speak with my wife?"

He might have phrased it as a question, but there was no doubt in either of our minds that I'd do exactly as ordered. I trailed behind him as he walked into the hallway.

Emmy stood up and came to the intercom, a smile tugging one corner of her lips before it slipped away.

"Do you want me to suit up and come in?" I asked.

"No, this works. Probably it's better to have the glass between us."

She rapped on the surface, but it was so thick the

noise barely registered on my side.

"Why? What's happened?"

"I have a tiny confession to make."

What kind of confession? She looked almost...almost contrite. "Okay."

"You remember when I came to Galveston to give you a hand packing?"

"I could hardly forget." A couple of the bruises Wade caused still hadn't faded completely.

"And we flew back on my plane?"

"Yes."

"We didn't hit turbulence."

"Huh?" What was she talking about?

"The vial of vaccine in the cooler didn't break because of turbulence or pressure changes. It broke because of me."

"You cracked it on purpose?"

"I did."

"But why?"

"Because I wanted the vaccine."

Honestly, she got more confusing by the second. Why on earth would she want it? To sell? Apollo represented my years of hope and determination, not a potential goldmine.

"I don't understand."

"Think about it."

So I did. And then I realised why she wanted the glass between us.

CHAPTER 41

"YOU VACCINATED YOURSELF?" I screeched. The glass may have been thick, but we didn't need the intercom for that part.

She nodded and gave me a look that was part apologetic, part...what? Pleased?

"It seemed like a good idea at the time. Now, it seems like a better idea."

"You injected an experimental drug barely out of its first stage trial."

And more than that, she'd injected *my* experimental drug. Apollo was everything I'd worked for—everything—and she hadn't even had the decency to discuss it with me.

Emmy shrugged one shoulder. "I had access to all the data. You'd have moved onto human trials soon. I just hurried things along a bit."

"Where did you even get the syringe?"

"First aid kit on the plane."

"Do you realise how many rules you've broken?"

"I've never paid much attention to rules."

Jed made me jump when he touched a hand to my waist. "Everything okay? I heard shouting."

"No, everything is not okay. This...this madwoman decided to use herself as a guinea pig for Apollo. My whole trial could get shut down!"

He turned to Emmy, eyes narrowed. "Is that true? You took Apollo?"

"What do you think?"

Jed leaned his forehead against the glass. "You crazy fucking bitch. Didn't you think of the implications for Chess?"

"I always think things through, believe it or not. And trust me; there won't be any problems with the trial, not with Black and James on our side."

"*Is* James on our side?"

"He will be."

The way she said that, I didn't doubt it for a second, and it scared me that a woman like her had so much leverage over somebody so important.

"We don't even know if it's safe or not," I said.

"Well, given that it's been a month and I'm still alive, I think we can assume it's not gonna kill me."

Jed's brow furrowed. "But where did you get the vaccine? I thought it was stored in a secure lab?"

Steam came out of my ears once more. "On the plane back from Galveston. She stole it out of the transport case on the seat right next to me. I can't believe I didn't wake up."

Emmy gave her annoying shrug again, and if the glass hadn't been there, I'd have slapped her.

"That was never going to be an issue."

Suddenly, I wasn't the only one shouting.

"You drugged my wife?" Jed yelled.

She stayed calm. "Girlfriend."

"Whatever. What the fuck did you use?"

"A roofie."

It was my turn again. "You gave me Rohypnol?"

"I always carry it in my handbag for those little

emergencies."

A voice came from behind me, low, bordering on dangerous. "What's done is done. Emmy understands your views, as do I, but her stupidity might just end up saving her life. The pair of you need to put your differences aside and treat this like the trial it is."

I swivelled my head and found those bottomless eyes boring into me. I could hardly say no to Black—he'd probably suck out my soul.

Emmy spoke up again, far more relaxed than me. "I left Abdallah alive to use as a control."

She glared at him through the glass, and he stared back sullenly. Seeing as he refused to cooperate, he was still cuffed to the bed, barely able to move.

Wow. She'd really thought this through, hadn't she? I took a handful of deep breaths and forced myself to set my emotions aside and think logically about this. Was I really surprised? I'd always known the ice queen skirted the boundaries of right and wrong. And by smashing every trial protocol known to science, she just might have helped a heck of a lot of people if Apollo worked.

Either that or she'd die within the month.

"Tell me what you need," Black said. "Funding, equipment, staff—I'll make sure you get it."

With those words, the anger boiling inside me reduced to a simmer. Black was right—what was done was done, and furious though I felt at Emmy's actions, I needed to look at the bigger picture. The people of Al Bidaya wouldn't care how a cure was found, just whether they'd live to see another sunrise.

"Fine. Emmy, you need to get back in bed while I write this mess into something that'll withstand peer review. And if you ever pull a stunt like this again, I'll... I'll..."

"She'll tell Bradley that those pink and silver tiles for your bathroom didn't really get discontinued. You called up and cancelled the order," Jed finished for me.

"Don't you dare," she said. "He'll paint my room beige in revenge."

"Then behave yourself."

The next morning, Emmy's husband came with me to explain to the rest of her friends what she'd done. One by one, they took turns to yell at her too, and I smiled inside. As Nate stomped back in and set up a laptop on one of those little tray-tables, another stranger walked in.

"Where's Emmy? I heard she only has a week to live."

His accent was French, and if I cared to admit it, which I didn't, sexy as heck.

Beside me, Dan muttered, "This has to be a record. Seven of Emmy's men in the same room. We only need one more for the full set."

"Who is he?"

"Gideon. Officially, he's an aide to the French president. Unofficially? Who knows?"

Black walked over and explained the situation, then I led Gideon to the glass corridor so he could tell Emmy she was an idiot too. At least, that was what I assumed he said. He spoke in French, but his hand gestures sure didn't look happy.

She grinned at him through the wall. "Thanks for

flying thousands of miles to tell me that."

"I can hardly take you out for dinner, *cherie*."

"I'll take a rain check."

He stayed for another twenty minutes, speaking quietly into the intercom, and after he'd retired to the conference room, I suited up and went to take the day's first set of blood samples.

Emmy held out an arm and sighed. "Guess I'd better get used to this."

"You know, when I first met you, I wanted to get myself a voodoo doll with your face on it."

"Looks like dreams really do come true."

"I changed my mind," I said quietly.

"Even after the whole plane episode?"

I rolled my eyes. "Even after that."

She smiled. "I'm glad. Mostly, I don't care what people think of me, but I've got a feeling you'll be around for a while."

I bit my lip as I clipped another blood collection tube onto the needle. "Do you really think so? This thing with Jed...it's so new, and I've never been in a proper relationship before."

"Yeah, it'll last. He looks at you differently—not just like you're dessert, but as if you're his whole world."

"I hope so, because he's mine."

On day three, the temperatures of both patients began to go up. First half a degree in the morning, then another degree in the afternoon. Abdallah was proving to be a nightmare of a patient. One of the male doctors dealt with him, and each time he took blood samples, four orderlies held the man down while another stood by with a Taser, just in case.

"How are you feeling?" I asked Emmy.

She flopped her head back on the pillow. "Not great. I've got a headache and my joints ache."

"Do you want me to get you a painkiller?"

"No. I'd rather not mask anything, and I don't feel much worse than I did after I took the vaccine—I got these symptoms a couple of days in."

I squeezed her shoulder. "Just rest, and make sure you drink plenty."

"Thanks, Mom."

"I'll analyse these samples and let you know what's happening."

"And his." She pointed at Abdallah. "I want to know how I compare."

Back in the conference room, everyone crowded around me once I'd been through decontamination.

"How is she?"

"Any sign of the virus?"

"Is the vaccine working?"

As I had for the last three days, I gave a quick update. "A slightly elevated temperature, although that could be due to Apollo fighting off Azrael. She's still joking around, which is a good sign."

The group dispersed to the edges of the room, which had been turned into an impromptu control room with phones, laptops, and video monitors. It seemed most people present had dug in for the foreseeable future and brought their work with them, the president included. He hadn't budged since Emmy arrived, and the media was full of speculation over his whereabouts. Whatever his relationship with her, it was clear how much he cared.

"You holding up okay?" I asked him.

"Yeah." He dropped an iPad into his lap. "The *National Enquirer* thinks I've been abducted by aliens, and my press secretary's threatening to resign."

"Maybe you could make an appearance?"

"Maybe." But he didn't move.

He hadn't shaved since he got there either, but far from looking unkempt, a few days of stubble only increased his appeal. Add jeans and a checked shirt, and we were talking hot lumberjack. Shoot. *Chess, stop thinking like that.* I glanced over at Jed, who was also rocking the bearded look. He may not have had James Harrison's power, but he certainly had more than enough sex appeal for me.

A shadow flitted across the room, and before I could focus, a man wearing a what I now knew to be a service uniform with a colonel's insignia put two fingers to the president's temple.

"Boom. Harrison, your security's fucked again."

Two seconds later, the newcomer was surrounded by a dozen secret service agents, guns drawn. I stumbled backwards until Dan caught me.

"Aaaand, we have the full set," she whispered.

Chapter 42

THE STANDOFF CONTINUED until Black waded into their midst. "Put the guns down. Rather than wasting your time on this man, I'd suggest you evaluate how he got in here in the first place."

A couple of the men in suits lowered their pistols, but the rest held steady until James waved them off.

"Like he said—find the holes and plug them. Now."

"Who's that one?" I whispered to Dan.

"Alaric. Sagittarius, ex-spy, and all-around sex god."

"How the heck did he get in?" Even I got questioned on my way back from the restroom once.

Dan rolled her eyes. "Who knows? He's invisible when he wants to be. The only surprise is that he didn't show up in quarantine wearing a hazmat suit."

Alaric tossed his hat onto a chair and clapped his hands together. "So, what's going on? I heard there was a biological attack, and I figured Emmy would be involved somehow. Where is she?"

"Quarantine," Black answered.

He looked far from happy at Alaric's arrival, and dare I say it, a tiny bit surprised.

"Fuck. She got exposed?"

"Yes."

"To...well, you're calling it Azrael?"

President Harrison stepped forwards. "What do you mean, *we're* calling it Azrael?"

"The Russians named it Likho."

"And how do you know that?"

Alaric shrugged. "I heard rumours flying around a few weeks ago and did some digging. Curiosity, if you must." He held his hands up. "But I don't work for Uncle Sam anymore, so I'd better not get involved."

"Look, if you have information—"

"I'll talk to Emmy about it, not you. Where is she?"

Black's face hardened. "For fuck's sake..."

But the president blew out a long breath and turned to me. "Chess, please can you escort this man to Emerson?"

"Okay."

"And don't let him out of your sight."

Every member of the secret service broke with their serious expression as I walked along the corridor beside Alaric. Their looks ranged from mildly annoyed to downright furious. I snuck a look over at him, and far from looking upset, one corner of his mouth quirked up in amusement.

But his expression grew grim as we neared the quarantine unit. "How is she? Is she sick?"

"A little achy." How much was I supposed to tell him? "She, uh, took an experimental treatment, so we're hoping it helps."

"Apollo?"

"How do you know about Apollo?"

He tapped the side of his nose. "I know a lot of things."

Emmy rolled off the bed and walked up to the glass when we arrived, eyes wide as she reached out to turn the intercom on.

"Ric? What the...?"

He tilted his head to the side and shrugged. "Remember that promise we made, Cinders? Whichever one of us died first, the other's supposed to pour a bottle of tequila over the coffin?"

Emmy thumped the glass, eyes narrowed. "You fuck! Six years without so much as a bloody phone call? For the first eight months, I didn't even know if you were still alive."

"After what happened, I didn't feel like talking to anybody."

"You're damn lucky there's a wall between us."

"Why?" He grinned, and his smile wouldn't have looked out of place on a Hollywood megastar. "Because I'm irresistible?"

"No, because I want to kick you in the balls for taking off like that."

"Cinders..."

"Stop calling me that. You lost the right when you walked out on me."

"I sent you a birthday card last year."

Emmy looked like she was about to start yelling, but Alaric stepped closer and put both hands on the glass.

"I'm sorry," he said softly. "But after what happened... I just couldn't deal with people. Haven't you ever wanted to run away somewhere nobody knows you? Make a fresh start?"

Her voice dropped too. "Yeah, I guess I have." A full minute passed in silence before one corner of her lips flickered upwards. "Nice uniform."

He gave her a bow and a grin. "Thanks. It's a little

tight across the shoulders."

"Who did you steal it off?"

"Colonel Schwarz."

"Figures. I don't think he goes to the gym so much anymore."

His voice grew serious as did his expression. "So, how are you feeling?"

"Not too bad. Kind of like I'm getting a cold."

"I hear you're trying a vaccine?"

"Yeah. I'm not exactly supposed to be."

He burst out laughing. "That's my girl. Well, if it works, you'll be one step ahead of the Russians. They shelved the program when their own vaccine didn't work."

"You found some information?"

I pricked up my ears too. Where did this virus come from? Whoever created it was undeniably psychotic.

"Not much. The scientist heading up the Likho project died three years ago, and his lab got sealed. But a few samples found their way onto the black market."

"How many are we talking?"

"My contact knows of half a dozen. One was used in Al Bidaya as a demo, and one got sold. Twelve million dollars. What's that—a couple of cents a life?"

"Four left. Fuck it, and I'm stuck in here. Anything on Lilith?"

"She's still in the wind."

Emmy paced up and down, and next door Abdallah's eyes followed her. That man gave me the chills. So much evil inside him, yet from the outside he looked perfectly normal.

"Will you keep looking?"

"I'll keep looking. Promise me you'll take care of

yourself."

"Don't have a lot of choice in here, do I?"

"Suppose not. You want me to stick around for a week or two?"

She paused in front of him, her hands on the glass. "Will you? Or are you gonna do a moonlight flit again?"

"I'll be here." He gave her a small smile. "Anything for you, Cinders."

The next day the air in the ward reeked of testosterone. For a room full of alpha males, they behaved remarkably well, but the underlying tension made me hesitate every time I stepped inside. Mostly, I hung out in one corner with Mack and Dan, plus Nate's wife, Carmen, who showed up every day after she'd taken their son to school.

Black had run a power cable down the corridor and set up his laptop outside Emmy's prison.

At seven a.m., I suited up and went to the quarantine unit. Despite being covered from head to toe, the hazmat suit felt less claustrophobic than being in the room I'd just left. I'd never thought I'd see the day when I went into the red zone to relax.

"Any change in how you feel?" I asked Emmy.

She stretched her arms above her head. "About the same. No worse."

"That's encouraging."

"And I'm doing better than old Amin." She jerked a thumb in the terrorist's direction. "He's already puked twice this morning."

I checked her vitals. "Your temperature's gone

down half a degree."

"Then we're heading in the right direction."

Over the next few days, Abdallah's health deteriorated. Without being surrounded by the sheer desperation of the hospital in Al Bidaya, I could spend more time studying him and his symptoms. He was the first man I'd watched Ebola destroy from infection to death. Emmy kept the same vigil, watching from the other side of her glass wall, at times with a faint smile twitching at her lips.

I was standing next to her four days later when he breathed his last, shuddered, and lay still.

Emmy pressed her face up to the glass. "I win, asshole."

Then she returned to bed and closed her eyes.

Her temperature had been normal for the last two days, and in the samples from yesterday and today, I hadn't been able to identify any viral RNA, which was an indicator of Azrael's presence in her system. It looked as if she'd fought it off. When I took a second sample and retested it, I got the same results. Nothing.

Apollo appeared to work, but since that conclusion was based on a sample size of one, I couldn't afford to celebrate yet.

After two weeks in captivity, Emmy paced her room like a caged tiger. Now that it looked as if she wasn't about to die, the ward outside had emptied out, with people stopping in to visit rather than sleeping there. The president's press secretary had announced his recovery from an unfortunate bout of norovirus, and

James Harrison had shaved and gone back to entertaining foreign dignitaries.

The one constant was Emmy's husband. He never left the medical facility, and at night he slept in the corridor next to his wife rather than in one of the empty beds. Emmy bedded down on the floor too, with only the sheet of glass separating them.

And she was driving me insane.

"More blood? Is there any left in me?"

"I need to monitor you. That's the whole point of the trial. Remember, the trial that you started all by yourself?"

"But I feel fine."

"Twenty-one days—that's what the protocol dictates. And the president himself signed off on that, so if you want to argue, you can take it up with him."

"Yeah, yeah. Already tried that."

She dropped back onto the bed and sighed. Some people might have been grateful for the rest—and Mack had set her up a laptop with every TV channel known to man—but it seemed the concept of relaxation didn't agree with Emmy.

The next day, her husband brought in a tank-like personal trainer who drilled her through the glass—squats, lunges, push-ups, crunches—until she crawled under the blankets and pretended to sleep.

"Better?" Black asked me.

"Better."

On day twenty-one, I gave Emmy the good news.

"Everything's still clear. You can go home

tomorrow."

I'd expected her to be overjoyed, but her glum expression didn't change.

"On second thoughts, do you mind if I stay here?"

I sat on the bed next to her. "Why? Yesterday you couldn't wait to get out."

"Mack came to see me. She's getting married in a week, and Bradley's having a meltdown over the last-minute arrangements. He saw this video of groomsmen dancing on YouTube and he wanted Luke's to do the same, only they all refused, so now he's decided the bridesmaids can do show tunes."

"And you're one of them?"

She buried her head in her hands. "My dress doesn't even have anywhere to hide my gun."

I burst into laughter, then quickly regretted it when the inside of my visor fogged up. "I probably shouldn't tell you, but I heard rumours that he's throwing you a 'welcome home' party too."

"Oh, fucking hell. If Black and I don't keep him in check, he runs wild." She gave a little cough. "I don't feel so good. Can you write that on the chart?"

"Nope. Have fun learning the choreography."

"I don't like you anymore."

But she smiled, and we both knew she was lying.

CHAPTER 43

THE TWO DAYS after Emmy got released were a whirlwind of activity. I'd been in touch with both Chet in Galveston and my new staff in Richmond by email, but I needed to visit the lab as well as catch up on correspondence.

Having friends in high places paid off because the funding and permission to run a wider trial of Apollo in Al Bidaya got pushed through without me having to print off a forest's worth of grant forms and write proposal after proposal. People were still dying, but the death rate had slowed markedly, and this new vaccination program for the surrounding area should ensure the disease was wiped out entirely. But the logistics still required a whole heap of work on my part.

"Anything I can do, darlin'?" Jed asked from the couch.

With the threat of Azrael temporarily lifted, he'd taken two weeks of leave and seemed to be spending most days asleep while I sat in front of my laptop.

Of course, that might also have something to do with the fact he spent most of the nights awake, like me. I yawned again. "Another cup of coffee would be great."

Minutes later, a warm mug found its way into my hands, and his lips found their way onto my neck. I loved this whole relationship thing, but it could be incredibly distracting. "If you want to go to the party tonight, you'll have to let me finish this document."

"How about we have our own party?"

"How about you go out and find me a box of donuts? I need a sugar fix."

He grinned and headed for the door. I watched his ass as he went, the soft denim of his well-worn jeans moulded to each cheek. How the heck had I ever chosen Wade over this man? I owed Emmy a medal for her intervention.

And for her help with Lottie, too. My sister was a different girl to the shell she'd been back at Bayview—fourteen pounds heavier, a whole lot happier, and with a new-found love of cooking. She'd be at the party tonight too, with Nigel, her friend-and-probably-more, and despite Emmy's assurances, I wanted to keep an eye on them. Although I had to admit, Nigel seemed like a sweet boy from what I'd seen of him. He'd even offered to colour-coordinate my wardrobe and teach me meditation.

Jed had offered up his spare room for Lottie, but it turned out Emmy had too. And Jed's apartment had no hope of competing with Palace Riverley and its swimming pool, so Lottie stayed put. Not that I was complaining. I couldn't deny the place was good for her, and secretly, I loved having the apartment to ourselves.

Anyway, I'd see her soon, if I ever got this damn equipment list written up. I forced myself to concentrate for fifteen minutes and think of everything we needed to ship to Iraq for the Apollo trial—syringes, slides, pipettes—we couldn't just pop to the store room if we forgot something.

At last, I managed to pen a coherent draft to discuss with the team tomorrow. Now I just needed to print it. In a rare moment away from the couch yesterday, Jed had installed the printer software on my laptop, but the darn printer had run out of paper. Did he have any? Or was that something I needed to go out and buy?

I rummaged around on the shelves in his study. Car magazines, old birthday cards, a box of condoms. I didn't even want to think about why he needed those next to his desk. A pile of papers fell to the floor and scattered, and I stopped to pick them up. Why was my signature on one of the pages?

I'd just began to read when the front door slammed, but I couldn't tear my eyes away. Were these what I thought they were?

Jed's voice drifted through from the living room before his shadow darkened the doorway. "I picked up donuts, plus brownies and cookies, but I bet none of them taste as sweet as you." He paused a few feet away. "Oh, shit."

"Shouldn't these be with the court?"

He took one step backwards, then another. "Yeah, I guess. I just hadn't gotten around to it."

"You mean to tell me we're still married?"

"Technically. On a scale of one to Emmy stealing your vaccine, how mad does that make you?"

I threw the papers, and they hit him mid-chest. "Why the hell didn't you say something?"

"I was worried you'd get upset. Looks like I was right."

I stomped over and jabbed him with a finger. "I'm not upset about being married. I'm upset because you didn't tell me!"

He grabbed my hand in both of his and brought it to his lips. "You don't mind being married?"

"Of course not. I love you, you idiot."

His shoulders slumped. "Thank fuck for that." He pulled me into his chest and wrapped me up in his arms. "I love you too, darlin'. Getting hammered in Vegas was the best mistake I ever made."

My husband, the romantic.

My *husband*.

"So what do we do now? Just stay married?"

"It would save me from asking you again in a couple of months. Plus it'd save us from a Bradley-esque wedding, and from what I've seen, that's something we want to avoid."

"I thought you got out of the dancing."

"Black threatened to fly Bradley to Abu Dhabi and leave him there if he mentioned it again. But now he wants us all to wear pink ties to match the flowers and pink fucking underwear."

"Who's going to see your underwear?"

"Exactly my point."

"Okay, so no Bradley. How about a honeymoon?"

Jed broke into a dazzling smile. "Oh, I'll take you on a honeymoon, Mrs. Harker. Anywhere you want to go."

"And the wedding night? I don't want to miss out on that."

He swept me off my feet, catching me by surprise. "Let's do that right now."

We were late to the party.

"Oh, wow." A rainbow of lights lit up Emmy's house, shining like a beacon in the darkness as we purred along the drive in Jed's Porsche. "It's beautiful."

"Not as beautiful as you."

I knew he was fibbing—the black wrap dress was a last-second purchase from the mall near his house when I realised if I didn't go shopping I'd be attending the event in jeans or a lab coat—but I appreciated his sentiment.

"I'm glad I bought a new outfit."

"You didn't need to. It's going to be carnage."

Really? The allure continued inside, with the silver horse twinkling under a galaxy of spotlights. A bevy of guests stood around, sipping champagne and nibbling on canapés, chatting quietly above elegant background music piped through hidden speakers. The parties Wade had taken me to were all networking shindigs with overly loud guests forcing business cards on everyone around them. I'd certainly never been to an event as elegant as this one.

Even Alaric had kept his word and hung around. I spotted him on the far side of the room, deep in conversation with Dan. According to Emmy, they all went way back.

A voice came from behind me. "Would you like a drink, ma'am?"

"I'd love a—" I spluttered as the waiter came into sight, holding aloft a tray of champagne. "Why are you wearing Tyvek?"

"All part of the theme, ma'am."

"Theme? What theme?"

Jed grabbed two glasses of bubbly, then took my elbow and led me into the great room at the back of the house. I spotted the Ebola-shaped cake straight away, and then the bedouin-tent-slash-bouncy-castle outside the windows.

Beside me, Jed burst out laughing, but I tried to straighten my face as Emmy walked towards us.

"Go on, laugh," she said. "It's either that or throttle Bradley. The bouncy castle was his idea."

"I was actually more amused by the Ebola cake."

"I know, it's in terrible taste, isn't it? He wanted to use biohazard canisters to serve the drinks in, but I put my foot down over that." She rolled her eyes. "He's using them in the treasure hunt later instead."

"Treasure hunt?"

"His new twist on laser tag. Girls versus guys. He's hidden canisters in the woods out the back with gifts in them, and he's sending us out to search for them."

"But it's pitch black."

"He's painted glow-in-the-dark biohazard symbols on them. Besides, it doesn't matter." She glanced at Jed, then bent to whisper in my ear. "Mack was watching him via satellite while he hid them earlier. We'll win easily."

A snort escaped, and I clapped my hand over my mouth. Emmy raised an eyebrow before taking hold of my fingers.

"Is that a wedding ring you're wearing?"

I'd had my Vegas ring in my purse the whole time, and it seemed appropriate to put it on again. Jed had rummaged around in his suitcase and found his too, so now we had a matching pair in classy silver.

"Somebody forgot to get an annulment." I glared at him, and he smirked back.

A shriek behind my back made me spin round, only

to find Bradley standing there with his mouth open.

"Bradley, you didn't hear that," Emmy said, her voice low in warning.

"I did. I absolutely did." He did a little jig. "This is now officially... What? An engagement party? A wedding reception? I have so much to do!"

He ran off, dodging waiters as he went.

"Oh my goodness, I'm so sorry. I didn't mean to hijack your evening."

She grinned. "No, no, this is great. I didn't want the party in the first place, but Bradley insisted. This takes all the heat off me."

The music stopped, and somebody tapped the microphone. Bradley had hopped up on the dining table at the far end of the room, resplendent in a silver tuxedo.

Emmy patted me on the arm. "Best of luck."

EPILOGUE

"I LOVE THE colour of your dress," I said to Mack as she stood before an antique cheval mirror wearing an elegant cream satin wedding gown with green detailing at the waist. "The accents match your eyes."

"Believe me, I know. Bradley spent an hour comparing them to the Pantone chart. Did you know my right eye is shade 576 and my left is 370?"

"He seems to have put a lot of effort into this."

"He has. I can't complain too much. If I'd been in charge of the organising, we'd still be living in sin twenty years from now. The only bit I did was the rings."

"What did you choose?"

"White gold bands, but they're engraved with our voice prints saying 'I love you.'"

"That sounds lovely."

Jed and I were still wearing our Vegas rings. We kept saying we'd buy new ones, but every time we were due to go shopping, we'd ended up in the bedroom instead.

Emmy walked past in a matching green dress, but the look on her face was black. "Bradley! There's no room for my gun in this outfit. We already talked about this. And if I can't wear a bra, I'll have to hide my knife in my hair."

Bradley skidded to a halt in front of her. His hair matched the bridesmaid dresses, his pocket square, and his socks. I stared down at my purple outfit, feeling slightly out of place, but also relieved I was only a guest at Mack and Luke's wedding rather than an integral part of the event.

Meanwhile, Bradley huffed. "We have snipers on the roof, most of the men have guns, and there's a ring of security guards around the whole estate. Besides, it's a wedding. You don't need a gun."

Dan joined her. "Of course we do. Haven't you seen *Kill Bill*?"

Bradley shuddered. "No! It has shooting in it."

Carmen walked by, carrying a bouquet of flowers. "I've stashed two pistols and a rifle under the altar, so we're covered."

"And I have a knife in my garter," Mack added.

Bradley put his head in his hands. "Why do I do this?"

"Because you love it."

A thin man wearing a tuxedo and an earpiece half-ran across the room, making a beeline for Bradley. As he stooped to whisper in his ear, Bradley went white under his tan. "Oh, hell."

"What's up?" Emmy asked.

"Trevor's escaped."

While Mack had vetoed most of Bradley's wilder ideas, including the show tunes, she'd agreed to his idea of using a hawk to deliver the rings at the perfect moment. Jed and I had attended the rehearsal dinner three days ago, and Trevor had performed flawlessly during the trial run.

Mack hurried over, holding up the bottom of her

dress. "Did he have the rings? Tell me he didn't have the rings."

Earpiece man gulped. "In a little pouch on his leg."

She let out a shriek, clutching at her hair until Bradley pulled her hands away. "Why didn't we just give them to the best man like normal people?"

"Because this is more fun," Bradley said, but he didn't look like he was having fun at that moment. In fact, he looked like he was about to be sick.

Emmy waved everyone quiet. "Do we know where Trevor is?"

"In an oak tree out the back, but he's really high up," earpiece man said. "How can we get him down?"

"Shoot him?" Carmen suggested.

Gasps sounded from all around.

"With a tranquilliser dart," she added hastily.

"But how will he deliver the rings?" Bradley asked.

Dan snorted with laughter, then quickly turned it into a cough. "Maybe we could strap him to a fishing pole? You know, kind of bob him along?"

"It's no good," Bradley said. "Someone's going to have to climb up and get him down."

All heads swivelled in Emmy's direction.

"Why is everyone looking at me?"

Fifteen minutes later, we stood in the woods behind Riverley Hall, Black's stunning home and the venue for Luke and Mack's nuptials. Mack and the bridesmaids had swapped out their pumps for wellington boots, and Emmy had changed into one of the Tyvek suits left over from the party last week.

We all craned our necks back and looked into the tree where Trevor stared impassively from a branch halfway up. His handler stood next to us, apologising every twelve seconds.

"I'm really sorry. Honestly, he's never done this before."

Emmy glared at him as she strapped on a pair of crampons. "He probably took offence at all the flowers. I hope none of the guests have hay fever."

"Only three, and they're all allergic to grass pollen," Bradley said.

"Good grief," Emmy muttered.

I must say, she was a very good climber. She shinned up the trunk in seconds and then disappeared into the foliage. After a bit of rustling, she popped out on the branch Trevor was sitting on and began to inch towards him. He watched her creeping along, and as she reached out an arm, he hopped up to a higher branch.

"You asshole."

Emmy wriggled backwards and repeated the process, only this time, Trevor took one look at her and flew back down to his handler. She pulled a twig out of her hair and threw it at Bradley.

"You'd better get the hairspray ready, party princess."

Bradley was still fussing with Emmy's up-do as everyone assembled outside the marquee.

"You got lucky with the whole Vegas thing," Dan whispered to Jed, loud enough for me to hear. "This could have been you otherwise."

Jed fidgeted with his tie. "I'd go through it for Chess."

I beamed at him. "You would? Because I was thinking..." Oh, the look of panic on his face was priceless. "Relax, I'm joking. After the hell my mother put me through with the whole Wade thing, a formal wedding is the last thing I want."

Although I was looking forward to the honeymoon. Emmy and Black had offered us the use of their private island off the Bahamas later in the year. Mack and Luke would be using it for the next week as their wedding gift, but apart from that, we had our choice of dates. Yes, Emmy had turned out to be far from the icy villain I'd first cast her as.

Jed was in the wedding party but I wasn't, so I took my seat in the front row next to Xav and Georgia. On my other side was Amy, who'd flown all the way from England with her boyfriend Mark, who was acting as Luke's best man.

"I've never been anywhere this posh," she whispered to me, looking a little nervous.

"Don't worry—it's all new to me too."

"I'd love a fancy do like this, but I'm not sure Mark would go for it. Not that he's asked, of course," she added hastily, then glanced at my hand. "What was your wedding like?"

"It really wasn't that interesting."

"No, seriously. I love hearing about these things. Did you have many guests?"

"I genuinely can't remember. We both got horrendously drunk in Vegas and the wedding was an accident."

Her eyes widened. "Wow. Your relationship must have been strong to withstand that."

"Uh, I'd never met him before that night, but it turned out better than I expected."

Amy's jaw dropped, but thankfully the string quartet in the corner struck up and saved me from having to explain further. Vegas quickie or not, the lump in my throat as Jed assembled up front with Luke, Mark, Nick, Nate, and Black was very real. I loved that man. He was everything.

Even in pink underwear.

Lottie and Nigel slid into their seats behind me, late, and I dreaded to think what they'd been doing together. But I couldn't be too upset. Nigel's cheerful outlook on life was exactly what my sister needed, and there was no doubting their fondness for each other.

The opening bars of the wedding march sounded, and Mack glided down the dusky pink carpet. Cream, green, pink—the colours Bradley had chosen—were perfectly coordinated, and everything from the flowers to the dresses to the earpieces the security guards wore matched. Although the number of guards seemed like overkill, given that most of the guests worked for Blackwood Security, Emmy and Black's company. Mack explained to me that they were her family as much as her blood relatives were, and I loved that idea.

Emmy, Dan, Carmen, Tia, and Nick's girlfriend Lara followed Mack down the aisle, clutching bunches of roses and carnations. As Emmy glided by, I caught the glint of something silver hidden in her bouquet and gave my head a little shake. She really had brought a knife with her, hadn't she?

The vows began, and then it was time for the

moment of truth. Would Trevor perform? The entire wedding party focused on the other end of the marquee when the pastor asked for the rings, and I noticed Mack was holding her breath. Trevor gave his handler a dirty look, then flapped his way down the aisle, pausing only to poop on the pink carpet. Bradley's gasp of horror was eclipsed by the collective sighs of everyone else.

And then they were man and wife. Luke kissed his bride, and after a minute Dan tapped Mack on the shoulder and cleared her throat.

"Guys, you have all night for that."

They pulled apart, both smiling and with eyes only for each other. For a moment, I really did regret missing out on that experience myself. But then Jed looked over at me and waggled his eyebrows, and I knew I'd gotten a good deal. I ran the tip of my tongue over my top lip, and he glanced at his watch before raising his eyes heavenwards.

Yes, no matter how wonderful this wedding was, my favourite part of the day would be heading home with my own husband.

I'd gone to Vegas, I'd gambled, and I'd won.

GET LUCKY

If you're wondering how Amy met Mark, I've written a short story about that, FREE to members of my reader group:

GET LUCKY

The stars say she'll get lucky, but will Amy's first date with Darryl be a dream or a disaster?

You can download *Get Lucky* here:
www.elise-noble.com/lucky

WHAT'S NEXT?

The Blackwood Security series continues with Seven's story in *Ultraviolet*...

A chance meeting in a frozen wasteland leads unwilling assassin, Seven, from Siberia to small-town Virginia. A new life in suburbia beckons. All she has to do is keep out of trouble as she tries to mend her broken heart.

Or so she thinks.

When Seven's world is torn away from her, she's left with no choice but to fight back, and help comes from an unexpected alliance. A deal is struck—If Seven helps Emmy Black to destroy the remaining stocks of a deadly virus, Emmy will assist with Seven's little problem.

But not only is Seven used to working alone, someone in Blackwood Security is keeping a secret from both of them, one with far-reaching implications.

Will life be the same when the truth comes out? Can Seven regain her old form and survive the operation? And how does disgraced CIA agent Quinn fit into the story?

Find out more here:
www.elise-noble.com/violet

The next Blackwood Elements book is *Lithium*...

Every girl loves ice cream, right?

Not Sofia. She's tried all the flavours, but plain old Vanilla was her downfall.

A trip to the Cayman Islands to give her ex what he deserves is made all the more complicated by her fear of water—not easy to handle at the best of times, but he's taken up residence on a yacht.

She cooks up a special recipe for revenge, and it's a dish best served chilled. But will handsome stranger Leo add some unwanted heat into the kitchen?

Find out more here:
www.elise-noble.com/lithium

If you enjoyed *Out of the Blue*, please consider leaving a review.

For an author, every review is incredibly important. Not only do they make us feel warm and fuzzy inside, readers consider them when making their decision whether or not to buy a book. Even a line saying you enjoyed the book or what your favourite part was helps a lot.

Want to Stalk Me?

For updates on my new releases, giveaways, and other random stuff, you can sign up for my newsletter on my website:
www.elise-noble.com

Facebook:
www.facebook.com/EliseNobleAuthor

Twitter: @EliseANoble

Instagram: @elise_noble

I also have a group on Facebook for my fans to hang out. They love the characters from my Blackwood and Trouble books almost as much as I do, and they're the first to find out about my new stories as well as throwing in their own ideas that sometimes make it into print!

And if you'd like to read my books for FREE, you can also find details of how to join my review team.

Would you like to join Team Blackwood?

www.elise-noble.com/team-blackwood

END-OF-BOOK STUFF

So glad this book is finally out in the world! I wrote the first draft a few years back, before the last ebola outbreak, and originally, the virus in the story was Ebola Zaire. But as governments threw money at the problem, it seemed like a cure was going to be found, and I figured I'd better create my own virus, Azrael, so the book didn't go out of date before it got published. But for now, Ebola seems to have retreated back into the rainforest, although it'll be back. It always comes back.

In Blue, I also wanted to show Emmy as others see her—her cold side, the mask she wears for the public. And James? There's a whole other story there...

Thanks as always to my team, because I couldn't make these books what they are without help. Abi, who drew the covers for the three Black books, stepped in again and put the picture in my head onto, well, not paper...screen. Amanda, for editing once again—I've learned so much since we started working together. My wonderful proof readers, Emma, John, and Dominique. And my beta readers for this book—Chandni, Harka, Jeff, Renata, Erazm, Helen, Terri, Musi, David, and Stacia. You guys rock!

Lithium
Carbon
Rhodium
Platinum
Lead
Copper
Bronze
Nickel
Hydrogen (2021)

The Blackwood UK Series
Joker in the Pack
Cherry on Top (novella)
Roses are Dead
Shallow Graves
Indigo Rain
Pass the Parcel (TBA)

Baldwin's Shore
Dirty Little Secrets (2021)
Secrets, Lies, and Family Ties (2021)
Buried Secrets (2021)

Blackwood Casefiles
Stolen Hearts
Burning Love (TBA)

Blackstone House
Hard Lines (TBA)
Hard Tide (TBA)

The Electi Series
Cursed

Spooked
Possessed
Demented
Judged

The Planes Series
A Vampire in Vegas
A Devil in the Dark (TBA)

The Trouble Series
Trouble in Paradise
Nothing but Trouble
24 Hours of Trouble

Standalone
Life
Coco du Ciel (2021)
Twisted (short stories)
A Very Happy Christmas (novella)

Books with clean versions available (no swearing and no on-the-page sex)
Pitch Black
Into the Black
Forever Black
Gold Rush
Gray is My Heart

Audiobooks
Black is My Heart (Diamond & Snow - prequel)
Pitch Black
Into the Black
Forever Black

Gold Rush
Gray is My Heart
Neon (novella)

Printed in Great Britain
by Amazon